# DON COYOTE

## THE AUTHOR

Whitman Chambers lives with his family in California and it is from the mountains that shadow his home that he draws the inspiration for most of his work. His stories of the West have won him an important name as a writer of virile, rapidly moving tales. In addition to being frequently represented in many of the larger magazines he is the author of these books:

"The Fighting Redhead,"

"Garber of Thundergorge" (in collaboration).

# DON COYOTE

*A Novel*

*By*
## WHITMAN CHAMBERS

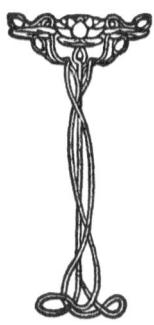

INTERNATIONAL FICTION LIBRARY
CLEVELAND        NEW YORK
Made in U.S.A.

# CHAPTER I

FATE must have been in a jocular mood that day. At least, so "Don Coyote" Lawrence reflected afterward. The matter of the riding gauntlet, for instance. A man might ride a thousand miles on the trails of the West and never see any kind of a gauntlet lying in his path. Yet there it had been, right in the center of the trail. Acting on impulse, he had picked it up. He had been interested at once. It was a woman's gauntlet, small and worn, and shiny on the insides of the fingers. Don Coyote had gazed at it musingly, a slow smile playing about the corners of his friendly, generous mouth. He had decided, without undue thought, that the glove must be returned to its owner. Again he had acted on impulse.

Donald Lawrence, be it known, was in many ways an impulsive young man. That, and a certain propensity for tinkering with refractory windmills, had gained him his appellation of Don Coyote.

It had come about in this wise: a certain bookish person of the gentler sex, having heard of several of Don's escapades and seeing him battle with a windmill that refused to function—this was in Texas, where windmills are of great importance in the scheme of life —had dubbed him "Don Quixote." Being a bookish person, she had pronounced the name of the famous knight "Don Key-o-te," as all bookish persons pronounce it. Don's friends, thinking that this was an easterner's pronunciation of the name of a certain well known western animal, had corrupted it to "Don Coyote" and the nickname had stuck—undoubtedly because his personality and character were no more like those of a coyote than they were like those of the Tibetan ovis poli, whatever that may be.

Don Lawrence was a mining engineer of parts, a graduate of the University of Hard Knocks. He had ridden out of Dos Pinos early that morning on a trail which, so he had been advised, would eventually take him to Chandler City. The distance between the two places was forty miles. The former town, a mining camp, was on the barren Nevada desert; the latter town, also a mining camp, was on the eastern slope of the Sierras, in California.

The migration, if so it might be called, had been the direct result of the pinching out of a quartz vein in the Little Papoose mine. The Little Papoose had never been much of a mine anyway, and Lawrence was glad to be shut of it. He hoped for bigger things in Chandler City. Hoping was as far as he dared go, for he knew that in California there were ten mining engineers out of work to every mine in operation. He knew, too, that he might be compelled to take a job as foreman, shift boss, driller or even mucker—and he didn't care greatly if he was.

A philosophical gentleman was Don Coyote Lawrence, with a happy-go-lucky nature that accepted good luck and ill with the same easy smile.

Noon found Don Coyote crossing the state line, under a blazing sun. As this was only a trail, and a poor one at best, there was no monument to mark the boundary—only a weather-beaten sign on a leaning post with "Nevada" painted on the eastern side and "California" on the western. The rider drew rein and paused a moment, staring back over his shoulder.

A great, level desert, dotted with clumps of sagebrush, stretched out behind him, sun-baked and uninviting. To the south, barely visible in the haze of dancing heat waves, he made out a fringe of low-lying hills, as harsh and barren as the desert. To the eastward he saw three mirages—three lakes as blue as the sky, cool-looking, pleasant, with white, sandy shores. Ten miles away they seemed, possibly nearer. Like three cool hands they beckoned him away from the heat and dust of the trail.

But Don Coyote shook his head with a slow, indulgent smile.

"Sort o' like life, ain't they now?" He spoke to his roan mare in a low voice, gently melodious. "They's three of them lakes. Fame. Fortune. Prestige. Nearly everybody in this h'yar world is runnin' toward 'em with their tongues hangin' out. They think they'll find water—which in the desert means life. But they won't. Not much, they won't, Cleopatra! All they'll find is heat and misery and more desert. They look pretty in the distance, but they don't mean nothing when you get there.

"You bet! We know, don't we, Cleo, old girl?" He stroked the roan's neck caressingly. "Yes, siree! We know, and that's why we're headin' away from them lakes. Fame, fortune and prestige. They don't mean nothing in our young lives, do they?" He touched the lean flanks with his spurs. "Cleopatra, let's be on our way."

The trail led slowly upward, keeping to the higher places, threading around coulees and dry washes. Ahead were the blue-tinged slopes of the Sierras, foot-hills close at hand, jagged granite peaks in the hazy distance. The country changed slightly as Don Lawrence wended his way along the faintly outlined trail. It became rougher. A few squatty digger pines were scattered among the sagebrush that sprinkled the brown slopes.

The heat, however, did not abate. Like a great woolen blanket it pressed down upon horse and rider. It was a weight that could not be shaken off. It rested heavily on the shoulders of the man, bowing them until he slumped lifelessly in the saddle. The mare's head, too, was bowed under that oppressive weight; though the pace was not fast, her flanks were foamy with sweat.

Shortly after one o'clock they breasted a little rise. Don Lawrence's eager gray eyes, peering ahead, caught sight of a dark brown patch in the lighter brown of a small flat. Mud! Water! The roan mare raised her head, whiffing the air, and quickened her pace. A few moments later horse and rider were drinking side by side out of the same water-hole. The water was brackish and warm. But it was water and it tasted infinitely good after more than twenty miles of sun-baked desert.

Lawrence got to his feet at last, brushed the water off his face and tugged at the mare's bridle. "Easy, lady," he cautioned. "You're mighty hot, you know. Take your time. We won't be leavin' for a few minutes."

He led the mare a step or two away from the hole, dropped the reins to the ground and untied a small parcel from behind the saddle. In the scant shade of a clump of sagebrush, where he was compelled to curl up almost into a ball to get out of the direct rays of the sun, Lawrence ate his lunch. Ten minutes later, after filling his canteen and allowing himself and the mare another long drink, he was on his way again.

Some three miles past the water-hole, where the trail led up through a narrow canyon toward the summit of the first range of hills, he found the gauntlet.

It was lying squarely in the center of the trail; it looked rather forlorn and abandoned. Don Lawrence drew rein before it, staring down at the bit of leather with a quizzical smile.

"Well! Who left you there?" he inquired. He scanned the trail minutely. Only one horse had traveled that route since the last rain, which had probably been weeks before. It had been a small horse, judging by the size of the hoof-prints, and it had thrown its left hind shoe. Lawrence dismounted and picked up the glove.

"H-m! You belongs to a lady, eh? Now I wonder if it wouldn't be the right thing to do to take you back to your mamma? Yes, I reckon I will—if I can."

He mounted again and headed up the trail, still regarding the gauntlet thoughtfully. "A right small hand your mamma has, hasn't she? Reckon we'll have to look her up. You're not very valuable. Still, she might think a lot of you. Let's see, now. Accordin' to Jimmy Marshall, this trail should hit a road about eight miles from here. If we go north on that road, we'll come to Chandler City in eight more miles. If we go south, we'll come to the Buckaroo mine and the end of the road in four miles."

Don Coyote nodded, apparently corroborating his memory. "It's a chance, that's all. If this h'yar three-shoed horse goes north, we'll lose his tracks in Chandler City. In which case we'll keep the glove as a souvenir of a long, hot, dusty ride. But if these h'yar tracks go south, toward that mine with the cowboy name, we ought to find the little lady without much trouble. And judgin' from your size, li'l ol' gauntlet, she's goin' to be a right small li'l woman."

Folding the glove carefully, he slipped it into the pocket of his coat and gave his attention to the trail. Four miles further on they reached the head of the canyon and, after a stiff climb, the summit of the first range. Lawrence drew rein and stared out over the panorama which unfolded before him. It was a wooded country he saw now, with tall yellow pines and firs and tamaracks banked against the hillsides. A good three thousand feet below him lay a long, curling blue ribbon, flecked with white—the Gila River. Ten or twelve miles away, nestling at the head of a long valley, he made out a cluster of buildings and tall chimneys—the mines and smelters of Chandler City. Near the river, far below, he caught an occasional glimpse of a yellow ribbon through the trees—the road from the town to the Buckaroo mine. Stretching across the western horizon, as far as he could see from north to south, were the jagged, saw-toothed peaks that formed the backbone of the Sierras, snow-clad even in July.

Don Coyote nodded, sighing gratefully. "This h'yar is more like it," he told Cleopatra. "This is our country. That stuff back there—" he waved his hand toward the barren, sun-beaten waste behind him— "them that wants it can have it. They can have it all. Ain't that right, lady?"

Touching spur to flank, he moved off down the trail toward the blue ribbon below him. The path was steep and the roan mare picked her way carefully. Nearly an hour had elapsed before they gained the road, which wound along the hillside a hundred feet above the roaring Gila. Lawrence dismounted hastily and scanned the deep dust of the highway.

"There's one," he said quickly. "And there's another. And another. All headin' south." He laughed, a gentle, boyish laugh, and patted the glove in his pocket. "Li'l gauntlet, you're goin' home to mamma. I wonder is she goin' to be glad to see you? Or is she goin' to throw you in my face and tell me to mind my own business? Oh, well, serve me right if she did."

Don Coyote mounted the mare. With a song in his heart he turned his back on Chandler City. Impulse again! Had he known what was in store for him at the head of that road he might not have been so ready to ride toward the south. Or, more likely, he would have headed up the road all the more eagerly.

For Don Coyote Lawrence was an adventurous young man.

# CHAPTER II

CLEOPATRA stepped out jauntily, glad that the steep, rocky trail was at an end. Indeed, so jubilant was she that shortly she broke into a canter.

"Suit yourself, honey," Don Lawrence grinned. "They's only four miles to go. Then, if we're lucky, I may be able to dig you up a square meal."

The dust lay several inches deep on the road. It was matted with pine needles. Above the roar of the river, the mare's hoofbeats could hardly have been heard at a distance of fifty feet. Suddenly Lawrence drew her up on her haunches.

"Steady, lady!" he cautioned in a low voice. "Somethin' funny here."

In rounding a bend in the road, he had sighted two mounted men a quarter of a mile ahead of him. The men themselves were not unusual. Their actions were. They had come to a halt in the center of the road. The taller of the pair was in the act of examining something that looked suspiciously like a revolver.

Now, contrary to popular opinion, the westerner of to-day does not consider a revolver as necessary a part of his wearing apparel as, say, his hat or his shoes. Many men appear on the public highways and byways without a sign of a holster. Indeed, at the risk of dispelling many fond illusions, one might say that side-

17

arms are no more common than grizzly bears, than which there are few things rarer.

When Don Lawrence saw that unmistakable glint of blue steel, he knew that these two men were either members of a posse in search of some desperado or they were bent on mischief. Accordingly, he swung his mare off the road into a grove of cottonwoods, threw the reins over her head and calmly dismounted. Picking up a large stone, he looked up quizzically into her brown eyes.

"Honey, does you whinny, Ah crowns you wid dis brick," he told her, grinning. Then he tossed the rock aside and crept out to the road, chuckling to himself. "That was plain enough language. I sure hope she understood it, 'cause I don't reckon these two hombres would take any too kindly to bein' spied on. Wish I had a gun, darn it!"

Peering out of the fringe of cottonwoods, he was just in time to see the two men disappear into a heavy growth of buffalo berry bushes. Lawrence watched a moment, saw that they did not reappear, and then slipped back into the cottonwoods. He sat down nonchalantly, leaned back against a tree and casually rolled a cigarette.

"H-m. The West is shore goin' plumb to the dickens." He shook his head mournfully. "Sort o' backslidin', as it were. Now who'd think that a feller could run onto a real, live hold-up these days? Now I wonder—" He half rose to his feet and then dropped back to the ground. "No, there wasn't no cameras showin'.

Couldn't be one o' them movie stunts. Yes, siree.
Must be the real thing. Guess I better stick around.
Always did have a hankerin' to see a genuine stick-up."

His cigarette lighted, he crawled forward on his
stomach until he reached a position that commanded a
view of the road ahead and which, at the same time,
was concealed by a heavy growth of brush. He waited
calmly, puffing on his cigarette. When it was gone he
rolled another, a rather difficult feat in his position.
The shadows lengthened and at last disappeared altogether as the sun went down behind the high range to
the west. His watch showed him that it was five
o'clock.

"Three hours more of daylight," he mused. "I wish
this stick-up would be pulled off. I'm gettin' hungry.
Besides, I got a date to match up a pair of ridin' gloves
with a li'l lady up the river."

Half an hour more passed. He moved restlessly,
half tempted to go on about his business. Those two
hombres weren't preparing to hold him up. Why
should he worry about the matter? Besides, he sensed
that it was rarely wise and that it was quite often extremely unhealthy to mix into affairs of this sort.

Then he discerned a lone rider moving briskly down
the road toward Chandler City. Lawrence strained
forward eagerly, anxious to miss not a single detail
of the drama that was about to be played for his special
benefit. At that, it all happened so quickly that he
missed half the play. Two shots from the berry
bushes, almost simultaneous, and the lone rider's horse

crumpled beneath him and skidded forward in a cloud of dust.

Don Coyote cursed softly. "The dirty skunks! If I had a gun I'd give 'em some of their own medicine, s'help me, I would. Ought to be ashamed o' their-selves, wastin' good hoss flesh that-away. Looked like a fair-to-middlin' sorrel, too."

The rider had fallen clear. But before he could get to his feet and draw the gun that was strapped to his side, the two bandits had leaped out of the bushes and had him covered. They were masked now and they disarmed him neatly and motioned up the road with their guns. For a long moment their victim, an elderly man with white hair and mustache, stood regarding them. Lawrence could see his lips moving and knew that he was cursing. One of the bandits prodded him in the ribs with his gun and the man at last swung about and started up the road.

The bandits worked swiftly. From behind the sad-dle of the wounded horse, which was spasmodically kicking its last, one of them unstrapped a heavy canvas sack. The other dashed into the bushes and appeared a moment later with their horses. The sack was lashed onto one of the saddles, the men mounted and were off down the road, flashing past Don Coyote's hiding place in a cloud of dust.

Getting to his feet, Don Coyote stepped out to the edge of the road, saw that the bandits were in full flight and then ran to his horse, mounted, and started down the road behind them. He did not ride fast, for

it was no part of his plan to overtake them. Indeed,
he had no plan as yet—he was again acting on impulse.
He felt that those two men should be apprehended and
brought to justice. They had stolen something; what
it was, he didn't know nor care. That was minor.
The important thing was that they had shot a perfectly good horse in cold blood, for no reason at all.
Any bandit worthy of the name could have pulled off
that stick-up without firing a shot. These men were
bunglers. More to the point, they had no respect whatever for good horse-flesh. They must be brought to
justice.

Though Don Coyote's mind was active, his eyes
were busy, too. He had already picked out the tracks
of the two horses the bandits had ridden; he had identi-
fied them and knew that he would recognize them again
if he saw them at the north pole. Accordingly he rode
leisurely, casting only a casual glance at the road now
and then to make sure that his quarry had not turned
off. He passed the point where the Dos Pinos trail
struck the road, saw that the bandits had not turned
east and rode calmly on down the river toward Chandler City.

"Makin' straight for the town," he mused after he
had covered a mile or more. "Think they'll be able to
hide their tracks. Well, if they's a paved street in that
burg, maybe they will. But if they isn't—boys, look
out! Li'l ol' Don Coyote is on your trail!"

He bethought himself suddenly of the riding glove
in his pocket. A frown wrinkled his tanned forehead

under the wide-brimmed hat.  He patted the pocket affectionately.

"Reckon you'll have to wait a while, li'l ol' gauntlet. I got more important business on foot than matchin' up gloves.  Cleo, keep movin'.'"

Riding casually around a bend in the road, he was suddenly confronted by the two bandits.  They were riding toward him and were not fifty feet away.  Don Coyote thought swiftly as he drew up his horse. They'd doubled back on their trail—riding on the edge of the road, too, where they would leave few tracks in the heavy layer of pine needles.  Two to one they were heading for the Dos Pinos trail, after first passing it up to throw off possible pursuers.

The two men drew up before Lawrence, regarding him with undisguised suspicion.  He met their frowns with an easy, guileless smile.

"Howdy, strangers," he greeted them cheerfully. "Am I on the right road to Chandler City?  I just come over the mountain from Dos Pinos an' I don't know much about trails in these h'yar parts."

The two bandits exchanged glances.  The taller one, a thin individual with a stubble of beard and ratty eyes, spoke at last.

"Didn't hear no shootin' up the road, did you?"

"Shootin'?"  Lawrence's surprise was well feigned. "No, can't say's I did.  What's the lay, stranger?"

"Some city feller's shootin' deer out o' season," the tall man replied, with poorly affected casualness. "We're out lookin' for him."

Lawrence shook his head. "No, I ain't seen a soul since I left Dos Pinos this morning. How far'd you say Chandler City is?"

" 'Bout six miles. Straight ahead." The speaker nodded to his companion. "Come on, Joe."

Without further words the two men rode off swiftly up the road. Don Coyote grinned broadly and headed down the road at an easy pace.

"That fast ridin' don't deceive me none a-tall," he remarked to Cleopatra. "I'd be willin' to bet my saddle against a last year's calendar that they're watchin' me from around the first turn. Half expectin' me to follow 'em and all ready to plug me if I do. Well, they ain't goin' to waste no ammunition on me. Not much. I craves to live a while longer."

Lawrence rode a full half mile without once looking back. Then he pulled off the road and hastily unsaddled the mare.

"Honey, you and me parts company right now," he told her. "No, it ain't 'cause I don't like you no more. But you can't go where I'm goin'. Besides, you've followed a tough trail and you're tired. You need somethin' to eat and a rest. As for me; well, I'm a wild coyote an' it's my night to howl."

He cached his saddle, and the few belongings that were tied to it, in a clump of alders. The remnants of his lunch he stuffed into his pocket. Slinging his canteen over his shoulder, he waved good-by to the mare.

"So long, lady. See you to-morrow—if I'm lucky.

If I ain't—well, take care of yourself an' be a good girl."

He swung off down the slope to the river, filled his canteen, took a long drink and forded the stream. He climbed the opposite bank until he was well up on the hillside, taking care to keep as much brush and trees as possible between himself and the road to the south. At last, when he had worked up some four or five hundred feet, he edged cautiously out into a little clearing and surveyed the opposite side of the canyon. From the eminence he had gained, it lay spread before him like a map in bas-relief.

"Let's see now," he mused. "There's the ridge that Dos Pinos trail comes down. There's another ridge this side of it and still another straight across from here. I'll take this one as far as the summit, cut over one ridge on the other side of the summit and beat 'em to that water hole. H-m. Somethin' tells me I got a hard night ahead of me. An' all because I started to return a lady's glove when I should have been mindin' my own business an' headin' straight into Chandler City."

"Oh, well," he added, as he started down the hill to the river, "it'd be a mighty dull old world if everybody minded his own business."

# CHAPTER III

Don Lawrence climbed swiftly, fighting to gain the top of the main ridge and a glimpse of the country to the east before darkness fell. Without that survey to fix it in his mind, traveling as he was without trail or landmark to guide him, he knew that he would never find the water-hole. The moon would be up about nine. It would make the country almost as light as day. But it would be a different kind of light than the daylight in which he had seen it last. Distances would be deceiving; ridges and peaks which had subconsciously registered on his mind that afternoon would take on another appearance.

Yes, he told himself repeatedly, he must reach that summit before dark. He had in the neighborhood of three thousand feet to climb, from the river. The trail had taken four miles to climb that three thousand feet. From the looks of the slope he was traveling, he'd gain the elevation in a little more than a mile—a stiff climb for any one, particularly for a man who has traveled more than thirty miles, most of it across a vitality-sapping desert.

But Don Coyote faced it with a light and willing heart. He was hungry and weary. At the back of his brain a small voice was telling him that he was a fool to mix into an affair which did not concern him.

Yet he had made up his mind, on impulse, and his mind having been made up, he faced the task before him with a smile on his lips. There was no turning back now. Don Coyote wasn't built that way. Besides, he had a hankering to settle matters with those two skunks who had shot down as nice a little sorrel as he had seen since he left the Panhandle.

Though he knew little about the country in which he found himself, he felt positive that the bandits' objective had been the Dos Pinos trail. They surely had had no intention of heading on up the river and overtaking the man they had robbed. They could hardly head west, for the country was too rough for horses— any one with half an eye could see that. They had gone north and then doubled back on their tracks. Only the east was left, and the easiest way out of the canyon in that direction was the trail Lawrence had traveled that afternoon. Five or six miles of that would put them in the desert, where travel would be limited to certain well ordered lanes which were marked by waterholes. And the only water-hole for miles was the one at which Don had drank earlier in the day.

"They'll hit for that sure," he told himself pantingly. "May not follow the trail all the way. May not even set foot on the trail. Be foolish if they did. But they'll make that water-hole some time to-night. An' I gotta get there first."

Thus committing himself, he steadfastly tried to put all thoughts out of his mind. It was one of his theories that thinking took energy. And he needed all of his energy right now if he was to gain the summit before nightfall.

Though his lungs ached for more air, though his heart pounded in his breast like a trip-hammer and the knives of fatigue cut cruelly into the muscles of his legs, he kept doggedly on, fighting his way to the top. Every step was a struggle. Every effort called forth all his will. If he had thought about the matter, he must surely have turned back. But resolutely he kept his brain inactive during the balance of that long climb.

At last the trees began to thin. The hillsides grew less steep. He knew that he was nearing the top. He paused long enough to glance at his watch.

"Five after seven. More than an hour—of daylight left. Better take it easy. Don't want—to give out—soon's I get—to the top."

He took the last five hundred feet at a slower pace and when he at last gained the summit and looked out over the broad expanse of desert and rolling hills his mind was clear enough to register them.

"Just like I thought. That water-hole is just about over there. I can head straight for it, where they can't. Leastwise, they won't. They'll go roundabout, keepin' to the bare places where they won't leave tracks. They'll travel easy, too, to save their horses. Yes, I reckon I can beat 'em—if I don't loaf none. Got to keep movin' an' movin' fast."

Suiting the action to the word, he took a last long look at the country before him and then swung off down the ridge which jutted out to the eastward. He traveled at a dog-trot, his fists clenched at his sides, his keen eyes searching out the easiest trail between the scattered clumps of sage.  Meticulously he kept off of the crest of the ridge, taking no chances of being seen by the fleeing bandits.

The great desert before him slowly changed color. The gray-brown sage became deep purple, the purple darkened to a deeper blue and the sage finally faded out as night came on.  Don Lawrence did not see these things.  His mind was intent on picking the most feasible trail and in keeping that image of the landscape clearly before him.

The moon rose and he knew that it was in the neighborhood of nine o'clock.  He knew, too, that the waterhole was not far away.  Several times he paused, listening for hoof-beats.  He heard nothing.  Not a sound broke a stillness so absolute that it seemed to beat upon his eardrums.  He plunged on, his mind swayed by one purpose; to get to the water-hole as quickly as possible.

He came upon it suddenly, a half mile nearer than he had calculated.  No one was in sight.  There was no sound of approaching horses.  He breathed a deep sigh of relief.

"Whew!  What a run!  Never so all in in my life. Water, come to your daddy!"

Dropping prone beside the spring, he buried his face gratefully in the water.  It was cooler than it had been that afternoon; it was unbelievably refreshing.  He drank deeply and filled his canteen, which was now half empty.  Then he rose and looked about.  Fifty feet away he saw a small digger pine. He walked to it, cut off a branch some three feet long and stripped it of bark and foliage. Going back to the spring, he rubbed the branch in the dark mud. Cocking his head on one side, he regarded his handiwork with a slow smile.

"Not very deadly lookin' at close range," he admitted to himself. "But at fifty or sixty feet it ought to get by right well. It ain't half so dangerous as a real gun, either."

He took another drink of water, washed the dust off his face and hands and hair, and then retired to a spot behind a bowlder some twenty paces from the water-hole. Here he sprawled out on his back and allowed his body and brain complete relaxation. Not a thought crossed his mind, not a movement stirred his form. He lay as one dead. Only his ears were attentive.

Five minutes passed, ten minutes, a half hour. Then he heard a low crackling sound, as of a horse's legs breaking through brittle sagebrush. Very cautiously he raised himself to one elbow and turned over on his stomach. He heard the unmistakable creak of saddle leather now and the low tread of horses' hoofs on sand. Then voices, low but clear in the still air.

" . . . Sure, I told him it was all or nothin'. We argued about it for an hour. He claimed he ought to get a share for tippin' us off. But I wouldn't listen to him. Not much. Finally, I says, 'Aw, dry up! You know blamed well the old man will square things with you.'

"Well, yuh should of seen his face. Tooken back?

Say, I never figured a big stiff like him could blush. But, by gosh, he did. Yes, sir. Blushed like a school kid. He never figured for a minute that I knew the old man was behind the whole game. Why, we could have held out an' made him pay us. The old man, I mean. Yes, sir! We could have kept the bullion an' made him pay us for pullin' the stick-up besides. I know blamed well we could. Only we didn't have no time to fix things up."

"What's the old man's game?"

"He's tryin' to bust Dorrington an' close down the Buckaroo. It's plain's the nose on yer face."

"Sounds funny to me. What'll he git out o' that?"

"Search me, but that's his game, just the same."

"But I don't see what good it'll do him to bust Dorrington an' close down the Buckaroo. He's got stock in it, ain't he?"

"Yeh. He's got stock in it, all right."

"Then what's his game?"

"Aw, how do I know? These big mining hombres are always up to tricks, ain't they? An' the old man's as crooked as they make 'em. Besides, I ain't runnin' his affairs."

"Yuh seem to know a lot about 'em."

"Aw hell! Dry up, will yuh!"

There was a moment's silence, save for the soft plup-p-p of hoofs and the creak of saddles.

"Hello! Here's the ol' water-hole. I was beginnin' to think we'd missed it. Don't think much of this business of travelin' in circles. Too blamed easy to go wrong. Let's tank up."

The two men dismounted, gave their animals their rein and flung themselves down on the edge of the water-hole. They drank audibly.

Don Lawrence rose, his pine branch in his hands. He did not speak at once, however. He waited until the two men, puffing and blowing, had gained their feet. Then he barked his order crisply:

"Put 'em up, boys!"

# CHAPTER IV

THE two men swung around as one. They hesitated an instant, peering through the faint light at Don Coyote. The latter literally trembled in his boots. Would they penetrate his ruse? Would they perceive that instead of a rifle he held only a muddy pine branch in his hands? Then they slowly raised their arms above their heads.

"Say, what's the idea, pardner?" the tall one demanded.

"Can't you guess?" Lawrence returned.

"You tryin' to hold us up?"

"I wouldn't be surprised, mister," Don Coyote grinned, holding his "gun" very steadily. "And if you try any tricks, I reckon I'll have to put a li'l daylight through yuh."

"Aw, say, now! We ain't got nothin'," the shorter man growled.

"No? Well, we'll see about that. Now you, Shorty, toss both your guns on the ground."

"Only got one."

"All right. Get rid of that."

The smaller man obeyed, cursing softly as he tossed his gun to the sand.

"You next, Slim," Don Coyote ordered.

Slim obeyed, holding a taciturn silence.

"Now, about face!" Lawrence barked. The men stared at him a moment and then slowly swung about. "That was rotten. You hombres certainly ain't never been in the army. Now see if you can do a forward march any better. Move!"

The bandits stepped out side by side, the tall one silent, the shorter one cursing under his breath. Lawrence waited until they had walked nearly a hundred feet. Then he called upon them to halt.

"If you boys turn around, I'll drill yuh!" he shouted.

Tossing his "gun" to one side, Don Coyote ran around the bowlder, crossed the intervening distance to the water-hole and retrieved the two revolvers. Slipping one of them into his belt, he covered the two men with the other. Then he laughed, loud and boisterously.

"Boys, the joke is shore on you! I once captured three Germans with a rifle that wasn't loaded, in the li'l war we had across the pond. But this is the first time I ever captured two bold bad bandits with a branch off a digger pine. Now if it'd been off a nice fir, or even a tamarack, but a measly ol' digger pine— Hey, there! Halt, damn yuh!"

The bandits, without glancing back, had suddenly scurried off into the sagebrush. Lawrence fired twice into the air, having no particular inclination to kill any one, even had he been able in the poor light.

"Halt, damn yuh!" he repeated, in the most threatening tone he could muster.

The bandits, however, were out of sight. One of

the horses, frightened at the sharp explosions, reared and plunged backward. Don Coyote saw the movement just in time. He dove for the bridle, caught it with his left hand and clung desperately.

"Whoa, boy! Whoa, old feller!" he pleaded.

The horse was high-strung and badly frightened. Several minutes passed before Lawrence got him under control. When the animal finally ceased struggling, Don Coyote looked about uneasily. Somewhere out in the sage those two men were watching him. One of them might have another gun. His position was none too secure.

Chagrined a bit, none too pleased over the way he had handled the situation, he pondered a moment. His heart had been set on capturing those two men and taking them into Chandler City.

"Oh, well," he ruminated, "I had to make 'em walk away from their guns. I shore couldn't walk up to 'em and let 'em see that I only had a stick in my hands, 'stead of a rifle. How'd I know they was goin' to bolt for the tall timber? Course, I might try to find 'em— and get plugged for my pains. Reckon my cue is to clear out pronto. I got the bullion—I guess that's what it was they stole—and I might's well call it a night."

He mounted the horse which was the least burdened of the two, tied the reins of the other to his saddle horn and loped off up the trail toward Chandler City. Piqued though he was over letting the bandits escape, he was nevertheless not a little proud of himself. He was looking forward to the return of that bullion to whoever was in charge of the Buckaroo mine.

Don Lawrence did not stop nor slacken pace until he reached the summit. Then he dismounted and, with the bright moonlight beaming down upon him, untied the heavy canvas sack from behind the saddle of the lead horse. He knew without looking into it that it contained bars of gold. Just to make sure, however, he untied the neck of the bag and glanced into it. He saw five bars gleaming dully in the moonlight. He secured the sack again and hefted it thoughtfully.

"Fifty pounds, more or less," he nodded. "Fifteen thousand dollars, maybe. And all mine if I wanted to keep it." He sighed regretfully. "Funny how some hombres is troubled with a conscience. Bet I'll wish I didn't have none—if I have to descend to mucking to get my three squares a day." He tossed the sack of gold bars onto the back of the horse he had been riding and lashed it there. "Bullion, you're goin' home to papa, whoever he is. Come on. Let's see if we can find him."

He mounted the other animal and started down the trail toward the river. The horses had hardly stepped out when three men rode into the trail some dozen paces ahead of him.

"Halt right where you are!"

Don Lawrence recognized a note of authority in the voice. He also recognized three rifles, glinting coldly in the moonlight. His heart skipped a beat as he realized his position. These men were members of a posse.

He was caught with the goods. In a strange country, without a friend to vouch for him, his story of how he gained possession of the bullion would fall flat. They'd laugh at him if he told them he was at that moment on his way to return it to its owner.

These thoughts flashed through his head in the twinkling of an eye. He was forced to make up his mind swiftly. It was capture or flight. Being constitutionally opposed to all forms of incarceration, he chose the latter, the rifles and the fresher horses of the posse notwithstanding.

With one movement he jerked loose the reins of the lead horse and slipped out of the saddle. He mounted the other animal with a flying leap, swung it around, drove spurs into its flanks and headed pell-mell toward the crest of the trail.

"Halt, you blamed fool! Halt or we'll shoot!"

"Shoot an' be durned!" Don Coyote muttered. "Can't hit nothin' in the moonlight nohow."

He bent low in the saddle, urging his mount to greater speed. A sharp report sounded behind him, then another and another. Half a dozen slugs whistled through the air about his head. He crouched lower, his head close against the horse's neck.

"Faster, baby!" he urged. "A little more an' we'll be over the top."

The firing ceased. In its stead came the swift rattle of hoofbeats as the posse swung into the chase. Don Coyote rode as he had never ridden before.

"A hundred and eighty pounds plus fifty," he computed thoughtfully. "That's two hundred and thirty. Too blamed much for this horse to carry. Looks like I've put my foot in it. If they ever catch me now, it'll shore go hard with me."

Then he laughed, softly, without too much humor.

"I shore wish that li'l lady, whoever she is, had held onto her darned ol' gauntlet. Now jus' look at the mess it's got me into."

# CHAPTER V

WILLIAM DORRINGTON, president and general manager of the Buckaroo Mining Company, bent over the table in the large living room of his home and stared at a long column of figures. Though he might not have been called old in years, his appearance was that of an elderly man, worn out by the battle of life, tired, disillusioned. His hair was thin and almost white as were his long mustaches. His gray eyes, a bit faded now, were rather wistful, the eyes of a dreamer. His chin was strong and aggressive, contrasting oddly with his eyes. The general impression he gave was of a fighter who has found the going a bit too hard and has gone down, almost but not quite beaten.

Dorrington at last leaned back in his chair, crumpled the paper into a ball and hurled it into the great fireplace behind him. He gazed abstractedly around the room, a baffled look in his eyes. He took in the details without consciously seeing them; the big table in the center; the Indian baskets, Gayle's most prized possessions, hanging on the walls; the wicker chair she had bought from the mail order house only a few weeks before; the thick rugs, so unlike those he was accustomed to; the blue chintz curtains at the windows; the magazine prints hanging here and there; the many little touches that were so distinctly feminine and which had changed this place from a huge room into a home.

Now they'd have to leave it all. He'd have to go down to Chandler City and find work. It wouldn't be easy, either, with the streets full of mining engineers looking for positions. Most of them young men, too. Rather hard, to go out and look for work when one is sixty-two—and feels eighty!

It would be harder still on Gayle, though. She'd hate to leave the house after she'd spent so much time fixing it up. And she'd been home only two months, too. Poor kid! Oh, well, he hadn't done so badly by her. Not many girls had gone through college when their dads had been in the circumstances he'd been in during the last few years. Seemed as though his luck would never break right any more. Take the Buckaroo. They should have been into those old workings a week ago. And not a sign of them yet. Not the slightest indication to show they were nearing them.

A sharp knock on the door startled him. He half rose from his chair and then relaxed again. "Come in," he called.

The door was opened by a huge man clad in the muddy blue denim and boots of a miner. He stood a moment, blinking his small blue eyes in the light. Inhumanly broad of shoulder, with a thick chest and arms that dangled almost to his knees, he seemed more like some sort of an animal than a man. He had no perceptible neck, his out-thrust chin resting on his chest. His head was bullet-shaped; the thick black hair was cropped close and stood up like the quills on an angry porcupine. Altogether, he was as uninviting and repellant a figure of a man as one would want to see. But he was an excellent mine superintendent—and Bill Dorrington judged his employees by their abilities, not by their looks.

"Come in, Burke," the old man invited, with a trace of weariness in his voice. "What did the boys have to say?"

Burke closed the door behind him and crossed the room to the fireplace. "Nothing doin', Mr. Dorrington," he answered, with a slow shake of his head. "They don't see it, not a-tall. The boys ain't got no faith in the proposition. They've seen that map you got and they know we'd be in the old workings by now —if the map was right."

"But it *must* be right, Burke."

"Well, they can't see it that way, Mr. Dorrington."

"Did you offer them the bonus?"

"Yeh, I told 'em about it. But they figure a month's pay in the hand is worth two bonuses in the bush, if you get what I mean. They got to have their money or they'll raise holy hell."

Dorrington looked into the fireplace, his shoulders drooping a bit. He spoke more to himself than to his foreman. "If we pay off the men, we'll have to close down the mine. We haven't enough money to pay them and keep going too."

The big superintendent did not answer. He stood with his cap in his hand, staring idly out of the window into the moonlight. Dorrington rose after a time. There was a little catch in his voice as he said:

"The men will be paid and the mine closed down in the morning."

That was all. Burke departed with scarcely a nod. Dorrington shrugged—it was as though he were shaking a load off of his shoulders. Well, he'd put up a good fight, anyway. And yet—

He crossed to a smaller table at one side of the room. Opening the drawer, he pawed through a number of blueprints and plans, and at last drew out a large roll of yellowed paper. He untied the string that was around it, took the roll to the larger table in the center of the room and spread it out, weighting down the corners with four ore samples from the mantelpiece.

He stared at it fixedly. It was the vertical plan of the original Buckaroo mine. The ink was faded. The lettering was in the flourishing, ornate script long ago out of date. The plan showed a vertical shaft and, branching out from it at the two thousand foot level, a long tunnel. At the end of the tunnel was pictured a great cavern, marked "ore chamber." The date of the map, printed under the name of the engineer who had drawn it, was 1869.

Dorrington looked at it for a long time; he made a few measurements with a ruler, several computations with the stub of a pencil. Then he shook his head and ran his thin fingers through his white hair.

"I can't understand it," he murmured. "According to all my calculations, we should have struck that ore chamber a week ago. And yet we didn't. There's not a sign of it. Why? . . . This map is authentic. I know that. It was drawn by a capable engineer. And I am certain my surveying of the new tunnel is correct. What is wrong? Why haven't we cross-cut that ore chamber?"

For a long time he sat in thought, puzzling over his problem. Finally he rose and, with the air of one definitely putting an end to a matter, rolled up the ancient map, tied it and returned it to the drawer.

An ore car rattled out of the tunnel a hundred feet away, thumped along over the rail joints to the dump and spilled its contents with a roaring clatter. Above the noise Dorrington heard the swift beat of familiar hoofs coming up the road from Chandler City. He went to the door and opened it. The hoof-beats stopped before the barn and a girl's voice called to him cheerily.

"Hello, dad! Be in as soon as I unsaddle."

Dorrington waited in the doorway. In a way he dreaded to face his daughter, knowing the disappointment his news would bring her. She had expected so much and hoped for so much—dreams of a new house on the crest of the hill above the mine, a car to drive down to town, an occasional trip to San Francisco, house parties for her former classmates from the university.

Gayle would be heart-broken. No, that wasn't exactly true. Gayle had courage. She'd met reverses before. She'd meet this one bravely.

After a few moments he saw her clean-limbed form

dashing across the clearing from the barn and up the steps of the rambling old house.

"Dad! Aren't you ashamed of yourself!" she cried laughingly, as she kissed him. "Wilcox and I waited dinner nearly an hour for you. Why didn't you come into town like you said you would?"

He looked at her quickly. Evidently she hadn't heard the news of the hold-up. "Didn't you come back by the road?" he asked.

"No. I took the trail on the other side of the river."

"Then you didn't see the sorrel."

"Babe, you mean? No." She looked at him narrowly and there was sudden alarm in her voice as she asked: "What—what happened!"

"She was shot out from under me this afternoon," Dorrington answered colorlessly. "About three miles up the road."

"Shot!" She clutched his arm. "But, dad! You weren't hurt?"

"No, no. They didn't harm me."

"They! Was it—a hold-up?"

"Yes."

"And the bullion?"

"Gone!"

# CHAPTER VI

"OH, dad!" It was a cry not of disappointment but of sympathy. Gayle threw her arms around her father, pressing his thin shoulder tightly against her cheek. Tenderly he drew her into the house.

"I'm so sorry, dad! After all the work you went to cleaning up those old tailings. And you needed the money so badly, too." She paused, staring at him. "But how did any one know that you were going to take that bullion into town to-day? You never told a soul, save me. I don't understand it."

"Neither do I," the old man answered feebly. "However, it is gone and we might as well face the consequences. I am going to close down to-morrow."

In the act of removing her hat, Gayle swung about and faced him. She was small, only an inch over five feet, but the way she carried herself gave her the appearance of being much taller. She was as straight and as perfectly formed as a young pine that has grown in a sheltered nook. Her eyes were dark and wistfully tender. They were large eyes and they gave her a childish look that was belied by her strong, firm little chin. Her cheeks glowed with color after the long ride from town.

"You're fooling me," she said hopefully.

Dorrington shook his head, forcing a smile. "No, I'm not, Gayle. We haven't the money to pay the men and keep working too. I told Chandler something of the situation when I 'phoned him to-night. Told him of the hold-up, too."

"He didn't tell me about it," the girl spoke up quickly. "I knew he talked to you. We were eating dinner at the time. But he didn't say a thing about the hold-up nor closing down."

"I guess he wanted you to enjoy yourself." There was a trace of bitterness in his voice that the old man could not hide. Gayle went to him, put her arm over his shoulders, brushed the rumpled white hair back from his forehead.

"I'm sure it isn't as bad as that, dad. We'll keep going some way. And we'll find that old ore chamber, too."

"I don't see how."

The girl looked away. She did not speak for a moment. Then, rather hesitantly: "I think Wilcox would help you out—if you'd ask him."

Dorrington shook his head with finality. "No. I can't do that. Wilcox Chandler and I have disagreed on this thing from the beginning. He has criticized my management time and again."

"I have never heard him, dad," the girl remarked in a low tone.

"Oh, he hasn't come right out and said anything

against me. It has just been little things. Little things that have gotten under my skin. No, I won't go to Wilcox Chandler. I'll give up the whole enterprise and start looking for a job at day labor first."

Gayle sat down, staring thoughtfully at the fire for a long time. "I think you're foolish, father," she said at last. "In a case like this you might—well, swallow your pride."

"This is just the kind of a case where I can't swallow my pride."

"But I am sure he'd be glad to help you," Gayle insisted.

"No! I shan't go to him!" Dorrington declared steadfastly. "Why, it would be just like—" He broke off, flushing.

"Like what, father?" the girl asked mildly.

"Well, it would be like bargaining my daughter for a few thousand dollars to put into this mine!"

The girl started back in her chair. Her dark eyes met her father's gaze, held it for an instant, and then lowered. The color crept slowly over her face, down her white neck. Her breathing was very fast for a few moments. Then, fighting to speak calmly, she said in a low voice:

"I don't think you are very fair, dad."

"No? Well, maybe I'm not, Gayle," he answered with a weary shrug. "But for the last month I have felt that only one thing has kept you from marrying Wilcox Chandler. That is my opposition. I have never expressed it before. But I know you have sensed it." Humbly he added: "Haven't you, Gayle?"

She nodded, neither speaking nor meeting his eyes.

"I haven't wanted you to marry him, Gayle, because I have never felt that he was worthy of you. You are young yet. You can't judge character as well as you will in a few years. You are dazzled by the attentions he has paid you and by his wealth. Right down in your heart you know that he is not the man for you. And yet, it it were not for me, you might marry him to-morrow."

He came to her and sat down on the arm of her chair. Putting his hand under her chin, he tilted it until her eyes met his.

"Isn't that so, Gayle?"

Weakly she made response. "Yes, I guess it is, dad."

He rose quickly, feeling suddenly very miserable and unhappy, and took a turn up and down the room.

"Do you see now," he asked a moment later, "why I won't appeal to Wilcox Chandler for money? If I accepted help from him, I would hardly be in a position to refuse my consent if he asks for your hand."

The girl sighed deeply and her chin sank lower on her chest. There was no sound for several moments save the distant roar of the river, in the canyon far below.

"Then if you fail here for lack of money," she murmured at last, "I am to blame."

"Gayle! Gayle! My dear!" Dorrington pleaded.
"Don't look at it that way. I—"

He broke off at the sound of a very feeble knock on
the door. Gayle rose from her chair. Dabbing hastily
at her eyes with a handkerchief, she crossed the room
and threw open the door.

A tall man stood limply in the doorway, bearing a
heavy canvas sack across his shoulder. He wore no
hat. His cheeks were sunken and flecked with dried
blood from many scratches. His clothes were torn.
He was covered with dust from head to foot. Blink-
ingly he stared into the room with bloodshot eyes.

"Three hours they been chasin' me," he muttered in
a hollow voice. "Three hours—three hundred miles,
more or less. Such white thorn an' mesquite I never
seen in all my life. Reckon I'm about torn to pieces.
They shot my horse—left hind leg. Had to take to
the brush and hoof it. But I got here. I brought
back—"

He paused. For the first time he seemed to take
cognizance of the slender figure before him. Then a
twinkle came into his gray eyes. A smile curved his
generous mouth. The canvas sack slipped off his shoulder and struck the porch with a thump. His right hand
went into the pocket of his coat and came out with a
small riding gauntlet.

"Ma'm, I reckon this h'yar glove belongs to you. I
done found it this afternoon on the Dos Pinos trail.
I thought as how you might be wantin' it, so I'm
bringin' it to you."

He extended the glove, bowed very low over it, lost his balance and pitched forward on his face. The girl stared down at the long, grotesque form.

"Why, dad! He doesn't move!"

# CHAPTER VII

On the sun-bathed porch of Dorrington's home, where the warm rays ironed the aches out of his muscles and filled his heart with peace, Don Coyote Lawrence told his story the next morning. It sagged a bit, that porch; it was unpainted and weatherbeaten. But altogether it was one of the most pleasing and comfortable spots in which Don Lawrence had sat in a long time. Built on a terrace several hundred feet above the roaring Gila, it commanded a breath-taking view of the foam-flecked river and the long, green canyon. Twelve miles away where the canyon widened into a little valley, gleamed the tiny houses of a toy town—Chandler City. Across the canyon, seeming hardly a stone's throw away, rose rank on rank of spired pines, like an army on parade. Behind them the snow-capped battlements of the Sierras stood out clean and sharp against the cloudless sky.

It was a picture of peace, this view, that met Don Lawrence's gaze, a picture that contrasted oddly with the activity and the myriad noises immediately behind him. For at the rear of the house were the mill, idle for the time being, the blacksmith shop, the cookhouse, the bunkhouse, the entrance to the tunnel, the dump— in short, the Buckaroo mine. And from these places came the clank of hammer on anvil, the rattle of ore cars, the hum of air compressors, the roar of rock on the dump—sounds to which the ears of Don Coyote were keenly attuned.

"Yes, it was the little lady's riding gauntlet that saved the bacon," Lawrence finished his story. Though he spoke to Dorrington, his eyes rarely left the slender form of his daughter, fresh and clean in starched gingham. "If I hadn't picked that up and decided to return it, I'd never have seen that stick-up. M'am, that was a lucky day you rode over an' lost your glove on the Dos Pinos trail."

The girl regarded him with twinkling eyes. "It was luckier than you think. Wasn't it, dad?"

Dorrington nodded slowly. "Fifteen thousand dollars may not seem like a great deal of money to you," he said. "But to us—it meant the difference between success and failure. It meant—just about everything."

Lawrence's searching gray eyes scanned the furrowed face of the old man and read much: a story of an uphill fight that was not yet over; confidence in a mine that was still unproven; undying gratitude for the recovery of a few bars of gold whose loss would have spelled failure. The younger man's heart warmed as he sensed the imminence of conflict and struggle.

"Briefly, the situation is this," Dorrington went on to explain. "I own fifty-one per cent of the stock in the Buckaroo mine and am president and general manager of the company. The mine is an old one. It was originally worked by an English company in the late sixties. Several million dollars of high grade ore was taken out of a single deposit at that time. The ore was packed out of here on mule-back and shipped round the Horn to England, where it was milled and smelted. That gives you an idea of how rich the ore was.

"Of course, there must have been thousands of tons of lower grade ore that was left behind because it would not pay to ship it so far—ore that by modern standards would be considered high-grade. Right now I am driving a tunnel toward that old chamber from which all this rich ore was removed. It was originally worked by a shaft and a long drift. They had so much trouble with water, however, and shaft mining is so expensive, that I decided to reach the ore deposit by a tunnel. The old shaft has caved, too, and it would cost as much to clean it out as it would to sink a new one."

"You got a map of the old mine, have you?" Lawrence asked.

The other nodded readily—and yet Don Coyote saw the faint shadow of uncertainty and bafflement that came into his tired eyes. "I have a map, yes. It was made by the engineer in charge when the mine was closed down. I got it from the heirs of the original owners, when I bought the claims from them. It is certainly authentic. It *must* be authentic—and yet—"

Lawrence regarded the old man thoughtfully. Dorrington was in trouble—he had known that from the first. Now, he sensed, he was getting at the seat of his difficulties.

"Well, I just can't understand it," Dorrington went

on after a moment. "According to all my figures, our tunnel should have cross-cut that old ore chamber a week ago. The map of the old workings is accurately drawn, or seems to be, and my surveying is correct. And yet we haven't found a single sign of that ore chamber."

The lines in his face had deepened as he spoke. He seemed at that moment a very worried and very disheartened old man. His daughter spoke lightly, in an obvious effort to cheer him.

"It will come out all right, dad. I'm sure it will. A few more days will see us into the old ore chamber. For that matter, now that Mr. Lawrence has recovered our bullion, we could work for weeks if necessary."

Dorrington forced a smile. "We'll hope we won't have to." To Lawrence, he explained: "I recovered that bullion from the old company's tailing pile. They used a stamp mill for a short time at first, but lost so much of the values that they later shipped everything to England. I milled their tailing pile and the bullion was the result. If we'd lost it—well, last night I ordered my superintendent to close down the mine, so you can see how important it was."

He paused a moment, regarding the younger man with undisguised respect and admiration. "Lawrence, you've pulled us out of a mighty bad hole, not without a great deal of risk to yourself. I won't try to tell you how grateful I am. Deeds speak louder than words. I'll do anything in my power to repay you."

Don Coyote slowly shook his head. "No, I ain't

lookin' for no reward. I ain't that kind. When I see somebody gettin' a crooked deal, I always feel a hankerin' to pitch in an' give 'em a hand. It's fun, kind of. That's the only reason I butted in last night. I was lookin' for some fun, an' I got it—plenty of it. But I don't want you to repay me."

"But isn't there something I can do to square accounts?" Dorrington insisted.

Don Coyote looked first at the old man and then at Gayle. He was interested in them both. More, he was interested in the situation at the Buckaroo. He could smell trouble farther than his namesake could smell a stray chicken and he sensed that trouble in some form hung over this mine. He had felt it from the first. It seemed to be in the very air. Though Dorrington's exposition of the situation had been frank enough, he felt that the old man had not told everything—possibly because Dorrington was himself in the dark concerning certain details.

The old map, Dorrington's failure to strike the ore chamber, the theft of the bullion—these things intrigued him. Everything, surely, was not as it should be at the Buckaroo. Then, like a forgotten voice from the past, certain words of the bandits the night before came back to him:

"He never figured for a minute that I knew the old man was behind the whole game. Why, we could have held out and made him pay us. The old man, I mean. Yes, sir! We could have had the bullion and made him pay us for pullin' the stick-up besides. . . . Tryin' to break Dorrington and close down the Buckaroo. Plain's the nose on your face."

Don Coyote suddenly came to a decision. "I'm lookin' for work," he said quietly. "I can do anything from muckin' to engineering and I ain't afraid o' hard labor. If you can take me on and give me a job, we'll call it square. If you can't—well, we'll call it square anyhow."

Dorrington's face lighted. Almost eagerly he asked: "Would shift boss be too low?"

"Considerin' the present state of my finances, nothin' would be too low."

"That's fine! That's fine! I'll be mighty glad to have you working for me, Lawrence. I need men like you."

Dorrington was smiling happily, but there was no answering smile on the lips of Don Coyote. The younger man considered a moment, wondering how best to approach the subject. Then, deciding that there was nothing to be gained by beating around the bush, he came out with the bold assertion:

"Mr. Dorrington, do you know that some one, known only to me as 'the old man,' is trying to break you and close down this mine?"

Dorrington sat up very straight in his chair. He did not reply at once. His eyes met Lawrence's level gaze, held it for several weighty moments. Then his own gaze shifted and he stared out over the river.

"I have known it from the first," he said finally. "Though for the life of me I cannot figure out why anybody should want to break me and close down this mine. And yet certain things have happened in the past, little things that did not amount to a great deal, that have made me suspicious that some one is working against me. Who it is, or why, I cannot understand. The robbery yesterday was the final straw. No one, save my daughter, knew that I was going to take that bullion to town. And yet I was held up by two men who knew what I was carrying."

Lawrence nodded. "You're right, sir. Those bandits were tipped off."

"I suspected as much. But how, or by whom, I haven't the least idea." Dorrington looked up suddenly at the other. There was a question in his eyes.

"Perhaps I'd best tell you all I know about it," Don Coyote spoke up quickly. "It's little enough. But it may give you some clue." Forthwith he narrated the conversation he had overheard between the bandits, adding, at the end: "Whoever this hombre is who's trying to beat you, he is a stockholder in your company. Leastwise, that is what them bandits said."

It was Gayle who spoke first. "But it is preposterous!" she exclaimed. "Why should any of our stockholders want to shut us down, when it would mean that they would lose what they have put into the mine?"

Don Coyote shook his head with a slow smile. "I reckon you'll have to answer that for yourself, Miss Dorrington. I'm sure I can't. An' from the way them bandits talked, it was somethin' of a mystery to them, too."

Dorrington sighed deeply. "It is all pretty much beyond me. As I say, I have suspected from the first that some one was trying to beat me, trying to force me to close down before I reached that ore chamber. But I never dreamed that it could be one of the stockholders."

"Ain't there no one you suspect?" Lawrence asked quietly. The younger man saw Dorrington glance quickly at Gayle. He saw the color creep into the girl's cheeks. "No," Dorrington said. "I suspect no one—primarily because I do not see how any one could hope to gain by closing us down."

"I reckon that's the angle we'll have to work from," Don Coyote replied thoughtfully. The "we," though quite unconscious, was natural enough. He was on the payroll of the Buckaroo mine now and, though only a shift boss, his primary interest was the success of the enterprise. "We'll have to look for somebody who stands to gain by closin' us down. I got a hunch that when we find the motive, we'll find the man."

"Yes, that is logical," Dorrington nodded. "Find the motive and we'll find the man. In the meantime, I'd like to have you meet my superintendent. Gayle, will you run over to the assay office and tell Burke I want to see him."

The girl nodded and departed for the office. Her face was a bit white now, and very serious. Apparently, Lawrence thought, she'd taken the unpleasant findings he'd brought very much to heart. Don Coyote glanced at her father. The old man sat slumped in his chair, a dejected figure. The whole thing seemed a bit too much for him.

"They's somethin' fishy goin' on round here," Lawrence told himself as he rolled a cigarette. "I got a hunch that there's more trouble in store for the ol' Buckaroo than this man ever dreams of. Oh, well, trouble an' me are ol' friends. Drag it on. I ain't had a real fight on my hands for six months. If I don't have one pretty soon, I'll be goin' stale. Bad luck, do your stuff!"

# CHAPTER VIII

AND trouble came. Mild at first, to be sure, but giving excellent promise of conflict in the very near future. It was in the form of a huge gorilla-like individual with a sloping forehead and a pugnacious chin whom Dorrington introduced as Ben Burke, his superintendent. Lawrence's dislike of the man was instantaneous and complete.

"Ben, Mr. Lawrence here is going to take Johnson's place as boss of the 'graveyard,' " Dorrington explained to the superintendent. "I have been dissatisfied with the work of Johnson's shift for some time. He has been averaging two feet a day less than the other shifts. Tell him he may either stay on the payroll as an ordinary miner or quit the job. Lawrence will go on to-night."

For a tense moment Burke's pale eyes traveled back and forth between Dorrington and Lawrence. There was hostility in his glance, hostility and half-veiled anger.

"I've always thought that the hiring and firing of the men was up to me," the superintendent said pointedly at last.

Dorrington shrugged wearily. "It always has been, Ben. But that shift has been loafing on the job and the fault is Johnson's. I decided several days ago that he would have to go."

The burly superintendent shuffled back and forth on his feet. Don Coyote smiled grimly as he noted that the man's fists were clenched.

"Me and Johnson are mighty good friends," Burke said finally. "I hate to fire him, Mr. Dorrington. It ain't been his fault he ain't made distance like the other shifts. He's got a lazy gang of men on the graveyard. I think you'd do better to fire the shift and keep the boss."

But Dorrington shook his head. "No," he said shortly. "If Johnson can't make his men work, he is not a good shift boss. He has got to go, Ben. That is final."

"Very well, Mr. Dorrington." The ponderous shoulders shrugged. With an effort at casualness, Burke swung about on his heel and started back to the assay office.

Lawrence made no comment as he watched him go. He had caught, however, the gleam of anger in those pale blue eyes and he knew that through no fault of his own he had made an enemy. He sensed, too, that Ben Burke would prove no ordinary enemy. A keen judge of character was Don Coyote—for character analysis is one of the most important courses in the curriculum of the University of Hard Knocks—and he knew that Ben Burke's powers for evil were commensurate with his great strength; the superintendent would hold a grudge; he would as readily hit a man in the back as in the face; his sense of honor, if indeed he had any, was badly warped.

And yet Don Lawrence looked forward only with anticipation toward the taking over of his duties as boss of the graveyard shift. He didn't like Burke; he didn't believe the man belonged where he was; he'd just as soon do battle with him as the next fellow, maybe a little bit rather.

Dorrington must have sensed the thoughts that were coursing swiftly through the mind of his new employee, for when he spoke his tone was slightly apologetic. "I suppose you think that Ben Burke is a pretty hard customer."

"I've worked under harder," Don Coyote shrugged his shoulders with an easy smile.

"Well, his bark is worse than his bite and he is really not as bad as he looks. He's a driver, to be sure. He works hard himself and he makes his men work hard. But that is what I need right now, when my funds are running low."

"I reckon you do," was Lawrence's ready comment. His thoughts, however, had gone off on a different tangent. Briefly, they were: "This feller Burke is no-good white trash. I'd lay two to one that he's crooked in the bargain. And with half a chance I'll prove it."

Dorrington rose from his chair. "Suppose you go over to the bunkhouse and get some more sleep, Lawrence," he suggested. "You lost quite a bit last night and you are going to work to-night. You'll probably need it."

Don Coyote laughed good-naturedly. "I won't argue with you, sir. From the way I feel now, I could sleep for a week and never wake up. However, somebody ought to do down the canyon an' round up my mare. Ol' Cleopatra will be wonderin' what's happened to me."

"I'll send one of the boys down right away," Dorrington offered.

"That'll be right nice of you, sir. The mare'll be somewhere around the first flat below the Dos Pinos trail. An' the saddle's in a clump of brush near a big rock right at the head of the flat. Can't miss it."

"I'll attend to it," Dorrington promised. "And by the way, I'll send for you this afternoon and take you over the mine. I'd like to have you look it over before you go to work."

"Yes, sir."

Don Coyote nodded to Gayle and strode off to the bunkhouse, where he rolled in on the first unoccupied bunk he came to. He did not go to sleep at once, however. He lay on his back, eyes closed, feeling very much at peace with the world and very pleased with himself. He had landed a job; he had made the acquaintance of a most charming young lady; he was in the vortex of what he sensed, and hoped, would soon be a maelstrom of conflict.

For an hour or more he lay on his back going over the hectic events of the past twenty-four hours. Piqued though he was at his failure to capture the two bandits, he was on the whole well pleased with the part he had played. He had lived up to his name of Don Coyote, and Don Quixote, too.

Two questions assailed his mind. Who was trying to break Dorrington and close the Buckaroo? Why hadn't Dorrington struck the old ore chamber as his map showed him he should?

They were hard questions to answer when he knew so little of the situation. He had a strong conviction, however, that the answers to those two questions were closely correlated. And he had a hunch, too, that Ben Burke was on the opposite side of the fence from Dorrington. Not the leader of a plot to break him— Burke hadn't brains enough for that—but certainly taking a hand in the plot.

"Boy, I shore 'nough drew a royal flush on this deal," Don Coyote mused with a grin. "A fabulously rich mine. An ol' man tryin' to play a game where the deck is stacked against him on every deal. As pretty a little gal as ever I set my eyes on. Pretty? That ain't no name for it. She's got the Mona Lisa looking like a decrepit Harvey house biscuit shooter. Somethin' tells me I'm goin' to like this job. Yes, siree! I reckon I'm goin' to have a right good time at this h'yar mine with the cowboy name."

It was mid-afternoon when the cook's flunky woke Lawrence and told him that Dorrington was ready to take him over the mine. When he went over to the house, however, he found Gayle waiting for him on the porch. She was clad in blue overalls and boots.

"Dad and Mr. Burke are checking over their surveying," she told him, smiling, "and I have been appointed a committee of one to take you over the mine."

Don Coyote smiled frankly into her eyes. "Ma'm, it'll make me most happy to accompany you."

The girl's manner was preoccupied as she took him through the various buildings of the mine. She was plainly worried. She spoke seldom and then only to make brief explanations to him. Her attitude puzzled him. It wasn't natural for a girl of her age, particularly *this* girl. Gayle Dorrington's lips were made for smiling, her heart for happiness. He felt immeasurably sorry for her—and his resolution to plunge into the thick of this fight was strengthened thereby.

After taking him through the mine buildings, she started up a steep path which led toward the top of the hill. "I thought you might like to see what is left of the old shaft house and the outcrops of the ledge," she explained.

Lawrence nodded readily, although at the moment he was far more interested in certain problems having to do with the Buckaroo than he was in shafts and ledges. Some distance up the trail they passed a small fan-house. Lawrence felt a rush of air and smelled powder smoke.

"This is our ventilating shaft," Gayle told him. "It cuts the tunnel three thousand feet from the entrance. The blowers at the tunnel mouth drive the air in through a twelve-inch pipe to the face of the tunnel, which has so far been run about thirty-eight hundred feet. The foul air is drawn back for eight hundred feet and out this shaft by the fan here."

Don Coyote nodded abstractedly. The workings of ventilating shafts were quite familiar to him—besides, he had no way of knowing what an important part in his life this particular shaft was soon to play. They passed on up the hill, casually inspected the ancient shaft and the outcroppings of the ledge, and were starting down again when Lawrence asked suddenly:

"Has your father any enemies that you know of?"

The girl looked up at him quickly, startled as well as puzzled by the question. "Enemies? Why, what makes you ask?"

His white teeth flashed in his tanned face as he smiled at her. "Maybe because I want to know," he replied evenly.

Gayle shook her head. "He hasn't an enemy in the world that I know of, unless—"

She broke off, dropping her eyes. Watching her, Lawrence saw her color rise slowly. He waited patiently for her to finish the sentence. Instead, she swung off down the steep trail ahead of him.

Don Coyote shrugged his shoulders regretfully, recalling an odd look that had passed between Gayle and her father that morning when he had asked if they suspected any one. So they were keeping something from him. Oh, well, after all, he was only a shift boss. Why should they confide in him? It was their funeral, not his.

Still and all, he wished mightily that there was some way he could help them. He knew intuitively that before long they were going to need help and need it badly.

# CHAPTER IX

GAYLE DORRINGTON did not speak again until they reached the foot of the trail. "Time enough for you to see the tunnel when you go to work to-night," she said.

Don Coyote nodded and accepted his dismissal, feeling vaguely disappointed. "Thank you, ma'm, for showing me around," he bowed politely. He was about to turn away when he heard the low roar of an automobile coming up the road toward the mine.

"That must be Wilcox Chandler," Gayle told him. "I'm sure I recognize the sound of his car."

There was warmth in her voice now, for the first time since they had started on their tour of inspection. A subtle change had come over her, so subtle that it was barely discernible. Yet Don Coyote felt it and wondered if the coming of Wilcox Chandler, whoever he might be, had brought it about.

"Next to my father, who owns the controlling interest in the Buckaroo, Mr. Chandler is the principal stockholder in our company," Gayle informed him. "I was talking to him over the telephone this morning and told him about your returning the bullion. I think he'd like to meet you. He was very interested. Mr. Chandler, you know, owns most of the mines in the

Chandler City district. The town was named after his father, who was one of the biggest mining men in the state."

Don Coyote nodded pleasantly, though his thoughts were at that moment hardly fitted to the smile that was on his lips. Don Coyote had certain fixed opinions regarding men who were born with silver spoons in their mouths. The mental picture that he formed of Wilcox Chandler was proved, when the mining man's car drove up to the house, to be not greatly in error.

In the first place, Don Lawrence didn't like the car. It was an expensive car and it might stand up on the rough roads of the mountainside; but it was a bit too ornate to suit his fancy. It had been chosen, he suspected, more because of its beauty than its wearing qualities. Don Coyote, it may be seen, also had certain fixed opinions about automobiles and the manner in which they reflected the characters of their owners.

In Wilcox Chandler himself, however, Lawrence was a bit disappointed. He had made up his mind, on the spur of the moment, that he was going to dislike him. He had decided that Chandler would prove bigoted and Ritzy and stand-offish, in short, a typical bloated plutocrat such as the wobblies took so much pleasure in denouncing. But Chandler, to all appearances, possessed none of these qualities.

He was a handsome fellow, a shade under forty. His black hair was touched with gray at the temples, his eyes were friendly, his mouth sensitive, his chin strong. He neither affected an important manner nor golf

trousers.  His greeting of Lawrence was cordiality itself.

"I'm mighty glad to know you, Lawrence," he acknowledged Gayle's introduction heartily.  "I've heard
a lot about you, even before this coup you pulled last
night.  One of my engineers, lad by the name of Bill
Couper, used to know you in Goldfield.  He never gets
tired telling me how you handled that strike at the
Morning Star, and the big fire in the Bluebird.  And,
at the risk of appearing to hand out a lot of soft soap,
I'll admit that I never get tired hearing about it."

And Don Coyote blushed.  It wasn't a habit of his;
indeed, he could hardly recall the last time he had
blushed.  But he felt his cheeks growing red and he
hated himself accordingly.  He wasn't quite sure
whether he should thank Wilcox Chandler for his com-
pliments or knock him down for making him blush before Gayle Dorrington.  Again, at the risk of being a
bit wearisome, it might be pointed out that Don Coyote
Lawrence had very decided opinions in regard to the
phenomenon of blushing among members of the sterner
sex.

"I won't try to thank you for getting that bullion
back for us," Chandler went on.  "Dorrington has already done that.  But I can assure you that we're all
mighty grateful to you."

"It wasn't nothin'," Don Coyote murmured un-
happily, still conscious of a red flush under the tan of
his cheeks.  "I was just lucky to see that stick-up, that's
all.  It was all luck, nothin' more."

Chandler shook his head, laughing softly. "Well, I can hardly agree with that, Lawrence. It wasn't luck that you chased those bandits. And it wasn't luck that you had the nerve to face them without a gun."

Lawrence shifted his feet nervously, anxious to get away. His first impression of Wilcox Chandler had been rather good. But this impression was undergoing a change—he didn't set much store by a fellow who appeared to take delight in making another man miserable.

"Miss Dorrington tells me that you are going to work as a shift boss here at the Buckaroo," Chandler went on.

Don Coyote nodded. "Yeh. On the graveyard."

Chandler shook his head hastily and glanced at the girl. "I don't like to take a good man away from your father, Gayle, but Lawrence isn't any shift boss. He's an engineer. And he's far too good an engineer, from all I have heard about him, to be wasting his time bossing a shift. How about it, Lawrence? Will you accept a position with me at ten thousand a year?"

Don Coyote was hardly prepared for such an offer and for the moment it staggered him. The highest he had ever been paid was eight thousand a year, and that was during a period when engineers were at a premium. A flash of intuition told him that something was wrong. Ten thousand was too high a salary. It was more than he was worth, considering the times and the many engineers who were out of work.

He had no time to analyze the offer. He sensed only

that Wilcox Chandler had misplayed his cards. And, considering the circumstances, his reply came promptly.

"Thanks, Mr. Chandler, but I reckon I'll stay here. I—well, I sort o' like it here at the Buckaroo."

In a silence that was almost tense with amazement, he excused himself and departed toward the bunkhouse. He carried with him two convictions. Both were, as usual, a bit impulsive and based more on intuition than on observed facts.

The first was that Wilcox Chandler was in love with Gayle Dorrington and she with him. Lawrence scowled as he thought about it. Darn fool that he was, what made him get an idea like that? Besides, whether it was true or not, what concern was it of his?

His second conviction—and this had a firmer foundation in fact than his first—was that Chandler's offer of a position came as a result not of his need for Lawrence's services but of his desire to get him away from the Buckaroo. Briefly, meddlers who delved into the affairs of other people were not wanted at the Buckaroo.

For an hour or more Don Lawrence thought over these two ideas, the net results of his meeting with Wilcox Chandler. Then he put them resolutely aside— shelved them, as it were, for future reference—the one because Gayle Dorrington's love affairs were so patently none of his business, the other because he could find no real motive for Chandler's wishing him to leave the Buckaroo.

Had Don Coyote observed Wilcox Chandler's last two acts before the latter left the Buckaroo late that evening, he would undoubtedly have been a bit pleased at the keenness of his perception, if at nothing else. And certainly he would have been interested in what those two acts revealed.

In the first place, Chandler kissed Gayle Dorrington good-by, an act that with some women might mean little or nothing and with others a great deal.

In the second place, Chandler spoke in a low, authoritative voice to Ben Burke, whom he encountered in the shadow of the blacksmith shop: "You've got to get this damned meddler out of the way. He balled up our game once by getting hold of that bullion. He'll do it again. He'll upset our whole plan if he stays here a week. He's that kind. I know, because I have heard of him before. Get him out of the way and do it in a hurry. Go the limit if you have to, but get him away from here. And if you wreck the mine in doing it, I'll add another thousand to what I've already promised you."

# CHAPTER X

At eleven o'clock that night Don Coyote Lawrence plodded into the tunnel with the graveyard shift, blissfully unconscious of the fact that no less a personage than Wilcox Chandler had decreed that his days at the Buckaroo mine were numbered. Even had he known of this fact, it is doubtful if he would have dwelt upon it to any extent. Though he was always ready to meet trouble half way, though there had been occasions when he had even stepped from his path to seek it out as witness his sojourn at the Buckaroo—he was not the man to cross his bridges before he came to them. Besides, there were other matters that for the time being engrossed his attention.

He saw at once that Johnson, the deposed boss of the graveyard, was going to give him trouble. The man was surly and ill-humored. Though he obeyed orders in silence, his work was slovenly and half-hearted. His influence on the other seven men of the shift was bad. Lawrence realized that sooner or later the man's hostility toward him would crystallize into something more serious than loafing on the job. Mining at best is dangerous work. A shift mate who bears a grudge is a constant threat; for a man may, without detection, encourage a rock to fall from the roof of a tunnel, a timber to be misplaced, an ore car to jump the track and crush the object of his enmity.

Don Coyote knew these things as well as the next man. Reckless though he was on occasion, there was still a cautious streak in his nature. Moreover, there was a certain discipline to be maintained.

For an hour or more he bided his time, watching developments and taking the measure of his men. Of the eight, three were openly in sympathy with Johnson. The others appeared to be good miners, interested only in the work of driving the tunnel. Then Don Coyote stepped to the side of the deposed shift boss and said coolly:

"I don't reckon I care to have you on my shift, Johnson. You can either draw your time or change over to another shift."

The man whirled on him with a snarl. "I'll get off this shift when Burke tells me to. Not until! Get that?"

The ex-boss was a burly individual, a good two hundred pounds of bone and muscle. Don Lawrence met his gaze steadily. "No," he decreed, "you'll get off now."

"Huh! Yuh don't say! Do yuh think you're big enough to make me?"

Johnson's inference was plain. If Lawrence let the insult go unchallenged, discipline would be shattered and his usefulness as a boss would be ended.

"I wouldn't be surprised," he remarked.

A right uppercut, rising from somewhere near his knee, caught the ex-boss squarely on the point of the jaw. The man staggered back against the face of the tunnel, more surprised than hurt.

Don Lawrence knew all the rules of rough-and-tumble fighting. He knew that the man who gets in the first blow has the big advantage—if he follows it up. Don Coyote followed that right uppercut with a vicious, whirlwind attack that completely smothered the larger man in a rain of blows. Fists flew from every direction and each fist landed on some vital spot of Johnson's anatomy.

In thirty seconds, without striking a single blow, the larger man went down in the muck of the tunnel. He rose groggily. A fist with one hundred and eighty pounds behind it caught him squarely in the midriff. He went down again and stayed down.

Don Lawrence acted with decision. Grasping the ex-boss about the middle, he picked him up and tossed him into a waiting ore car. "Haul that out to the dump," he ordered one of the muckers, and turned back to his men.

"All right, boys," he grinned cheerfully. "Show's over. Reckon we'll get back to work."

It was all over so quickly that the men could hardly realize what had happened. And yet Don Lawrence knew that he had made at least four friends on the shift. He knew, too, that discipline would not in the future be lacking on the "graveyard."

At two o'clock the crew knocked off work to eat their lunches. Lawrence took his pail from the shelter of a timber, where he had cached it, and sat down on a large rock to eat. The other men started toward the mouth of the tunnel.

"Wait a minute!" he called. "Where you goin'?"

"Out to get our lunches," one of the men answered.

"Out to get your lunches! Say, what kind of a mine is this? Didn't you bring your lunches in with you when you came on shift?"

"Naw. Johnson always let us go out to the cookhouse an' eat."

Lawrence shook his head. "A fine kind of a boss he was, lettin' you men waste time by goin' out of the tunnel to eat!" He hesitated an instant, decided that there was such a thing as overplaying his hand and then said: "All right. Go ahead this time. But tomorrow night you'd best bring your lunches when you come on shift."

The men shuffled off down the tunnel. Lawrence watched their flickering lights until they merged into the darkness. He ate his lunch thoughtfully, oppressed by the weight of his self-imposed responsibility. Though actually he was only a shift boss, the problems that confronted Dorrington had already become his problems. He was as interested in the Buckaroo as though it were his own mine.

For one thing, he meant to make a new survey of the mine, on his own initiative and his own time. Dorrington had said that the tunnel should have cross-cut the old ore chamber, and the ledge of high-grade, several days before. Either the map which he had been following was inaccurate or his figures were in error. Dorrington was no fool and he knew mines—Lawrence was convinced of that. And yet if Burke had had any hand in the surveying, it was quite possible that the discrepancy lay in that direction. Don Coyote meant to find out, anyway.

Another thing that he intended to investigate, as soon as he had the time, was Wilcox Chandler's connection with the Buckaroo. His impression of the mining magnate was not as clear-cut as it might have been. He'd been too embarrassed by Chandler's praise and the proximity of Gayle Dorrington to form an accurate judgment of the man.

The more he thought about it, however, the more convinced he became that Chandler might be the person who was fighting Dorrington. It was quite possible, particularly in view of what he had heard of the tactics used by the elder Chandler in building up his fortune.

"Might be a chip off the ol' block, at that," Lawrence mused as he munched a sandwich. "Either that or he don't know much about the scale of wages for minin' engineers. Ten thousand a year! Huh! If he's heard anything about me at all, he's probably heard that I'm a meddlesome sort o' cuss an' a square shooter in the bargain. An' I got a hunch that that's just the kind of a hombre he don't want on this h'yar job. Yes, siree! That ten thousand looks phoney to me. If he'd made it five thousand, I'd never got suspicious. But ten thousand—h'm! Blamed phoney lookin' to me."

Don Coyote finished his lunch and rolled a cigarette. He took a deep puff and leaned back against the wall of the tunnel.

"Now let's see. Didn't I hear Dorrington say somethin' about the little lady bein' in town with Chandler the afternoon of the stick-up? Seems to me he did say somethin' about it, one time or another. And I know darned well he said that him and the girl was the only ones that knew he was goin' to take that bullion into town."

Lawrence pursed his lips thoughtfully and blew a smoke ring toward the roof of the tunnel. It was whisked away by the strong draft from the air pipe. He nodded.

"Yeh, I'll lay two to one that that's what happened. The li'l lady spilled the beans to Chandler without knowin' she was doin' any harm. Told him her dad was bringin' the bullion to town that afternoon. And Chandler tipped off them two bandits, prob'ly indirectly."

Don Coyote jumped to his feet. "By the Lord, I must be right! Fits right in with what them two stick-up men said out there at the water-hole." He recalled the words of the bandits, as nearly as he could remember them: "He claimed he ought to get a share for tippin' us off. But I told him the old man would

square that with him. That took him back a little.
Never figured fer a minute that I knew the old man
was behind the whole game . . . The old man is
tryin' to bust Dorrington and close down the
Buckaroo."

Don Coyote slapped his knee elatedly. "Plain as the
nose on yer face! This Chandler is the 'old man' them
hombres was talkin' about. Couldn't be nobody else.
He's the boss of Chandler City and bosses are always
known as the 'old man.' Shore now, it's simple as
A, B, C. For some reason Chandler wants to bust
Dorrington. To do it, he's got Burke in here. Burke
is crooked. He probably tipped off Burke about that
bullion and Burke tipped off them two bandits. Shore,
that fits in."

Lawrence took a few steps up and down the tunnel,
running a nervous hand through his thick, dark hair.
"H-m, I don't reckon I'll wait till morning to look
into this thing. I'll get Dorrington out o' bed and talk
things over with him to-night. Mañana may be a right
good word for some folks, but as far as I'm concerned,
it ain't in the dictionary."

He started down the tunnel at a swift pace, murmuring from time to time: "Ten thousand a year! Ten
thousand a year! The big dub! If it hadn't been for
that, I'd never o' got suspicious. Ten thousand bucks!
Huh!"

He passed the ventilating shaft, three thousand feet
from the mouth of the tunnel, and hurried on, busy

with his thoughts.  He had covered another thousand feet or more when he suddenly stopped short, sniffing the air.

Smoke!

# CHAPTER XI

DON COYOTE had known fear before. Not the fear of a bullet or the fear of a fist harder than his own. The fear that every miner knows, paralyzing, blood-chilling. The fear of fire!

Now he knew it again. His heart seemed to rise in his throat. His breathing quickened. His pulse raced. He broke into a run. The smell of smoke grew stronger. Then, rounding a slight turn in the tunnel, he felt a sudden nausea in the pit of his stomach.

Scarcely two hundred feet away the dry timbers of the tunnel were burning fiercely. He stopped, staring bewilderedly at the flames. There was a low rumble. He knew that the roof of the tunnel had caved, its timbers weakened by the fire. Sparks swept toward him. He could almost feel the hot breath of the flames. Dazedly he swung about, knowing that his exit in that direction was definitely cut off.

The only alternative was the ventilating shaft. It was provided with a ladder for just such an emergency. He knew that he could get out that way—provided that the men on the surface had foresight enough to re-verse the fan. As he had observed that afternoon, the ventilating system of the Buckaroo consisted of two fans. The one at the mouth of the tunnel drove fresh air into the workings through a twelve-inch pipe that ran from the entrance to the working face. The other fan, located high on the hill, sucked the foul air out of the tunnel through the ventilating shaft.

The air pipe leading into the tunnel had, of course, been broken by the cave-in, Don Coyote reasoned. The fan on the hill, however, still functioned. Its action was to draw the smoke and the fatal carbon monoxide gas from the fire and up the shaft. Unless it was reversed, and quickly, the shaft would be filled with gas long before Lawrence would be able to gain the surface.

He raced back through the tunnel, his eyes and lungs smarting from the acrid fumes. By the time he reached the shaft, he was puffing, not from his exertions but from lack of oxygen. Grasping the lower rung of the ladder, he swung himself upward like a monkey. The current of air was still upward. The shaft was rapidly filling with smoke and the "white damp" that is the dread of every miner.

Don Coyote fought upward for fifty feet or more. Then, his eyes streaming tears and his lungs choked by the smoke, he realized that he did not have a chance of gaining the surface. The air was becoming more unbreathable every second. His only hope was in descending to the tunnel and taking refuge at the face. There he would have a chance for a few hours. Maybe the fire would burn itself out or some one would think to reverse the fan.

He dropped back down the shaft as fast as he dared,

fell in a heap on the floor of the tunnel and started to crawl toward the face. His head was whirling dizzily. Only by a supreme effort of will could he force his lagging muscles to move.

"Got a touch of white damp already," he told himself. "Gotta get out o' this pronto. Don't take much o' that stuff to knock a man."

The air grew better swiftly. At last he was able to get to his feet and stagger the remaining distance to the face of the tunnel. Here the atmosphere was unpolluted. He sat down on a rock to think the situation over.

Two courses were open to him. He could build a barricade of timbers, chinking the cracks with mud and strips of his clothing. Behind it he would be safe for some time, at least until the oxygen was exhausted —the fire would hardly work that far into the tunnel without fresh air to feed it. The alternative was to wait until some one had the presence of mind to reverse the fan and flood the mine with fresh air, thereby forcing the smoke in the opposite direction and giving him a clear outlet through the shaft.

He decided on the latter course. In the first place he had the strong man's horror of being shut up in the face of danger. And in the second place it was doubtful if he had the strength to build a barrier, weakened as he was by the poisonous fumes.

He settled himself to wait and while he waited a murderous anger took possession of him. The fire in the Buckaroo tunnel had been set deliberately. Of that he was certain. Johnson, Burke, Chandler. One of these men, or all of them, were responsible. Don Coyote swore that he would some day settle accounts with those three gentlemen.

An hour passed. From time to time he walked down the tunnel a ways, eager for the first breath of fresh air that would tell him the fan had been reversed. But it did not come. The air steadily became more visciated, more difficult to breathe, more deadly.

Don Coyote became weaker with every passing moment. He knew now that he had made a mistake. He should have built that barrier, he told himself. Shouldn't have credited anybody around there with any presence of mind. Shouldn't have trusted anybody to think of reversing the fan. Damned fools! Why couldn't they use their heads?

A horrible fear suddenly took possession of him. Suppose Dorrington had refused to reverse the fan, knowing that to pump fresh air into the shaft would prolong the fire until the entire workings were gutted. Don Coyote cursed weakly. Was he to be sacrificed on an altar of selfishness? Was he to die like a trapped rat because Dorrington would not risk his mine to save him?

"No, no, no! Dorrington ain't that kind," he strove to bring reassurance to his rapidly failing heart. "He's been a miner himself. He knows what it means to get trapped. He wouldn't leave me here, without a chance o' gettin' out. He'll reverse that ol' fan. Sure he will. He'll get me out if it wrecks the whole damn' mine."

But time passed, with sickening celerity, and still the rush of air was up the shaft.

It was nearing four o'clock when he made the trip to the shaft that he knew would be his last. His miners' lamp had burned out now and he was too weak to fill it, though the darkness and the roar of the flames and the faint smell of smoke filled his heart with terror.

For five hundred feet he groped his way along between the tracks. The gas was growing worse. Not a breath of fresh air met his parched lungs. He cursed, sobbingly, as he realized that the fan was still drawing the fumes up the shaft.

He stood still a moment, leaning weakly against the wall of the tunnel, summoning strength to take him back to the face. Almost subconsciously he took in the situation. The flames were now within a few hundred feet of the shaft and burning fiercely. Once they reached the shaft and started toward the surface, it would be too late to reverse the fan. To do so then would only force the flames on into the face of the tunnel.

Don Coyote turned weakly and felt his way back along the tunnel. He walked in a daze now, stumbling, falling, recovering himself with difficulty. At last he reached the face, flung himself down in the muck. For a time he fought the wave of lassitude that was creeping over him. At last he gave up, murmuring weakly:

"Damn that li'l lady's ridin' gauntlet!"

# CHAPTER XII

DORRINGTON was awakened shortly after two o'clock that morning by the voice of his superintendent. The man had apparently knocked on his door and, getting no response, had poked his head into the room.

"Mr. Dorrington! Mr. Dorrington!" he was calling excitedly.

The old man sat up hastily, blinking the sleep from his eyes. "What is it, Burke?" he asked.

"There's a fire in the tunnel. Out of control. Looks like a bad one." The voice was high-pitched, almost hysterical.

Dorrington leaped out of bed. "Fire! Good God!" he exclaimed, reaching for his trousers. "Is everybody out?"

"Yes, sir!" came the unsteady response.

"Where is it? How did it happen? Tell me all about it," Dorrington ordered tersely as he flung into his clothes.

"The graveyard came out of the tunnel at two to eat their lunches," Burke began.

"Came out!" the old man barked. "What's the idea of coming out to eat?"

"Johnson always let 'em do it, sir," the superintendent answered apologetically. "I guess Lawrence done the same thing. Anyway, they started back a few minutes ago and found a big blaze about two thousand feet in. They tried to put it out but it had too much of a start on 'em. They battled with it for a while. But the smoke got the best of 'em an' they had to come out. Looks like the whole workings is gone, sir."

Dorrington cursed softly and started toward the door. "Come on," he ordered gruffly.

In the living room he encountered Gayle, who had thrown a bathrobe over her shoulders and hurried out of her room. "What's happened, dad?" she asked in a small voice.

"The workings are afire. You'd better go back to bed, girlie. There's nothing you can do."

"Is—every one out?" the girl asked quickly.

"Yes, so Burke says."

The two men dashed out of the door and around the corner of the house to the entrance of the tunnel. Scantily clad miners were running from the bunkhouse, gathering around the tunnel, talking excitedly. Snatching a light from the cap of one of the men, Dorrington plunged into the workings. Burke followed him, along with several members of the graveyard shift.

The old man did not pause nor speak until he had covered a thousand feet or more. Then he stopped, staring ahead at the wall of flames which blocked the tunnel. He swung around at last.

"No use," he said brokenly. "We'll have to seal her up."

They started back to the surface in silence, hurrying along the runway between the tracks.

"You're positive every one is out?" Dorrington asked after a time.

"Yes, sir. I checked 'em over myself," Burke answered.

"Any idea how it started?"

"Well, I got kind of a hunch," Burke replied evasively.

"Out with it!"

"I'd rather not say right now. I'd like to investigate a little first."

"Where's Lawrence? He ought to know something about this."

"He's gone."

"Gone!"

"Yes, sir. Cleared out."

They had reached the entrance of the tunnel now. Dorrington swung about and regarded the burly superintendent. "Just what do you mean, Burke? Are you insinuating that Lawrence set this fire and then cleared out?"

Burke shrugged his great shoulders. "That's the way it looks, Mr. Dorrington. I ain't makin' no accusations, mind you, but Johnson and two or three of the boys say they saw him headin' down the road on his horse a few minutes ago."

Dorrington glanced over the miners. "Where's Johnson?" he demanded.

The former shift boss elbowed his way through the throng. "Right here, Mr. Dorrington."

The old man scanned him narrowly. "What happened to your face, Johnson?"

Several of the miners snickered. Johnson scowled. "Had a little ruckus with one o' the boys," he answered.

"H-m. Well, how about this? Burke says you saw Lawrence ride away a few minutes ago."

Johnson nodded. "I wouldn't swear it was him. But I'm pretty sure I recognized that roan mare. And nobody else could have been ridin' her because she ain't that kind of a mare. Couple o' the boys tried it this afternoon an' got throwed."

Dorrington turned to one of the men. "Thompson, run over to the barn and see if that roan mare is gone."

The man departed on the run. Dorrington observed another figure trotting along behind him toward the barn; it was Gayle, fully clothed now. The two returned very quickly.

"She's gone," Thompson announced, and Gayle nodded confirmation.

The old man felt suddenly very weak and disheartened. The damage to the Buckaroo was bad enough, coming as it did at a time like this. Very likely it would close them down for good. And yet, somehow, the wreckage of his hopes hurt less than the knowledge that he had misjudged Don Coyote Lawrence. He had liked that young man from the first moment he had seen him, staggering into the living room. The man's personality had drawn him more strongly than any person's he had met in years. The conclusion that he was forced to draw—that Lawrence had fired the Buckaroo—hurt deeply.

"Shut off the fan at the tunnel," he ordered wearily. "No use feeding more air to those flames."

"How about the fan on the hill?" some one asked.

"Let it run. It's not doing any harm."

Dorrington ran a weary hand across his forehead. He seemed dazed, so completely disheartened that he did not care what happened to the mine. Everything was lost anyway, the mine, the possibility of realizing his dreams, his faith in mankind, everything. He tried to rally, tried to bring himself to take steps toward getting the fire under control. But he had lost heart completely, seemingly irrevocably.

Then a small arm went around his waist. A small hand grasped the lapel of his coat. "It can't be so bad, dad," Gayle whispered cheeringly. "Let's fight it, dad. They've got us down, but we aren't beaten yet. Let's show them that we know how to fight. Won't you, dad?"

He looked down at her slender face. In spite of himself he smiled at her insistence. "Of course we'll fight, girlie," he said, not without some effort. "We'll put that fire out first and then we'll go ahead and reach that ore chamber. Sure we'll fight."

"That's the old spirit, dad," the girl applauded.

Dorrington turned to his men, whom Burke had herded away from the tunnel. The superintendent was talking to them now. Dorrington didn't catch the words but he did catch the tone of the big man's voice —it was threatening, decidedly so. He wondered at the incident for a moment and as quickly forgot it as plans for combating the fire crowded into his mind.

"Burke, get your men on the job," he ordered tersely. "There's no time to waste. Get planks and board up the entrance to the tunnel. One layer of planks as close together as possible. Nail tarpaulins over that, blankets, anything. Several thicknesses of them. Then another layer of planks. Hurry now!"

The men scattered as Burke bawled his commands. All but two of them. These two hesitated in front of the superintendent. Had Dorrington's perception been a bit keener, he would have recognized them as members of the graveyard shift. They said something to Burke and like a flash the big superintendent's fist shot out, once, twice. The men dropped like logs.

"After this you obey orders, see?" Burke bellowed. "Now go get them planks like I told you."

Dorrington's jaw set. He didn't like that sort of thing. There were other ways to maintain discipline besides brute force. He made a mental note to speak to Burke about it later. Then he turned about to take a hand in the sealing of the tunnel.

The work progressed slowly, far slower than it should have. The nails, which should have been in the blacksmith shop, were mysteriously missing. Half an hour passed before they were found in a corner of the cookhouse. Burke was excited and knocked the cook down, though that individual protested vehemently that he had had nothing to do with moving the nails.

There was a shortage of suitable planks, too. Several had to be ripped off the side of the mill and pressed into use. Though apparently trying his best to speed the work, Burke got in the way of the men and actually slowed it down. All in all, it was a nerve-wracking job and its completion found Dorrington and his men on edge. The old man sighed with relief and shook his head.

"If that's the type of superintendent I've had on my payroll," he told himself, "I think I'd better get a new one. He works hard but he seems to do more harm than good."

He glanced at his watch. It was nearly four. The sealing of the tunnel had consumed almost an hour. The ventilating shaft, he knew, should be sealed, too, although it did not make a great deal of difference so long as the fan was drawing the air out. He decided, however, that it might as well be done then as later.

He had given the order and started the men up the hill with the necessary materials, when he saw Gayle running across the flat from the direction of the barn.

"Dad!" she called to him. "Come here quickly."

There was something in the tone of her voice that made Dorrington run anxiously to her side. "Gayle! What is it?"

She met his eyes. He saw that her face was white and tense in the moonlight. "Don Lawrence's mare has come back to the barn!"

"Come back!" Dorrington exclaimed. "Did Lawrence come back, too?"

"Lawrence didn't come back," the girl told him soberly, "because he never went away."

"Gayle! What do you mean?"

"Lawrence is in the tunnel!"

Dorrington was conscious of a bulky form at his side.

"Lawrence ain't in the tunnel, miss," Ben Burke contradicted flatly. "The boys seen him ride away just before they discovered the fire."

The girl whirled on him furiously. "Burke, you keep out of this!" she cried angrily. "I'm talking to my father and I don't care to be interrupted!"

The superintendent took a step backward, plainly amazed at her fury. Gayle went on. "Lawrence didn't ride that mare away from here. No one rode her away. She was led away. I know because I looked at the cinch on her saddle. And it was fastened as no man who ever saddled a horse before would fasten a cinch. And it was loose, so loose that a man couldn't ride in that saddle without its sliding off."

Dorrington stared at her, pondering deeply. "Possibly—Lawrence was thrown. The cinch—many have worked loose."

"No, no, no!" the girl expostulated. "That mare could never have thrown Lawrence. He's not that kind. Besides, I tell you that no man who knew the first thing about riding would fasten a cinch like that one was fastened."

Dorrington's shoulders squared. "How long has the mare been back?" he asked quickly.

"I don't know. One of the men told me she was in the barn. I won't tell you who it was—" she glanced scornfully at Burke— "but he said he was almost certain that Lawrence never came out of the mine."

The old man whirled on the superintendent. Though Dorrington was a small man, the other took an involuntary step backward. "You hear that?" Dorrington cried. His face was white with fury. The accusing finger that he raised was trembling. "You blundering fool! If we don't get Lawrence out of this mine alive, so help me God, I'll kill you, Burke!"

# CHAPTER XIII

DORRINGTON thought swiftly. There was one chance that Lawrence might yet be alive—if he had taken refuge at the face of the tunnel. It was a slim chance, to be sure, considering the time that had elapsed since the fire started. It was very probable that the deadly white damp had seeped into every part of the workings by this time. Nevertheless, he was determined to do everything in his power to effect a rescue. Reversal of the fan might result in the total destruction of the mine's timbering; it might result in the tunnel's caving in a hundred places; it might result in the wrecking of the whole enterprise. Dorrington knew these things as well as the next man. But he did not give them a thought—there was no price that could be set on a human life.

"Burke, get up the hill and reverse that fan," Dorrington ordered. "Take half a dozen men with you and wait for me at the head of the shaft."

Burke shifted uneasily. Even in the moonlight Dorrington could see that his small eyes were feverishly ·bright. "If you reverse the fan and fill the mine with fresh air," the superintendent reminded haltingly, "that fire'll gut the whole workings."

"Let it!" Dorrington shot back. "What do we care

about the workings when a man's life is in danger? Now get up there and do as I tell you. And take plenty of lights with you. We're going down the shaft."

"We!" It was a gasp, almost a cry of anguish.

"You heard me! Now move!"

While Burke stumbled up the hill, Dorrington ran back to the tunnel. The men were still grouped about the entrance, talking in low tones.

"Tear that cover off, men," Dorrington ordered. "Lawrence is in that tunnel and he may still be alive. Burke has gone to reverse the fan. We've got to have a draft through the tunnel or the gas will be forced into every part of the workings."

The men fell to with a will, urged on by excitement and Dorrington's crisp words. The old man watched them a moment, saw the work well under way and then ran over to the house. He disappeared for a moment. When he returned, he found Gayle waiting on the porch. She saw him slip a revolver into his pocket.

"What are you going to do?" she asked, her voice trembling despite her efforts to be calm.

"I am going to force that yellow dog Burke to go down the shaft with me," Dorrington returned coldly.

"You think there's a chance—of finding him alive?"

"Yes. A chance—that's all."

Suddenly the girl threw her arms about him. "Oh, dad, you'll be careful, won't you?" she pleaded. "It's so dangerous—that white damp. You can't smell it. You can't see it. You don't even know it's there until it's too late. Won't you let me telephone to town?

We could send for masks. They could be here in no time at all."

"No, dear. There isn't time. Every minute counts now. We'll have to go in without masks."

He bent down and kissed her hurriedly, and then broke away and started up the hill. He knew she was following but he did not look back.

When he arrived at the shaft, breathless after the swift walk up the trail, he found Burke and half a dozen miners grouped around the little shack that housed the fan. He put his hand over the exhaust, saw that the fan had been reversed and was pumping air down the shaft, and turned to Burke:

"Come on, Burke," he ordered in a low voice. "We'll start down now."

Burke shook his head wildly; his eyes were wide, staring. "I ain't goin'. I ain't goin' to risk my life when it's ten to one he ain't in there. No, sir. Not me."

Dorrington whipped out his revolver. "You'll go, Burke, and you'll go now. If you don't, I'll kill you where you stand."

The statement, without doubt, was an exaggeration —Bill Dorrington was no killer. But even in the moonlight, Burke could see the fury that blazed in the older man's eyes. He hesitated, doubtless deciding which was apt to prove the least dangerous, Dorrington's gun or the white damp in the mine. He chose to face the latter. Turning without a word, he stumbled into the fan house and started down the shaft. Dorrington accepted a proffered lamp.

"If any of you men are willing to come with us, I'd like to have you," he said. "I shall not order you down, however. Not *you.*"

Three of the miners stepped forward without hesitation.

"We'll go with you, Mr. Dorrington," one of them declared. "If an old man like you is game to face it, I guess we ought to be. Let's go."

Dorrington's heart warmed with gratitude as they started down the shaft. He well knew the respect in which a miner holds the white damp which forms in a burning mine. Of all the dangers he is called upon to face, he fears this the most. The constant handling of high explosives, the ever-present danger from falling rocks, the possibilities of being entombed alive—these are nothing compared with his dread of gas. Care, proper timbering, good workmanship may reduce all other dangers to a minimum. But white damp may be combated only with gas masks—and there were none available.

The five men moved down the ladders slowly. Burke first, then Dorrington, then the three volunteers. Though haste was urgent, Dorrington did not dare go too fast. It was imperative that the fan be given time to clear every bit of gas out of the shaft—one breath of the deadly carbon monoxide would cause death.

By the time they reached the foot of the shaft, all five of them were exhausted, as much by the uncertainty and suspense and fear as by their exertions. The fire had burned to within twenty feet of the shaft. They could feel its hot breath on their faces as, fanned by the sudden rush of fresh air, it flamed fiercely.

Though the current of air was toward the mouth of the tunnel, away from the shaft and the face of the workings, Dorrington knew that there was not a moment to waste. The fire would creep back. Five minutes might see their escape cut off.

"You men wait here," he ordered the miners. "Burke and I will go in to the face."

The huge superintendent literally cowered at the words. "We ain't got time," he groaned. "The fire'll be here in a minute or two. We'll never get out. Besides, there's gas in there. I know it."

Dorrington did not need to draw his gun this time. His hand moved toward his pocket and Burke swung around. Holding his light high above his head, the superintendent raced toward the face of the tunnel, with Dorrington hard put to keep at his heels.

Burke had been right. There was gas in that section of the tunnel. Not a great deal, probably only the most minute quantity. But there was enough that Dorrington felt it. His head reeled, a great weariness seized his muscles. Burke felt it, too. He was staggering now, glancing over his shoulder appealing from time to time, plunging on when he saw no signs of relenting in the old man's set face.

They found Don Coyote lying on his back at the face of the tunnel. He did not move as Dorrington bent over him and called his name. The old man did not take time to feel for a pulse. He straightened up hastily, gritting his teeth when he found his legs hardly strong enough to support him.

"Bring him along," he ordered.

"But he's dead!" the superintendent gasped. "It's all I'll be able to do to carry myself out."

Dorrington dared not take time to argue with the man. He bent down and grasped Lawrence's feet. "Help me, damn you!" he commanded.

Burke did as he was ordered now, probably because he was too dazed by gas and fear to resist. He caught hold of Lawrence's arms and together the two men started down the tunnel toward the shaft. They had traveled only a few feet when Dorrington stumbled and fell. He got up slowly, finding the task almost too much for him.

Burke took one glance at the old man. Then he shouldered the lifeless form. "Carry him—by myself —faster," he muttered, and plodded off down the tunnel.

How Burke gained the shaft with his burden Dorrington never knew. He saw the superintendent's light dwindling into the distance and started out to follow it—he had lost his own lamp when he fell. Only half conscious, he stumbled along between the rails, tempted every moment to lie down and give up the ordeal of trying to save himself. Minutes passed, during which he staggered forward dazedly.

Then two lights loomed up suddenly before him.

He saw two vague forms. He felt himself picked up and rushed along through the tunnel. Then a blast of cool, pure air struck his face. He gulped it down. His senses cleared with surprising rapidity. He saw Burke leaning weakly against the ladder, gasping like a fish out of water. Lawrence's form still draped grotesquely across his shoulders.

"You'll be all right in a minute, Mr. Dorrington," one of the miners was assuring him. "Just got a touch of gas. Fresh air'll fix you up. But we better get out o' here. The fire'll be on top of us in another minute."

"I'm ready," Dorrington smiled weakly. "Let's go. You boys help Burke with Lawrence. The lad's heavy. I can get along by myself now."

The superintendent, however, shook his head when the miners stepped toward him. "Carry him myself!" he muttered doggedly. "Lemme alone."

"Better let us give you a hand," one of the men advised. "You're all in, Burke. That gas got you."

"Gas be damned! I'm all right."

There was a wild look in his eyes, a queer twist to his thick mouth. He seemed almost like a madman as he stared at them belligerently, blinking very rapidly, gulping great lungfuls of air. Then he turned around, caught the ladder with his huge hands and started upward. One of the miners tapped his head and nodded significantly to Dorrington.

"Nutty," he decreed. "Better let him have his way."

Dorrington nodded, feeling all at once a great rush of pity for the big superintendent. The man deserved no pity, he knew that; he deserved no sympathy, no consideration of any kind. And yet Dorrington was unaccountably sorry for him as he fought up the ladder with his heavy burden.

The old man and the miners started up behind the superintendent. As Dorrington climbed, inhaling deeply of the pure air which rushed down the shaft, he felt the lassitude leaving his muscles. They worked up slowly, knowing that they were out of danger even though the mine by now might be a flaming furnace. If the fan should break down—well, Dorrington put the thought out of his mind. The fan wasn't going to break down.

The climb was a long one, a thousand feet or more, and long before he reached the top, Dorrington realized that he was a very weary man. Doggedly he refused help from his men. If Burke could make it with a hundred and eighty pounds across his shoulders, he could certainly do it alone. Nevertheless, he was several minutes behind the superintendent when he gained the fan house. He paused there a moment, catching his breath, and then hurried out into the moonlight.

He found a wide circle of men. Gayle was at the edge of it. In the center was Burke, methodically applying artificial respiration to Don Coyote.

"Is he—alive?" Dorrington asked anxiously.

The superintendent did not respond. He was muttering to himself, unintelligibly, awesomely, as he worked over Lawrence. Gayle was at her father's side by now.

"Don't go near him, dad!" she pleaded, in a terrified whisper. "He knocked three men down who tried to help him with Lawrence. I believe—he's mad!"

"Nonsense!" Dorrington scoffed. "He's mad, all right. Mad with anger."

He crossed the intervening space and knelt at Burke's side. "Any signs of life, Ben?"

Without for an instant losing the rhythm of his task, Burke's heavy arm flung out and knocked Dorrington backward into the dirt.

"Lemme alone!" he muttered, in an odd, strained voice. "Lemme alone, damn yuh!"

Dorrington recovered himself and got to his feet. He stared at Burke for a moment and then shrugged his shoulders. The man was doing his work well; no one could have applied artificial respiration more efficiently. Best to let him alone until he recovered from his tantrum, or whatever it was that possessed him.

"You men get down the hill and seal the tunnel again," Dorrington ordered quietly. "Stop the fan first. As soon as you get the tunnel sealed, come up here and close up the shaft. Hurry now, boys. Every foot of timbering you save means dollars to the company."

The men hurried off down the hill, leaving Dorrington and his daughter alone with Burke and Lawrence. The old man and the girl stood side by side, saying nothing, watching the slow, even movements of the big superintendent as he drew Lawrence's arms over his head, paused, brought them to his side, paused, moved them over his head again, in endless, monotonous repetition.

"He moved!" the girl whispered suddenly, straining forward.

Dorrington nodded. "I think he's coming to now."

"Oh, I'm so glad!" Gayle breathed fervently. "It would have been terrible if he'd lost his life in our mine, after all he did for us."

A moment later they saw Burke draw Don Coyote to a sitting posture. Lawrence blinked a moment, rubbed his eyes, took a slow, deep breath. Then they saw his lips curve into a smile.

"Hello, Burke," he said, rather feebly. "I guess— I'm all right—now. Is the—fire out?"

The huge superintendent grunted and got to his feet. He grinned broadly, a grin that was half a sneer. Then, with a wave of his arm as though he were washing his hands of the whole affair, he stumbled off down the trail chuckling to himself.

A few moments later, as the old man and Gayle were helping Don Coyote to his feet, a burst of demoniac laughter floated up the hill.

# CHAPTER XIV

FOR several minutes Don Coyote stood regarding Dorrington and his daughter. The overpowering anger he had felt a short time before, when he reached the conclusion that the tunnel had been deliberately fired, had passed. He was dizzy now. His head was whirling. It ached fearfully. And as he met the level gaze of the old man a feeling of shame came over him. He suddenly held out his hand.

"Mr. Dorrington, I want to apologize," he said unsteadily. "When I was trapped down there in the tunnel, waitin' for somebody to help me out, I got the idea that you refused to reverse the fan for fear o' destroyin' the whole workings. I was wrong, o' course. I should have knowed better than to think you'd be that onery. I begs your pardon, sir."

Dorrington took the outstretched hand warmly. In the moonlight, Don Coyote could see a sheepish smile twist the corners of his mouth. "Lawrence, if you are honorable enough to apologize for misjudging me," the old man said, "I guess I should do the same thing by you. Some of the boys told me they saw you riding away from the mine just before the fire was discovered. Your mare was gone and I naturally got the idea that you had set the fire and escaped."

Don Coyote's tall figure straightened. "My mare was gone!"

"Yes. Some one had led her off. It wasn't until she came back to the stable that it dawned on me that you might still be in the mine."

Lawrence nodded wearily. He was still too weak from his experience to think coherently. The conclusion, however, was so obvious that no great mental effort was required. He had been the victim of a plot, engineered most likely by Burke or Johnson, to wreck the mine and get him out of the way at the same time. He said as much to Dorrington as the three of them started down the hill.

"Yes, it begins to look that way," the old man admitted reluctantly. "Some one, whoever is trying to wreck the Buckaroo, is afraid of you."

Don Coyote smiled, though there was little of humor in the situation. "I reckon they've heard that I'm a pryin', inquisitive sort of cuss."

"I'm glad you are," Dorrington returned. "And I only hope that this affair to-night won't scare you out. I think I need you here and need you badly. You won't leave us, will you?"

"Leave yuh?" Don Coyote came back. "Say now, you couldn't drag me away from this h'yar mine with a ten-mule team. No, siree! I'm with yuh to the end."

"Thanks, Lawrence," Dorrington said with quiet heartiness. "If I make a go of this mine, you won't regret your action. Though as things stand now, it looks mighty dubious. This fire will set us back

months. If we pull through at all, it will be a miracle."
They had reached the clearing before the house. "You
two go in and wait for me. I want to see that the
mine is properly sealed."

Lawrence started to protest but the old man waved
him aside. "No, you've got to rest awhile. Go on
in and sit down and take it easy. A man can't get
knocked out by that white damp and go back to work
the next minute. Wait till your head clears a bit and
you feel better. I'll be along shortly. I want to talk
things over with you."

Without further protest Lawrence followed Gayle
into the house. The girl switched on a light and
motioned to a chair. She watch him as he sat down
and smiled commisseratingly when she saw that his
movements were rather feeble.

"You're feeling pretty shaky, aren't you?" she suggested.

"Well," he grinned, "I've felt a lot worse in my life
—and a lot better, too."

"Will you let me make you a cup of coffee?"

"Oh, don't trouble yourself. I'll be all right in a
few minutes."

"It won't be a bit of trouble," she said quickly.
"Besides, I could drink a cup myself. Excuse me and
I'll put it on the stove. It will only take a few minutes."

His mind was in an odd turmoil as he watched her
leave the room. He knew that he should be angry.
He knew that there should be no room in his thoughts
for anything save Burke and Johnson and Chandler,

and the wrong they had done him. His thoughts now, he told himself, should be centered on squaring accounts. There was no doubt but that one or all of those men had had a hand in the plot to kill him and wreck the Buckaroo. His self-respect demanded that he settle matters as soon as he felt able, that very night if possible.

And yet, strangely, he had difficulty in keeping his thoughts on that particular problem. Persistently they strayed to Gayle Dorrington. Though she had left the room, her face remained before him, wistful, tender, altogether adorable. He found himself growing restless waiting for the reappearance of her slender form.

Don Coyote sighed, very deeply. "Shore now, I can't be fallin' in love," he told himself. He considered the thought. "Or am I? Somethin' is shore wrong with me. Either it's love or that blamed gas. Pretty hard to tell. Reckon they both affect a feller the same way."

Then she was back. "Just a few more minutes," she told him.

The girl stood in front of him a moment, tilting her head to one side and looking quizzically into his eyes. Don Coyote's heart skipped a beat as he met her gaze. She was so near, so irresistible, it took all his will to keep from reaching out for her.

"You are coming around fine," Gayle smiled. "Your color is much better."

Which observation, considering that Don Coyote

was at that moment blushing furiously, did not require unusual powers of perception.

"Wait! I'll put a pillow behind your head. You'll be more comfortable."

Don Coyote gulped. A pillow! A woman putting a pillow behind his head! It was almost too much. He struggled for words as she ran across the room to the old sofa, picked up a bright-colored cushion and returned to his chair. Talkative though he was by nature, he found himself suddenly stricken dumb by the mere proximity of a beautiful woman. The realization angered him.

He raised his hand in protest. But her slender fingers were already on his head, moving it gently forward. He felt the pillow slide down behind him. He looked up, a bit dazed now, certainly not himself. Her face was but a few inches from his. His outstretched hand met hers, quite by accident. He caught it, gripped it so tightly that the smile on her lips was suddenly swept away. Slowly, irresistibly, he drew her toward him.

Don Coyote saw her dark eyes widen with surprise, consternation, fear. He was suddenly overcome, releasing her hand as abruptly as he had taken it. He was utterly ashamed. He, Don Coyote, had brought fear into a woman's eyes. He wanted to flee, never to see Gayle Dorrington or the Buckaroo again as long as he lived.

Coolly came her voice, as from a great distance. "I think the coffee must be ready now. I'll get it."

He was too dazed by the enormity of his crime—and to Don Coyote it was a crime, no less—to realize what she had said. He knew only that she was hurrying out of the room. She was going to call her father, he reflected. The old man would kick him off the place— and it would serve him right, too.

"What a consarned fool I turned out to be," he groaned, writhing in his chair. "As decent a little girl as ever came over the pike. And me tryin' to kiss her —when I've only known her about twenty-four hours. How in the name of tarnation did I get that way?"

# CHAPTER XV

Don Coyote started to rise from his chair and then sat down again abruptly. No use running away, he told himself. Might as well stay and face the music. He started as he heard her step and saw her hurrying into the room with two cups of steaming coffee. She placed them on the mantel, crossed the room to the table and pulled it over in front of him.

Don Coyote stared up at her dumbly, incredulously. Apparently the calamity he feared had, for the time being, been miraculously averted. And yet her attitude toward him was different. He saw that immediately. Her smile was not cold—but it was not warm. Her manner, although not exactly distant, was polite rather than friendly. ·

"Will you have cream and sugar?" she asked, as she moved the cups to the table.

"Thanks, ma'am," he answered miserably. "I'll take it black."

As he gulped the fiery liquid, quite oblivious to the fact that it burned his throat, he realized that she was scrutinizing him thoughtfully. He colored under her direct gaze and immediately hated himself for his show of emotion. Vaguely he felt that he should apologize for his actions. And yet how could he? There was no excuse he could offer. Besides, he had wanted to kiss her. He still wanted to, for that matter.

Then she spoke, and her words were like a cool mountain breeze to a man who had been long on a sun-drenched desert. "Do you think that was a deliberate attempt to kill you?"

He wanted to shout for joy. Commonplace though her words were, they showed plainly that she had chosen to overlook his gross breach of etiquette. Not forget it—no, she wasn't that kind. Just overlook it, possibly forgive it.

"It was an attempt to kill two birds with one stone," he answered brightly. "Me and the Buckaroo."

"But why should any one want to kill you?" Gayle asked.

"Because I have a reputation for not mindin' my own business. It's a habit o' mine, always prowlin' around buttin' into somebody else's affair. Like returnin' that glove to you. An' like goin' after them two road agents. It shore wasn't no business o' mine and yet there I was, little Johnny-on-the-spot."

The girl smiled whimsically, in a way that made Don Lawrence's heart flutter.

"You're sort of a Don Quixote, aren't you?"

Lawrence gulped and a beaming smile illumined his ruddy face. "Miss Dorrington, you're the second little lady that's called me that," he told her elatedly. "Fact is, I'm known all over the southwest as Don Coyote. That's what the boys down there called this Quixote feller that used to ride his cayuse round the range takin' pot shots at windmills."

He rushed on volubly, overjoyed at the way she had

hit upon his nickname. "Funny feller, that Quixote person. He must have been loco, don't you reckon? I never could figure why he went around shootin' up windmills. But I've heard tell that was his favorite game. Liked it better'n poker. Maybe you could tell me, Miss Dorrington. You've read about him a lot, I guess."

She nodded seriously, trying valiantly to keep from smiling. "Yes, I've read quite a bit about Don Quixote. And the more I think about it, the more I realize how fittingly this little lady, as you call her, named you. Don Quixote was quite a Lothario."

The young man blinked and thought a moment. Then he shook his head bewilderedly. "Nobody ever called me that before," he told her. "I reckon if you were a man I'd have to fight. Is it much worse than a pole-cat?"

She laughed at this and was immediately penitent. "We ought to be ashamed of ourselves, sitting here, joking when the Buckaroo is in flames."

Don Coyote jerked erect. "That's right, ma'am. I'm sorry. Reckon I better get outside and lend a hand."

"No, you sit still," she interposed hastily. "There are plenty of men. You've done enough for one night. You stay right here until dad gets back. He said he wanted to talk to you."

Lawrence relaxed constrainedly. Now that she called it to mind, he felt a bit conscience-stricken. There was nothing wrong with him now. He should be out there with the men. And yet her tone had been authoritative. He didn't quite know which would be worse, to shirk when the others were working or disobey her direct orders. He sensed, somehow, that Gayle Dorrington wasn't used to being disobeyed.

Before he could make up his mind footsteps sounded on the porch and Dorrington poked his head through the doorway. White and strained he looked, very old and weary.

"Haven't seen Burke, have you?" he asked anxiously.

Lawrence and Gayle shook their heads.

"Why, dad?" the girl asked.

"I'm afraid he's lost his mind. He met one of the boys down by the cookhouse and jumped on him for no reason at all. Almost killed the poor fellow. Then he disappeared."

Gayle's face paled. There were few things she feared. But an insane man—

"You think he is dangerous, dad?" she asked hesitantly.

The old man shrugged. "Never know about a crazy man, Gayle. Burke always has been a bit light-headed, you know. Never too steady. I guess that trip into the mine was too much for him. If a man is a coward at heart, fear is liable to do most anything to him. But don't worry. I think he's cleared out. I just thought I'd take a look around to make sure."

"You'll be back soon?" Gayle asked.

"Just a few minutes. We're going up on the hill to close the shaft now. It won't take long."

Don Coyote started to rise from his chair. "Reckon I better go with you."

Dorrington shook his head and glanced meaningly at Gayle. "I'd rather you stayed here," he said casually. "You can't be any too strong yet. Besides, I have more men than I can use." He smiled reassuringly at his daughter. "I'll be back in just a few minutes, girlie."

He closed the door and they heard his hurried footsteps retreating across the porch. The man and the girl looked at each other across the table. Gayle's face was white now. The look in her wide dark eyes was almost the same as he had seen there when he had tried to kiss her.

Don Coyote smiled reassuringly. "There ain't nothin' to worry about. Burke'll come out of it all right. I've seen lots of 'em go loco from fear. And they haven't always been cowards, either. Fear is a dangerous thing if a man has got a bit too much imagination. An' fear of that white damp that you can't see nor smell nor taste is the worst kind o' fear I know of. I ain't backward about admittin' that I been afraid of a lot o' things in my life."

He might have added that at the present time he was more afraid of a certain woman's smile than he was of a dozen Ben Burkes. But instead he said: "I wonder if you wouldn't tell me somethin' about this Don Quixote feller that you two little ladies named me after. I never heard much about him, 'ceptin' how he always hankered to shoot up windmills. Who was the hombre? What range did he ride?"

She smiled in spite of herself. "Don Quixote was a knight, a very famous and very valiant knight. And his range was—well, most of Europe, I suppose."

"But these h'yar windmills now—"

"Oh, that was just one incident in a long and variegated career. He did lots of other things besides—"

The girl broke off. Glancing up at her, Don Coyote saw the pupils of her eyes dilate. He saw her lips part. He even saw the rapid beating of the pulse in her white throat.

He did not turn at once. He knew without turning that the door had been noiselessly opened and that Ben Burke stood watching them.

# CHAPTER XVI

PERHAPS for the first time since his rescue, Don Lawrence came to an acute realization of the fact that his unpleasant experience in the mine had weakened him greatly. At another time he would not have shrunk particularly from an encounter with Ben Burke. The man was larger and heavier than he by sixty or eighty pounds. In fact, he was one of the largest and most sturdily built men he had ever seen. Still, there were other things that counted more in a fight than weight—agility, speed, skill, fighting spirit.

At the present time, however, Don Coyote felt that he possessed none of these qualities. He knew, too, that it would be useless to call for help. Dorrington and the men were far up the hillside, working noisily. His cries would go unheard. He was not without hope, however. He might be able to talk Burke out of any intended violence, or at least put him off until Dorrington returned.

Don Coyote rose from his chair and very casually turned around. Though no man had ever accused him of being a coward, his courage ebbed when he saw the look in Burke's face. The man was crazed, there was no doubt about that. His pale blue eyes were wide and glassy. His thick lips were parted in a snarl, showing discolored, uneven teeth. His breath hissed with every quick, labored exhalation.

For a long moment the eyes of the two men met. Neither moved while they measured each other carefully. Then Don Coyote smiled mildly and nodded.

"Come in, Burke," he invited. "How's the work gettin' along?"

As casually as possible, though the strain brought the perspiration out in little drops on his forehead, Lawrence turned his back on the intruder and resumed his seat.

"Care for a cup of coffee?" he asked, without looking around. "I reckon there's some left. Would you mind goin' out and gettin' it, Miss Dorrington?"

The girl caught her cue and rose. But something in her movements, her white face, must have warned Burke.

"You stay where yuh are!" he ordered sharply.

Don Coyote heard the door close, the latch click, and then a stealthy tread behind him. He waited, racking his brain wildly for some ruse that would stay the huge superintendent. But his mind seemed an utter blank. It whirled dazedly, like a circling buzzard, refusing to come to earth. He heard another step behind him. Then Burke's hoarse voice.

"You move an' I'll kill you, Lawrence. I got no fight to pick with you. It's with that damned woman. She—"

Don Coyote rose quietly and turned toward the big superintendent. "No fight to pick with me?" he repeated calmly. "That sounds kind o' funny, considerin' that you tried to murder me a short while ago."

Burke accepted the statement without argument. "That was different. I tried to get you out o' the way, mebbe, but I'd never have been dragged into that mine if it hadn't been for that woman there. She found out about your horse comin' back. She told the old man that you was still in the tunnel. And he dragged me into that—that—" his voice rose shrilly—"that damned white damp! It's her fault, by God! It's her fault!"

Burke strode toward the table, his great fists raised over his head. Don Coyote stepped out of his path, watching him closely. The man had no eye for anything save Gayle. He reached the table, swung around it. Eyes wide with terror, the girl crouched in her chair. Her lips were parted but no sound came from them.

Don Coyote swung suddenly around, grasped his chair and raised it high in the air. With one leap he was on the table. Before Burke had time to dodge or ward off the blow, Lawrence brought the heavy chair down over the superintendent's head with every ounce of strength in his body.

It was a terrific blow, a blow that would have felled an ox. It smashed the chair to fragments. Burke staggered under it, slipped to one knee, rocked back and forth for a brief instant and was on his feet again.

Lawrence gasped, hardly able to credit his eyes. A blow like that would have killed an ordinary man. And yet it had not so much as knocked Burke off his feet.

The man was inhuman. He had no nerves, no sense of pain.

The unexpected attack, however, had diverted his attention from Gayle. He whirled around. With a growl like an enraged animal he leaped at Lawrence. The latter jumped backward and landed on the floor on all fours. He squatted there an instant, waiting to see which way Burke would come around the table.

But the big superintendent did not come around the table. He picked the table up in his great paws, raised it high overhead and hurled it with all his might at Don Coyote. The latter sprawled flat on his face, the heavy piece of furniture missing his head by inches. He was on his feet again in an instant, but he saw at once that it was no longer possible to evade a hand to hand encounter.

He squared off warily, knowing that if Burke once got those huge arms around him, the big man could crush the life out of him with hardly an effort. The superintendent lunged toward him wildly, his knotted fists fanning the air. Don Coyote sidestepped neatly, lashed out with his right fist and caught Burke squarely on the point of the jaw. The blow was not a gentle one; his whole weight, backed by desperation, was behind it. Yet it glanced off the big man's iron jaw like a drop of rain on a tin roof.

Burke whirled and came at him again, his eyes staring with an insane light, his arms flailing. Again Don Coyote dodged the sledgehammer blows that were aimed at him. From the corner of his eye he saw that Gayle was moving. She was taking something down from a nail on the wall. A gun? No. It was something round.

Then Burke was on him again. The big man was more wary now. He did not come at him in a whirlwind rush. He stalked him slowly, driving him toward a corner. Don Coyote retreated cautiously, never daring to take his eyes from Burke. If only Gayle would get out. She had a chance now. Burke's back was to her. But she made no move toward the door. She was fumbling with something. Don Coyote dared not raise his glance from Burke to see what.

The superintendent swung. Don Coyote blocked the blow, though it jarred him from head to foot. He countered swiftly, aiming at the other's solar plexus. The blow was accurate but he might as well have smashed his fist against the side of an oak barrel, for all the effect it had on the crazed superintendent.

Don Coyote became a bit panic-stricken. He wasn't used to this sort of fighting. When he struck a man as hard as he had struck Burke, he was used to seeing him go down, or at least show that he had felt the blow. But not so this berserk gorilla. Three blows he had received, any one of which would have knocked out an ordinary man. And yet they had had no more effect on him than the playful taps of a four-year-old child.

Don Coyote was against the wall now. He did not aim another blow at Burke. He knew it was useless. The superintendent came toward him slowly, one cautious step at a time, his two arms outstretched like a man stalking a calf in the corner of a corral. Lawrence gritted his teeth and waited. Then, when Burke was almost upon him, he lowered his head and sought to dive under the man's arm. But Burke was too fast for him. He caught him around the waist, enfolded him with both of those thick arms and drew him in slowly against his steel-ribbed chest.

Don Coyote did not give up easily. His heavy boot beat a swift tattoo on the other's shins. He had the satisfaction of feeling Burke wince. That was all. The vice-like grip grew tighter, crushing the breath from his lungs. With his face pressed tightly against Burke's neck, he could see nothing. He prayed that Gayle had fled the room. It might be possible for her to get help before his ribs were crushed in that inhuman embrace.

The world whirled about him dizzily. The smell of sweat was strong in his nostrils. Fight against it as he would, he felt himself slowly losing consciousness.

# CHAPTER XVII

Don Coyote was nearly out when he felt Burke's form suddenly relax. The big man screamed shrilly, a scream that was cut off almost at its inception. He released Lawrence and the young man dropped to his knees. He was on his feet again almost at once. Hazy though the scene was at first, it crystallized after a moment like a motion picture brought suddenly into focus.

Burke was clawing frantically at his neck, which had been caught in the loop of a lariat. Gayle, at the other end of the line, was valiantly throwing all her weight on it. The big man lunged toward her and the rope grew slack. The loop was jammed, however, jammed so tightly that Burke was for the moment unable to free it from his neck.

Don Coyote saw the situation at a glance. Left to himself, Burke would be able to get free before the line strangled him. The young man leaped toward the superintendent, raining blows on his face and head as fast as he could hurl his fists. The attack was so sudden and so vicious that Burke for an instant forgot the danger of that rope around his neck.

He fought back at Lawrence, while Gayle jerked the rope tighter. The big man's breath came in shrill wheezes, like a drowning man gasping for air. For several moments they fought toe to toe. Then, seeing that Burke was growing weaker, Don Coyote dove and caught him by the knees. They went down in a struggling, squirming heap.

"Tighter, Gayle!" Lawrence shouted. "Haul on it, li'l lady!"

Gayle hauled, with the strength of desperation. The giant's movements grew more feeble. Claw as he would at the rope, he could not tear loose the knot that had jammed at his throat. He relaxed suddenly, rolled over on his back and lay still. Don Coyote leaped to his feet. Taking the lariat from the girl's unsteady fingers, he passed the free end around Burke's wrists and knotted it. He took a couple of hitches around the man's ankles.

"He'll come to in a minute," he remarked. "Couldn't kill him if you tried."

He released the rope from Burke's throat and bound him carefully. When he straightened up, his face was beaming.

"Ma'm, you're a li'l lady after my own heart," he said with a bow. "I couldn't have pulled that trick better myself."

Though Gayle's face was full of color now and the look of fear had passed from her eyes, she had not yet completely recovered. She swayed slightly and Don Coyote put out his hand to steady her. She was very close to him. The contact with her warm arm sent a wave of emotion sweeping over him.

Then she was in his arms. He never knew how she

got there. One moment she was staring into his eyes, her shapely lips parted as she tried to force a smile, tried to speak. The next moment she was in his arms, trembling, her face pressed tightly against his shoulder. His hand touched her shining black hair, stroked it gently.

The world rushed away like a receding wave in a tide rip. They were utterly alone, Burke's trussed form, the house, the mine, the whole world forgotten.

"There, there, li'l lady," Don Coyote whispered unsteadily. "It's all right now. He can't hurt you. There ain't nothin' to be scared of. Buck up, li'l lady."

He paused, while his arms drew closer and his trembling lips reverently touched her hair. She moved then, slowly raising her head and meeting his gaze. For a long, unforgettable moment their eyes met. Then he kissed her, breathlessly, full on the lips.

The latch of the front door clicked. For an instant neither moved. Then a suave, unruffled voice:

"I beg your pardon. I didn't mean to intrude."

They turned then, Don Coyote releasing the girl reluctantly. Wilcox Chandler was standing in the doorway. Apparently he had not yet seen Burke's bound form, which was on the other side of the room, for he stood regarding the two with a faintly cynical smile.

"One of the men 'phoned in that there had been an accident," he explained imperturbably. "I came right out, thinking there might be something I could do."

"Come in, Wilcox," the girl said in an odd, still voice.

Lawrence glanced at her. A rosy flush had crept over her face and down her smooth neck. She was almost pathetic in her embarrassment and disconcertion. Don Coyote felt a surge of anger sweep over him. The hectic events of the night had left his nerves shattered, on edge. He'd have liked nothing better than to have been able to plunge his fist into the center of Chandler's smooth face. He took a step forward, angrily.

"Aren't you in the habit of knocking before you enter a room?" he demanded.

Chandler was maddeningly apologetic, his very humility serving as tinder for Don Coyote's rage. "I am very, very sorry, Mr. Lawrence." His tone was deeply penitent, almost mocking. "If I had realized for an instant that anything like this—"

"Oh, dry up!" Lawrence grunted, advancing threateningly another step.

The girl was beside him now, her hand on his arm. "Please, Mr. Lawrence," she pleaded. "Please don't —have any more—trouble."

For the first time Wilcox Chandler seemed to take cognizance of the disordered state of the room, the overturned table, the shattered chair. His jaw set and he snapped the door shut behind him.

"What in blazes—" he began angrily, and as quickly broke off as he caught sight of Burke in the far corner of the room. He stared at the unconscious form for a long moment and then shifted his glance to Lawrence and Gayle. He made no demand for an explanation, merely asking: "Where is your father, Gayle?"

"On the hill. Superintending the sealing of the shaft. The tunnel is still burning."

Chandler considered this for a moment, while his eyes rested on Burke. Don Coyote writhed inwardly, longing to throttle the man.

"Burke lost his mind!" the girl suddenly burst out. "He fired the tunnel, Wilcox. He admitted he did. He trapped Mr. Lawrence in it. Father made him go down the shaft after him. The fear of the white damp was too much. He carried Mr. Lawrence up and brought him to. Then he lost his reason completely. He attacked one of the men and almost killed him. Then he disappeared. He showed up just a few minutes ago. He was going to kill me."

"You!" Calmly though he had listened to the explanation, Chandler could not hide his surprise at the girl's last statement. "Why should he want to harm you?"

"Because I discovered that Mr. Lawrence was still in the tunnel. His mare had been led away and we thought at first that he had set the fire and fled." Her voice broke a little and her eyes were oddly repentent as she glanced at Don Coyote. "Then I found that the mare had come back to the barn and I knew that Mr. Lawrence was still in the mine."

"Burke was terrible," she added after a moment. "Like a beast. Utterly bereft of reason. I was frightened almost to death. There was a terrible fight."

Chandler smiled a bit skeptically. "And Mr. Lawrence subdued Burke? Single-handed?"

"No. I helped," Gayle admitted. "With the lariat. I caught him around the throat. We almost had to choke him to death before he lost consciousness."

Chandler hastily crossed the room and knelt at the big man's side. Don Coyote watched him closely, missing not the slightest movement nor change of facial expression. Wilcox Chandler was worried. He showed it as plainly as though he had said so in as many words. And Don Coyote knew that he was not worried about Burke's condition—whether Burke lived or died, regained his sanity or became a raving maniac, meant little or nothing to Wilcox Chandler.

But if Burke regained consciousness and chanced to tell but a few of the things he knew—ah, that was a different story, Don Coyote reflected.

Chandler rose to his feet again. "He's breathing, all right. But none too steadily. We should get him to a doctor immediately. He may be badly hurt."

Don Lawrence laughed shortly. "You couldn't kill that man with an ax. Believe me, I know."

Chandler ignored the statement. "Besides," he went on, speaking to Gayle, "he is dangerous to have around here. We'd better get him to town as soon as possible and lock him up. It doesn't pay to take chances with a maniac, particularly a giant like Ben Burke." He turned to Don Coyote, at last speaking to him directly. "Lawrence, run up the hill and tell Dorrington to come down here at once."

The peremptory tone was too much for Don Coyote. Cool and unruffled though he was ordinarily under even the most trying circumstances, this was an occasion when he lost his temper.

"If you want Dorrington, run up the hill and get him yourself," he came back heatedly. "And if you want your employee"—the inference was unmistakable —"taken to town, you can take him there."

For a space that seemed minutes the two men glared at each other. The masks were down. As surely as he knew his own name, Don Coyote knew that Chandler was behind the plot to wreck the Buckaroo.

And, half crazed by anger and weariness, Don Coyote took no pains to conceal his knowledge. It shone patently in the level, sneering gaze of his steel-gray eyes.

# CHAPTER XVIII

IT was quite within the realms of probability that Chandler and Don Coyote would have come to blows then and there had there been no intervention. Certainly they hated each other enough to have forgotten the bonds of propriety and the accepted standards of conduct, and flung themselves at one another, the presence of Gayle notwithstanding.

Born to hatred, these two men; as unlike they were as the midday sun and the darkness of a mine shaft.

Success had polished Chandler until outwardly he was as smooth as a quartz pebble in a creek bottom; but though he glistened with worldliness and the pride of achievement, he was as barren of "color" as a ledge of porphory.

No shining light was Don Coyote Lawrence. The proverbial silver spoon had been conspicuously absent at his birth; and the struggle with life had served only to roughen him and sharpen the corners of his uncouthness. It had not hardened him, however; nor did his outward roughness conceal the nobility of character that was his only heritage.

The impasse that might have ended in a primitive struggle was broken by the sudden arrival of Dor-

rington, who threw open the door and strode into the
room.

"Oh, hello, Chandler! Thought you might come out.
Good—good Lord! What's happened?"

Seeing that Gayle was too wrought up to make
another explanation of the fight with Burke, Don Coyote tersely told the old man what had happened. Dorrington's face paled as he listened to the recital.

"Lawrence, I wonder if we'll ever square our debt
with you," he said feelingly when Don Coyote had finished. "This is the second time you have come through
in the pinch."

"Don't give me too much credit," Don Coyote
smiled, his old, carefree manner coming back to him.
"The li'l lady had more to do with puttin' Burke out
than me. I was just about done for when she dropped
that rope around his neck."

"Well, I'm proud of you both," Dorrington said,
glancing pridefully from one to the other. "Some day,
if we ever get this mine to paying, I'll try to settle accounts. In the meantime—"

"Don't you think we'd better get Burke into town?"
Chandler put in coldly. "The man may be badly hurt.
It would be rather unpleasant if he died on your hands."

"He's all right," Don Coyote stated calmly. "If
you'll look at him, you'll see he's come to."

All of them turned then and saw that Burke was
regarding them balefully with his small, pale blue eyes.
Chandler became suddenly insistent.

"We'll have to have him locked up. Jail is the only

place for a man like that. We'd better get him out of
the way before he breaks loose."

Don Coyote smiled inwardly. The man's anxiety
was so patent that it was laughable, at least to one person in the room. The new mood that had come over
Lawrence with Dorrington's arrival made him inclined
to bait the mining magnate.

"He may be all right in a little while," he remarked
easily. "Temporary insanity, yuh know. Like as not
he's himself again right now. Don't see no use in
draggin' him to jail."

Chandler seemed almost to grit his teeth as he turned
to Dorrington, ignoring Don Coyote's remark. "You
may use my car to take him in if you wish, Dorrington."

Dorrington nodded thoughtfully. He was almost
apologetic as he glanced in Don Coyote's direction.
"Yes, I guess it will be safer to get him out of the
way. He should be under a doctor's care, anyhow.
If you'll give me a hand, Lawrence, we'll see if we
can carry him out."

"You bet!" Don Coyote nodded. Odd, he reflected,
how differently two men could give an order; where
Chandler's tone was designed to put a man in his place
as a menial, Dorrington's manner just as clearly estab-
lished a man as an associate.

When they bent over Burke, however, they saw at
once that two men could not handle him. The man
started to struggle silently, ferociously, threshing about

on the floor like a freshly-caught trout. Lawrence
hastily pushed the older man aside.

"Don't get too close, sir," he cautioned. "No use
takin' chances with them feet o' his. Wait a minute.
I'll get a few of the boys. This ain't goin' to be any
easy job."

Lawrence hurried out of the house and across the
clearing to the bunkhouse. Picking out four of the
men whom he felt could be trusted, he told them the
situation and brought them back with him. At that,
it was not a wholly one-sided struggle. Tightly bound
though he was, Burke still had plenty of fight left, as
more than one of the miners learned before they got
him into Chandler's car.

"Lawrence, you go on in and go to bed," Dorrington
ordered when the task was completed. "You've done
enough for one night. Besides, I want you on hand
early in the morning. Want to talk some business with
you. You won't be able to stand on your feet if you
stay up much longer."

Don Coyote nodded wearily. "You're right. I'm
about dead." He nodded to all of them, as they stood
grouped around Chandler's car. When he spoke, however, his voice was for only one. "Good night, folks.
An' pleasant dreams—if possible."

Dorrington watched him drag his weary feet across
the clearing and disappear into the bunkhouse. He was
glad of the faint light, for his eyes were a bit misty.
"There's as brave a lad and as true a lad as I ever
met," he said quietly, as much to himself as to the

others. "I think we're mighty lucky to have him on our payroll."

Neither Chandler nor Gayle made any comment. Dorrington turned to the mining magnate. "Would you mind putting up with us for the balance of the night?" he asked. "I have some matters I'd like to talk over with you in the morning. I'll take Burke in, if you don't mind my driving the car. I'll have to go anyway, I guess, for I suppose it will be up to me to make some kind of a formal charge. You might just as well stay here and get some sleep."

Chandler hesitated; then, apparently unable to think of any excuse for refusing Dorrington's request, he nodded. "All right, thank you."

"Gayle will put you up in the spare room," Dorrington said, as he climbed behind the wheel of the car. "It's not quite as modern as you're used to, but I guess it will do. It's almost dawn now."

"It will be perfectly all right," Chandler assured him.

Gayle and the mining magnate stood very close together as they watched the automobile out of sight down the winding road. When its headlights had disappeared, they turned and walked silently back to the house. The stillness was oppressive to the girl; it seemed to bear her down like a weight upon her shoulders. Not a sound came from the sealed mine. The fans were stilled. No ore cars rattled down the track to the dump. There was no wind; the tall trees that surrounded the clearing stood black and grim and motionless. Even the moan of the river was faint and far-off.

It was a silence of disaster, of defeat, of crumpled castles and shattered hopes.

The girl shivered slightly, as much form nervousness and weariness as from the early-morning chill. Chandler took her arm as they reached the porch.

"You're cold, my dear," he said gently.

"Not particularly," she murmured.

"Maybe something warm to drink will make you feel better. Shan't I run over to the cookhouse? I can rout out the cook—"

"No. I can get some coffee. There is some already made. I can warm it up."

She spoke listlessly, almost docilely, like a child who has done wrong and is waiting for punishment. Wilcox Chandler smiled to himself. This meddling young Lawrence had his uses after all. Chandler thought he knew what had caused the girl's mood, and he was not far wrong in his surmise. He resolved to play his cards very carefully.

"If you'll clear up the living room a bit, I'll get some coffee for us," Gayle told him as they entered the house.

She disappeared into the kitchen and Chandler set about putting the room to rights. He lighted a fire with some kindling which lay on the hearth and tossed on the pieces of the broken chair, which was beyond all hope of repair. He retrieved the table from where it had been tossed, righted it and moved it to the center of the room.   He placed a chair on either side of it and stood back regarding them thoughtfully.

The setting for the little drama he planned was complete.

# CHAPTER XIX

GAYLE DORRINGTON did not return to the living room for more than fifteen minutes. Chandler began to grow a bit restless. Though he needed only to open a single door, he knew better than to follow her out to the kitchen or show the slightest anxiety about her absence. He knew quite well that she might easily have put the coffee pot on the stove and returned to the living room to wait for it to heat. The fact that she did not, the fact that she waited in the seclusion of the kitchen, told him many things—chief among them being that she was already repentant.

When Gayle at last appeared with the coffee, Chandler saw that she was more nearly herself. She had a smile for him and a measure of her usual calmness had returned. He held a chair for her with meticulous politeness, saw her comfortably seated and then took the chair across the table.

"It has been rather a hard night for you, hasn't it?" he remarked sympathetically. "The fire in the mine and the rescue of Lawrence and that terrible fight with Burke. You're just about used up, aren't you?"

She nodded, smiling a bit ruefully as she sipped her coffee. "I am very tired."

Chandler talked on casually, asked about the fire and the rescue. Deliberately he made no mention of the thought that was uppermost in her mind: his own untimely entrance when he had seen her in Don Coyote's arms. Carefully he evaded any mention of the incident, well knowing that in so doing he forced her to bring it up herself. At last she did, as he knew so well she would.

"Just what are you thinking of me, Wilcox?" she asked finally. Her voice was none too steady as she put the question. Her eyes seemed disinclined to meet his.

"What am I thinking of you?" he repeated. His hand rested ever so lightly on hers. "I am thinking you are altogether the most adorable little woman I ever knew. And I am thinking that I love you with all my heart."

"No, no, no!" she shook her head. "I don't mean that way. I mean what did you think when you walked in—and—"

"Oh, come, come!" he interrupted graciously. "Let's forget about that. It was nothing."

"Nothing?" Her eyes met his now; they were vaguely reproachful. "Do you think that I allow every man who comes along to put his arms around me?"

"No, of course not," Chandler made haste to reassure her. "But I rather imagine you didn't *allow* that fellow to take you in his arms. He just did it."

She smiled faintly at this remark and Chandler's heart glowed warmly. Could she fail to see his magnanimity in offering her this loophole?

"You are very kind to me, Wilcox. But you must

have seen that I offered no resistance to his attentions."

Chandler shrugged and glanced down at the table. His acting was excellent; Gayle could see very plainly that he was hurt. "I am sorry you brought this thing up," he said softly. "Now that you force me to it, I shall have to admit that I was—well, a bit disappointed. I thought—oh, let's forget about it, my dear."

She shook her head slowly. "No, I don't want to forget about it. I don't want you to think that I allow that sort of thing from an almost total stranger. Why, I have only known Mr. Lawrence a little more than twenty-four hours! What must you think of me?"

"I told you what I think of you," Chandler replied gently. "You are the most adorable—"

"Oh, bother!" she interrupted. "Won't you listen to me? Won't you let me explain!"

"I will, yes. If you insist. But I am sure I will think just as much of you if you don't. After all, no harm has been done."

"I'd rather tell you," the girl said, lowering her eyes, "even if my explanation does sound a bit unconvincing. It was just after that terrible fight with Burke. Mr. Lawrence and I had fought together, you might say. I hadn't done much—but when you come right down to it, I saved the day. If I hadn't thought of the lariat and known how to throw it, there is no telling what would have happened."

She shivered slightly at the memory and then went on more softly. "The reaction after that terrible fright was almost too much for me. I almost fainted. Mr.

Lawrence put his hand out to steady me. Then I was in his arms. I was so frightened and my nerves were so shattered that I—I just had to go to some one. I didn't mean to let him kiss me—and still—when he did—"

"I know, I know," Chandler said consolingly. "You hardly knew what you were doing, you were so worked up. I was a little disappointed when I saw you because —well, as you say, you are not that kind of a woman. Now suppose we forget all about it."

"I shall," she said, smiling. "Will you?"

"I certainly shall," he nodded. "Now don't you think it is time you went to bed?"

"Yes, I guess it is," Gayle admitted. "Though I don't feel the least bit sleepy."

"You're tired, though. You'll feel better for a little rest."

They rose from the table. "You know where you're to sleep?" she asked.

"Yes. I'll turn in shortly. I think I'll have a smoke first."

"Good night," she murmured.

"Good night, dear."

He walked with her part way to her door. Then, as by common accord, they moved toward the window and stood for a moment looking out over the canyon. The faintest touch of rose was in the eastern sky. The pines on the far side of the canyon were just emerging from the murk of darkness. Far below, barely visible, was a winding ribbon of tarnished silver. A hush as of death was everywhere.

Chandler's arm was round her waist. He drew her close to him, raised her face until her eyes met his. He did not kiss her.

"Gayle, you mean more to me than anything else in the world," he told her very earnestly. "Won't you marry me?"

Her form stiffened ever so slightly in his arms. She did not reply at once.

"I'll be very good to you, Gayle. I'll give you anything in the world you ask. I am very rich. I have more money than I know what to do with. It will be yours, to buy you every happiness."

"You are very kind," she said softly.

"Gayle, dear. Won't you marry me?"

She sighed, so faintly as to be hardly audible. "Some day—I think—I shall."

Then she was gone, slipping out of his arms like a wraith. The room seemed to have grown colder with her going.

For half an hour Wilcox Chandler stood before the window, watching the dawn break over the canyon. His heart was warm; he was very pleased with himself. The Buckaroo was wrecked; only a miracle could save it now. And Gayle Dorrington had said that some day she would be his wife. He smiled as he thought of her words. Some day. He was quite certain that that "some day" would be soon.

Another person saw the dawn break over the canyon

that morning. Lying sleeplessly on his cot in the bunkhouse, his bloodshot eyes staring out of the window, was Don Coyote Lawrence. His soul was troubled and his heart was angry. But from time to time he touched his lips with a reverent hand. They seemed still warm with Gayle Dorrington's kiss.

And in her room in the big house, sleepless with exhaustion, Gayle Dorrington watched the coming of the dawn. Her soul, too, was troubled. And the cause was hard for her to understand. She had told Wilcox Chandler that she would forget a certain incident. But she knew that she would not forget it, could not forget it. Were the game to be played over again, she knew that her part would be the same.

How, oh, how, had this unknown, smiling wanderer gained such a hold upon her heart?

# CHAPTER XX

DON COYOTE awoke that morning with a splitting headache and, unusual for him, a grouch. He lay for several minutes thinking over the events of the night before. Save where they touched on Gayle Dorrington, his thoughts were not pleasant. The timbering of the Buckaroo was probably a total loss; from statements Dorrington had made about the financial condition of the mine, it was quite probable that work on it would never be resumed. That in itself, he reflected, should cause him little uneasiness. It was not his mine. He was a mere shift boss, and a rather blundering one at that. And there were plenty more jobs in other mines.

And yet he got little consolation from the thought. He didn't want to work in another mine. He wanted to stay with the Buckaroo. He wanted to see old man Dorrington beat the interests that were fighting him and win to the top. Dorrington's fight had become his fight. Why? Because he was built that way. Reason enough.

And Chandler. Don Coyote scowled as he thought of the man. How a supercilious ass like Chandler could get over with Gayle Dorrington! It was beyond him. Still, he was forced to admit, the man had his points. He had almost liked him himself when he had first met him. If it hadn't been for Chandler's obvious interest in Gayle he might like him yet—if he hadn't learned so much about him.

Well, what had he learned? When you came to put your finger on it—nothing. Suspicions, circumstantial evidence, intuition. That was all he had to go on. Nothing tangible. Nothing that he could throw up to him and tell him to clear off pronto if he didn't want to see smoke belching from the business end of a six-gun.

Damned mess, that's what it was. That map, now. Dorrington had vowed it was authentic. Why hadn't they reached the old ore chamber? The map showed its location. According to Dorrington's calculation, they should have cross-cut it a week ago. And yet there had been no sign of reaching it. Funny. The old man's surveying might be wrong. That was a possible explanation, but not a probable one. Dorrington knew his business when it came to mining, even if he wasn't much of a judge of the company he allowed his daughter to keep. Something was wrong somewhere. Either the map was loco or the surveying was out. He meant to look into it—when and if ever the mine was opened again.

Damned mess, that's what it was. If it hadn't been for the li'l lady's riding glove he'd never have been mixed up in it. He swore under his breath. Mixed up in it! He wouldn't trade places with any other mining engineer in California. He wouldn't miss this ruckus for a thousand dollars, no, not for ten thousand dollars! What was money compared to the chance of getting into a good fight! Huh!

"Hey, you! Goin' to stay there all day?" It was the voice of the rotund cook. "If you want any breakfast, yuh better make tracks."

Don Coyote rolled out of bed. He felt better already. His grouch was disappearing fast. "I don't care no more about breakfast than I do about my right eye," he told the cook earnestly. "But if I miss out on it, I'm liable to climb your frame."

"Huh! You an' how many?" the cook grunted, and rolled out of the bunkhouse.

Don Coyote grinned broadly as he slipped into his clothes. "Looks like I've made a friend already," he told himself. "It ain't everybody that that ol' cook would take the trouble to call to breakfast. If you're there, yuh eat. If yuh ain't, yuh don't. That's the rule of every cook I ever knew." He started toward the door. "Water, where is you? I need cleansin'."

Don Coyote was busily working on his fifth helping of hotcakes, one eye on his plate and the other on the swiftly diminishing stack of cakes in the center of the table, when the beefy cook hove into sight.

"Old man sent word over he wants yuh, Lawrence," he announced. "You're through eatin', so clear out an' let the yallerjackets move in on that syrup you spilled."

"Me? Through?" Don Coyote looked up in surprise.

"Yuh had fifteen cakes, ain't yuh?" the cook roared.

"Fifteen! I been keepin' tabs. An' that's too consarned many for any one man."

Don Coyote nodded regretfully. "Yeh, you're right,
li'l ol' lard pail. Fifteen is too consarned many," he
paused, guilelessly, "when they're like these h'yar
cakes."

Dodging the broom that hurtled across the room,
paying no more heed to the cook's roaring imprecations
than he would to the lazy buzzing of a fly, he moved
casually out of the dining room. Don Coyote's knowledge of women might be classed as sketchy in the ex-
treme; his knowledge of cooks was quite thorough and
complete.

Don Coyote's hearty breakfast had left him in good
humor, as witness his little by-play with the cook. As
he walked across the clearing toward Dorrington's
home, however, a feeling of depression came over him.
The mine was silent. But it was a different silence than
the silence of "change day," when the men changed
shifts and the mine was idle for eight hours. This was
an oppressive silence, the silence of calamity.

The bright morning air was contaminated by the
faint, unmistakable smell of burning timbers.

He mounted the stairs, crossed the wide veranda and
knocked at the door. His heart began to pound. He
was suddenly hungry for sight of Gayle, her deep eyes,
her glistening dark hair, her tenderly wistful face.
Would she answer his summons? Or would her father
come? Then she was standing before him, smiling
faintly, bidding him good morning.

But it was a different Gayle than he had expected. Shadows of sleeplessness lay under her eyes. Her face was pale and oddly thin; accentuated was the wistful quality that had first drawn him to her.

"Good mornin', ma'am," Don Coyote smiled. "How are you this morning?"

"Tritely speaking, I'm as well as might be expected," she laughed, a bit shakily.

Don Coyote shook his head ruefully. "It was a hard night, for more than one of us. The cook was tellin' me your dad wanted to see me."

"Yes. Come in and sit down—Don Coyote."

There was a hint of merriment in her eyes. It sent the blood coursing through his veins, warming his heart, dispelling his depression like boiling water melts a snowdrift. Don Coyote! Rather a reprehensible nickname to one who did not know. But from Gayle—a compliment, a challenge, a plea.

"Dad and Mr. Chandler are just finishing breakfast," Gayle added as Lawrence entered the house. "They'll be in in just a moment."

The words were a shadow crossing the sun, darkening the world and Don Coyote's brow. Chandler. The mention of a name. What a little thing to bring the gloom!

He took the proffered chair in silence, sat down, rolled a cigarette with fingers that were not too steady. He glanced up for her permission before he lighted it. She nodded quietly.

"By all means," she said. "Please make yourself at home."

"Thank you."

Gayle sat down near him. She must have sensed the feeling of restraint that had come over him, for she made no attempt at conversation.

"Maybe some time you'll tell me the story of Don Quixote," Lawrence suggested at last. "Seein' as I been named after him, I reckon I ought to know somethin' about him."

"I'd be glad to," Gayle responded. "But surely you've read something about him, in school, perhaps."

He shook his head; the reflection of a weary smile crossed his lips. "No, I ain't never been to school much. Never even got through the eighth grade. Had to go to work when I was thirteen. Been workin' ever since."

"But you're a mining engineer."

"University of Hard Knocks," he told her. "At that, I'm better than some I've known who had the right to use a lot of letters after their names. It ain't the school that counts so much, it's—it's—"

"The man," she supplied.

He nodded, with a quiet shrug of his broad shoulders; oddly, there was nothing of conceit in his manner. The girl scanned him narrowly. Mayhap she was comparing him with some one else. If she did, if she went beneath the surface, she must have found him flattered by the comparison.

Don Coyote rose and nodded good morning as Dorrington and Chandler came into the room. The old man looked better. Though he had had only a few hours sleep at best, his eyes were clear and the fighting, aggressive tilt had come back to his chin. He might be down, the younger man reflected, but he was far from out. He'd give a good account of himself yet.

Chandler's greeting was friendly, if constrained. The three men sat down, while Gayle left the room. Dorrington filled and lighted his pipe before he spoke.

"Well, Lawrence, I guess you know the position we're in here at the mine," he said at last. "I took that bullion into town last night with Burke; got it in safely, thank heaven! It will run about fifteen thousand. Not much when you consider that we may have to retimber the whole workings. However, we're going ahead as soon as the fire is out. We're going to go as far as we can. It will be close scraping. We'll have to make every dollar count. Anyway, be that as it may, I want to ask you if you will accept the position of superintendent?"

# CHAPTER XXI

Don Coyote was surprised and pleased. It was not the first time he had been promoted from shift boss to superintendent of a mine, but ordinarily it was a process which took months or even years. The quiet announcement that he had been placed in charge, after only four hours of actual work, took him back for a moment.

"I just got word from one of the doctors who was called in to see Burke that he appeared to be hopelessly insane," Dorrington went on. "Of course, it may be only temporary. He may come out of it in time. But I don't believe I would care to employ him here again. A strange case, Burke's. You'd hardly expect a man to go insane through fear, particularly a huge, hulking fellow like Burke."

"They are just the kind it gets," Chandler put in, "because they have so rarely known fear. Unless Burke has been in a mine disaster, I'll wager he never knew the meaning of fear before. Certainly he was never afraid of any human being."

"Ah, there you are," Dorrington pointed out. "Burke went through the Bellingham disaster nine years ago. If you happen to remember, forty-eight men died of gas in the old west drift of the Bellingham. Burke and two others were the only ones who got out alive. They say Burke was out of his head for nearly a month after that experience. Since then he has had a deathly fear for any form of fire."

"Explanation enough," Chandler commented.

"More might be added," Don Coyote remarked casually.

Chandler glanced at him quickly, his dark eyes searching the other's frank countenance.

"What do you mean, Lawrence?" It was Dorrington who asked the question.

"I mean just this," Don Coyote answered. "I ain't no psychiatrist, or whatever you call them insanity experts, but I got a hunch that somethin' else was weighin' pretty heavy on Burke's mind. Burke was rough and he may have been mean and may have liked to use his fists, but he wasn't the kind that could commit a deliberate murder an' keep his head while he was doin' it."

Chandler started in his chair at the bald statement. Dorrington, however, evinced no surprise.

"Murder!" the mining magnate exclaimed. "That's a pretty serious charge, Lawrence. Perhaps you'd better explain yourself."

"I don't reckon there's much explainin' needs to be done," Don Coyote answered, his voice very cool. "Anybody that knows the facts could draw only one conclusion—that Burke tried to murder me."

Chandler's eyes narrowed. "Maybe you'd better state the facts, Lawrence."

"Sure. That's easy. Here they are. I was the only man in the tunnel at the time the fire broke out. The miners had just gone outside to get their suppers and they passed the spot where the fire started not more than fifteen minutes before it was discovered. It wasn't smolderin' then, like any fire started by accident would be doin'. Yet when they came back fifteen minutes later, maybe less, it was a roarin' conflagration."

"But possibly a cigarette butt, an unextinguished match—" Chandler began.

"No," Don Coyote interrupted with a shake of his head. "Lighted matches and cigarette butts don't ignite mine timbers without doin' a lot of smolderin' and stewin' around first. No, that fire was set. Burke just the same as admitted it last night. Then there was the business of runnin' my mare out of the stable and some of the boys sayin' they saw me ridin' away just before the fire was discovered. My mare's pullin' out couldn't have been no accident, because she was tied. All right. What's the conclusion you draw? It's this: that Burke set that fire an' had an accomplice run off my mare, makin' it look like I'd set the fire an' cleared out. There you are. Take it or leave it."

Chandler nodded thoughtfully. "Yes, there may be something in that. It looks odd, I'll admit."

"You're damned right it looks odd," Don Coyote grunted.

"But," Chandler came back promptly, "you can't prove anything on Burke. The man was insane when he came in here last night. Besides, what motive could he have for trying to kill you and wreck the Buckaroo?"

"That's another easy one," Don Coyote paused, staring Chandler straight in the eye. He had presented all the facts he had. His next move was pure bluff, nothing more. To be sure, it was backed by a mighty strong hunch. Several things pointed vaguely at Burke, none of which, however, could be regarded as conclusive evidence. And yet he spoke with quiet conviction.

"Burke was the man who tipped off them two bandits that Dorrington was taking the bullion into town day before yesterday."

The quiet statement took Chandler unawares. He blinked twice and his gaze wavered for an instant—the only indications that Don Coyote had hit the nail on the head. But the latter noted them and smiled inwardly. Chandler wasn't so blamed steady after all, he reflected. Had any one offered to bet on the matter at that moment, Don Coyote would have offered pretty high odds that his hunch was correct. Ben Burke had tipped off the two bandits, he had set fire to the Buckaroo tunnel—and Wilcox Chandler was behind the whole business.

The mining magnate's eyes narrowed as he regarded Lawrence. He did not speak for a moment. When he did, his voice was steady, almost casual.

"How do you know that, Lawrence?"

"Because I overheard some palaver between them bandits when I was layin' out by that water-hole,

waitin' to hold 'em up. Fact of the matter is, I heard
a lot of interestin' things. And I reckon the *least* important thing I heard was that Burke tipped them off."

Don Coyote was full of confidence now; he had the
feeling of a poker player who is betting his stack on a
pair of deuces and bidding fair to get away with it.
The actual information unwittingly divulged by the
bandits amounted to little; some one, identity unknown,
had tipped them off; and some one else, known only as
"the old man," was attempting to wreck the Buckaroo.

Chandler's self-possession, that tiny part of it that
had been lost, had returned. He questioned Lawrence
casually; his manner was that of an attorney who al-
lows a witness to offer hearsay evidence, knowing quite
well that it will be given no consideration.

"What else did you hear of interest to us, Lawrence?"

"I heard that a certain person is tryin' his durnedest
to wreck the Buckaroo and bust Mr. Dorrington," Don
Coyote answered promptly.

"Who is this certain person?" Chandler queried, not
greatly interested.

"I reckon that's somethin' I better keep under my
hat for the time bein'," Lawrence returned coolly.

"Suit yourself," Chandler turned to the old man.
"Do you believe this, Dorrington?"

The manager of the Buckaroo methodically filled his
pipe, lit it and sat regarding the burning match for a
moment. He blew it out when the flame touched his
fingers.

"Frankly, Chandler, I do," he admitted wearily. "There have been many things that point to that conclusion. Not only the robbery and the burning of the mine, but other things. I won't try to go into them. They didn't amount to much for the most part. Taken singly, they mean little. But taken altogether they seem to lead to the very conclusion that Lawrence has pointed out. Some one is trying to break me and wreck the Buckaroo."

"And I'll say this much," Don Coyote put in. "That some one is a stockholder o' this company."

"Oh, but that's absurd," Chandler smiled indulgently. "Why in the world should a stockholder of the company try to wreck the mine? It isn't logical. Where's the motive, man?"

"That is something I would give a good deal to know," Dorrington answered.

The mining magnate shook his head with finality and rose abruptly to his feet. "You are allowing your imagination to get the better of you, Dorrington. The fire, I'll admit, looks peculiar. But as for the rest of these charges, they simply won't hold up under logic. Stockholders don't attempt to wreck their own mines. And even if these two bandits made the statements Lawrence credits to them," he paused the briefest instant to allow the connotation of his remark to penetrate, "it can be nothing more than idle, unwarranted gossip."

Don Coyote rose to his feet too. His tanned face

was dark now and his gray eyes were glittering menacingly, like points of steel. His attitude was belligerent, though calm.

"Are you meanin' to insinuate that I lied about this thing?" he demanded slowly.

"I am not insinuating anything," Chandler answered, plainly taken back by the other's manner. "I am merely characterizing the conclusion you and Dorrington appear to have drawn as completely unwarranted and absurd."

"It's just as well," Don Coyote drawled, " 'cause the last hombre that called me a liar didn't wake up for more than an hour."

Chandler drew himself up with dignity. "Are you attempting to threaten me, Lawrence?"

"Aw, shucks!" the younger man grunted, and strode to the window. He did not turn around until Chandler had departed and he felt Dorrington's friendly hand on his shoulder. Then he faced the old man with a slow grin.

"What do you think?" Dorrington asked.

"Think! I know! He's guilty as hell!"

The old man frowned and shook his head wearily. "Why, Lawrence? Why? What in the world can he hope to gain by wrecking the Buckaroo? My God, man, what is the answer?"

"That's somethin' we got to find out," Don Coyote smiled. "I got a hunch it won't be easy, either. Still,

I'm willin' to stake my little mare Cleopatra against a plug o' chewin' tobacco that in the end we knock that holier-than-thou, swell-headed Wilcox Chandler for a row of brick garages."

## CHAPTER XXII

DORRINGTON walked slowly back to the center of the room and sat down again. Don Coyote followed him after a moment. He felt suddenly very sorry for this old man who was waging an uphill battle, in the dark, against unknown enemies. More than anything else in the world he wanted to aid him, to encourage him, to show him that he for one was ready to fight to the last ditch to help him win out. But there were certain situations in which Don Coyote found himself bereft of words. This was one of them. To save his life he could think of nothing encouraging to say.

And, when he came right down to it, there was little about the situation that could be considered encouraging. Without doubt, the fire was still raging in the sealed tunnel. It would smolder there for days. The timbers of the entire tunnel and shaft might be destroyed before the fire burned itself out. Don Coyote knew what that would mean. The country rock was soft. The tunnel and shaft would cave in innumerable places. It might take months to muck it out and retimber it. Fifteen thousand dollars, which appeared to be all the money Dorrington had, might not even see the job to completion. And even if it did, there was still the matter of the unlocated ore chamber. That, in itself, might prove an unsurmountable obstacle in the way of the success of the Buckaroo.

All in all, the situation was anything but encouraging. Dorrington knew it; the new lines of worry in his face showed that. Don Coyote knew it, too. But there were no lines of worry in the younger man's face, though he told himself that the success of the Buckaroo had come to mean everything to him. Don Coyote was not the worrying kind.

"Lawrence, have you any idea what can be behind Chandler's plan to close us down?" The old man asked the question abruptly.

Now Don Coyote had certain ideas on the subject. He had given it no end of thought and he had come to the point where he believed he saw a glimmer of daylight ahead. But, under the circumstances, he dared not voice his suspicions to Dorrington—for the very reason that Gayle played too important a part in them. Besides, he might be wrong, and the matter was far too personal to be discussed without something more than suspicions to back him up.

Accordingly he shook his head. Lying came hard for Don Coyote, but he did his best. "That's what defeats me. I can't figure his game either. But I wouldn't worry about it if I was you, Mr. Dorrington. We're onto him now, leastwise, we think we are, and we can be on the lookout for his tricks. Only this: we got to keep our suspicions to ourselves. If I was you, I wouldn't tell nobody, not even your own daughter, that we suspect Chandler. I think it'll be better that way. Eyes and ears open, mouth shut and nose to the grindstone—that's the program that'll bring a man out on top whether he's runnin' a mine or raisin' hogs or sellin' bootleg likker."

Dorrington smiled. "I guess that's good advice, Lawrence. We'll stick to it anyway. Now to the more immediate business at hand. How long before you think we dare enter the mine?"

Don Coyote considered a moment and suddenly gave birth to what, for the moment, seemed a brilliant idea. "You got any water up the hill, above the shaft?" he asked quickly.

"There's a creek in the canyon about a quarter of a mile south of the shaft."

"How much water in it?"

"Oh, it's quite a stream. It might fill a two-foot pipe."

Don Coyote slapped his thigh jubilantly. "Great stuff! We'll flood the workings. I should have thought of that before. Only reason I didn't is because it's usually impossible to flood a tunnel. Here's the idea. If we leave the fire to burn itself out, it's liable to gut the whole workings. No matter how tight you seal her, air is bound to work in an' feed the flames. The tunnel will be full of gas for weeks and weeks. And any time you start the blowers to clean it out, you're just goin' to start up the fire again. Here's what we'll do. We'll put five or six men to work at the mouth of the tunnel, buildin' a water-tight door there. We'll put the rest of the crew to work on the hill and run a ditch from this h'yar creek to the shaft. Then we'll flood her. How's that?"

Don Coyote's face was beaming as he explained his plan. His enthusiasm must have been contagious, for Dorrington's eyes lighted as he listened.

"It sounds reasonable, at that," he admitted. "At least, it can't do any harm. By heaven, we'll try it."

Without wasting any further time in discussion, they hurried out of the house and across the clearing to the bunkhouse. They found the men standing about idly, discussing the fire, Burke, the situation at the Buckaroo and the poker game of the night before. Dorrington explained the plan hastily, ending with:

"It may take us ten hours to get that water to the shaft and it may take twenty. But we are going to work now and we aren't going to stop until it is there, if it takes a week. Double time for overtime and a fifty dollar bonus to the man who, in my judgment, makes the best showing with a pick and shovel. Anderson, you pick out four men and go to work to make that barrier watertight. The rest of you boys get your tools and start up the hill."

Dorrington and Lawrence led the way with their transit and surveying outfit. It was not a time for guesswork. They surveyed the proposed ditch accurately, drove their stakes to mark it and then laid their transit aside and took up pick and shovel with the rest of the crew. The idea of a superintendent and a manager working side by side with their men was new. Leaving out of consideration the need for haste and the

fact that every shovel counted, Don Coyote and Dorrington could have done nothing which would have
served more to win the admiration of the men.

The miners worked like demons, bending to the job
at hand with a will. It was not an easy task either,
particularly for men used to working in the cool depths
of the Buckaroo. The hillside on which they worked
faced west and long before noon the sun reached
around the ridge and beat down upon them pitilessly.
Perspiration ran from their faces in streams. It was
gruelling, back-breaking toil and the tempo was far
from slow. One by one they shed their shirts, stripping
to the waist. Don Coyote smiled as he glanced over
the crew.

"They look like a bunch of stokers in the boiler room
of a liner," he grinned to himself. "And to-morrow
they're goin' to feel like a bunch of parboiled lobsters—
if I know this h'yar sun!"

He warned them but they laughed at his warnings
and the dirt flew faster. At noon the cook and his
flunkey arrived with lunch. Four times they toiled up
the hill with grub, the fat cook grumbling with every
step. They piled it up in the shade of the fanhouse.
There were twenty-six men at work on the ditch and
there appeared to be enough food for a hundred and
twenty-six. But when the crew went back to work,
not a crumb was left. Even the squirrels went hungry
that day.

The work progressed swiftly, faster even than Don
Coyote had dared hope when he saw the length of the

litch and the rocky ground through which it had to be
lug. When it was necessary to blast, as was the case
n a dozen or more places, only the shortest of fuses
was used and the men were swinging their shovels almost before the rocks stopped falling out of the air.
The miners had caught the spirit of the thing; they
knew the need for speed and, in a measure, the serious
predicament of the Buckaroo. Every minute saved now
meant dollars to the company, and every dollar saved
for the company would stave off ruin, and the loss of
their jobs, just that much longer.

"A good crew you got," Don Coyote commented to
Dorrington along about the middle of the afternoon.
"The average miner will work just so fast an' no faster.
Follow him around jabbin' him with a darning needle
if yuh want to, but you can't get him to speed up a bit.
These boys are different—most of 'em."

"Most of them are old friends of mine, boys who
have been with me for years, on other jobs," the old
man told him. "They're loyal and they'll work their
heads off if they see the need for it. The others—"

Don Coyote nodded. "Workin' well enough right
now, because we're watchin' 'em and they know they
have to. They don't dare to lay down on the job. But
I been keepin' my eyes open. I know which ones have
been puttin' their hearts into this job an' which ones
ain't. There's Johnson an' five others that'd like to
quit. An' soon's we get this h'yar ditch dug, they're
goin' to quit—by request."

At five the men knocked off work for another meal,

which was laboriously packed up the hill by the cook and his flunkey. They lost less than fifteen minutes. Back at work again, with the sun hanging low in the heavens and the air growing cooler, they plunged into the task at hand like new men. The ditch was to be approximately five hundred yards long. A little more than three hundred yards had already been completed. The work was progressing fast, so fast that at times the winding line of fresh-turned earth seemed almost like a long snake crawling out of its hole.

Before dark Jimmy Tubbs, the mine's electrician, a worried-looking, earnest little man, rigged a dozen or more big lights above the line of the ditch. And with darkness the men, dog-tired though they were, instead of slacking up, fell to with renewed vigor. The night air was keen and bracing. They drank deeply of it and their weary arms moved faster.

It was midnight and a huge yellow moon was just peering over the tops of the trees on the high eastern slope when the job was finished. With a sigh of relief Don Coyote called off the men and gave the order to turn in the water. He watched it run down the ditch, darkly sparkling, gurgling pleasantly, and plunged his head into the first wave that reached the fanhouse. He rose, sputtering and shaking the water out of his hair.

"You boys have done noble," he told the men proudly. "Ain't I right, Mr. Dorrington?"

So weary that he could hardly stand, the old man nodded vigorously. "You certainly are, Lawrence."

"And who gets the fifty-dollar bonus?" Don Coyote asked.

"Suppose we let the men decide that?" Dorrington suggested. "How about it, boys?"

A wave of muttering passed over the group of miners. Then, as though prompted by a stage manager, came the decree in unison: "Swede Jenson."

Now Jenson may have done more work that day than any other man of the crew; then again he may not have. It was a matter that might have been argued in the bunkhouse for weeks. But the fact was—though Don Coyote did not know it at the time—that Jenson had a buxom sweetheart back in the old country whom he was very desirous of bringing to California, object matrimony. He had been saving his money to that end for several years and always required just a little bit more. His favorite saying had become, "Wal, Ay ban nading only fifty, saxty dollars more to send for my Katrina." Indeed, so long had he been saying this that the boys had become a bit skeptical about the Swede's intentions. However, they had him where they wanted him now— there would be romance at the Buckaroo if it had to be dragged there by the straw-colored hair of her head.

"Three cheers for Katrina!" some one shouted.

They were given with a will, while Dorrington murmured a few words of explanation to Don Coyote. The latter grinned, enjoying the Swede's discomfiture immensely.

"Now, boys," Lawrence went on when the cheering had subsided. "This h'yar ditch has got to be watched

every minute. New ditches have a habit of breakin'
and we ain't goin' to take no chances with this one. I'll
stick up here for two hours. Then I'll count on you to
have somebody up here to relieve me. Fix it up among
yourselves. Now get below an' tell the cook to give
you somethin' to eat an' then turn in. You can sleep
as late as you want in the mornin'. You've earned it."

The miners trooped off down the hill, all but John-
son. The deposed shift boss hung behind a moment.
"I want my time," he told Dorrington and Lawrence.
"I ain't used to being driven like a damned mule."

"Fair enough," Don Coyote said quickly. "Do yuh
want it to-night?"

"Yeh!"

"Can you give it to him, Mr. Dorrington?"

"Yes," the old man answered wearily.

"Good." He turned back to Johnson. "So long as
you're goin', you might as well take the rest of your
cronies with you. He named five men. "Those men
are fired, see? And they can clear out with you—to-
night. Mr. Dorrington will pay the whole gang of you
off."

Johnson grunted and strode off down the hill.

"I'll go into town in the mornin' an' hire some more
men," Don Coyote told his employer. "Now you go on
down an' go to bed, sir. It's been a hard day for you."

Dorrington smiled. "It has been just as hard for
you," he reminded.

"Yeh, but I'm used to 'em hard," Don Coyote

grinned. "The harder they are, the better I like 'em. Good night, sir."

"Good night, Lawrence. You're a brick." The old man stumbled off down the trail.

As Don Coyote watched the bent shoulders out of sight, his thoughts were on his trip to Chandler City the next day. He was rather anxious to see this town that was practically owned by Wilcox Chandler—he was more or less keen to brave the lion in his den, as it were. He might have been surprised, he most certainly would have been interested, had he known the far-reaching effect that that trip would have on himself and on the Buckaroo.

# CHAPTER XXIII

Don Coyote swung a shovel over his shoulder and started off along the ditch, watching carefully for breaks in it. Not until then, after the inaction of the last few minutes, did he realize how dead-tired he was. Every muscle in his body ached; every movement sent sharp needles biting into his legs and arms and chest. It had been daylight before he had gone to sleep that morning and he had worked almost steadily for fifteen hours.

He chuckled softly. "I reckon more people have killed themselves by over-confidence than over-work," he soliloquized. "I got too blamed much confidence in myself. I might just as well have told one of the boys to take the first trick at standin' guard here, one of 'em that got some sleep last night. But no, I got to show how good I am an' do it myself. I got to tell 'em, as it were, 'Me, I don't never sleep an' I eat up work like a donkey engine eats wood. That's me, Don Coyote Lawrence.'" He grunted. "That's also a consarned fool."

He reached the intake of the ditch and turned back. "Oh, well, maybe some day I'll learn. Wish I'd thought to have 'em send up a bite to eat."

He reached the fanhouse again, saw that the water was pouring down the shaft in a steady stream and leaned his shovel against the wall. "Here's where this h'yar sentry takes a rest for a minute or two." He dropped down at full length on the hillside, staring up at the diamond-studded sky. "Thank the Lord there ain't no corporal of the guard in this man's army," he grinned at the moon.

For a space of perhaps five minutes he lay there on the hillside, going over the exciting events of the last few days. Don Coyote had never led a quiet life; indeed, one might almost have called him an adventurer. As has been stated before, his indisposition to mind his own business, his ever readiness to mix into the affairs of others, particularly if it promised excitement, had caused him to diverge widely from the straight and narrow path of an ordinary, humdrum existence. He had been in many tight places and up against many tough situations. But never before, in all his life, had as much action been crowded into as short a space of time as the few days since he had first caught sight of Gayle Dorrington's glove on the Dos Pinos trail. Several times during those few days he had regretted seeing that glove. But those times had been brief. Excitement was meat and drink to Don Coyote, as necessary a part of his life as the air he breathed.

Save for the overpowering weakness that threatened every minute to send him off to sleep, he was quite content with life and with himself. He had a good job; he hadn't learned yet what it would pay, but that didn't matter—money was one of the things he worried least about. He faced a situation that gave promise of plenty of excitement, plenty of action and a good fight occasionally. And, more pleasing than everything else put together, he felt that he was aiding some one who was not only worthy of aid but was sorely in need of it.

So it may be seen that the little lady who first named him Don Quixote—or Don Coyote, as his friends had it—was a character analyst of the first water.

Lawrence got to his feet finally, humming a little tune under his breath, picked up his shovel and started along the ditch. He had taken but a step or two when he heard his name called by a voice that set his heart to thumping. He swung around, to see Gayle coming up the trail. She was carrying something on a tray. Eagerly he ran to meet her.

"Li'l angel of mercy!" he cried, when he saw that she was bringing something to eat. "This reminds me of that little ruckus we had across the pond. It was a good ol' war, that one, one of the best li'l wars I ever fought."

He helped himself to a sandwich from the tray. "But there was times when the eats was few and far between. I rec'lect one night I was standin' sentry duty behind the lines."

He helped himself to another sandwich. "Hadn't had no supper nor nothin'. Been out queenin' with some li'l frog, I reckon, an' missed out. I forget. Anyway, I was pretty close to starvation. Hadn't started to gnaw on my belt yet, but I was just about comin' to that."

He swallowed gratefully and took a third sandwich. "Well, here I was, walkin' along my beat, when all of a sudden I spotted one o' them li'l Salvation Army ladies headin' toward me. Doughnuts! Say, I ate a whole dozen of 'em. And say, do you know that since then I ain't never been able to look a doughnut in the face without comin' to attention and salutin'?"

Don Coyote took his fourth sandwich from the tray and chuckled deeply. The chuckle slowly died in his throat, however, as he looked into the girl's face. She wasn't laughing. She wasn't even smiling. She was staring at him fixedly and she was thoroughly exasperated. No doubt about it.

"Uh—uh—did I get off on the wrong foot takin' these h'yar sandwiches?" he asked. "If I did, I'm sorry. But I can't—very well—put 'em back. Not now."

"Don Coyote, you're a fool!" the girl stated.

"Fool? Me? Why?"

"Because you stayed up here to-night," Gayle answered shortly. "Haven't you any sense? Haven't you any regard for your health? Why didn't you let one of the men watch the ditch? You didn't get any sleep last night and you must be almost dead. You wouldn't even have had anything to eat if I hadn't thought of you."

"An' for that, ma'am, I'm deeply grateful," Don Coyote bowed with the utmost gravity.

"But you're not made of iron. You're not able to stand such a pace. No man is. Now you march down the hill and get some one to take your place up here."

Don Coyote looked at her gravely; the faint light hid the twinkle in his eye. "Ma'am are you plannin' to get married?" he asked abruptly.

"Married!" The question startled her. "What makes you ask such a thing?"

"Well, I just thought mebbe you was practicin' on me," Don Coyote returned soberly. "When a li'l lady starts orderin' folks around—"

"Oh, don't be foolish!" She smiled in spite of herself. "Have another sandwich and here's a bottle of coffee. You must have been a terrible trial to your mother."

"Reckon I was. . . . Good coffee. Did you make it yourself? . . . Still am somethin' of a trial, I reckon. Only she don't hear much of me 'cepting when I get shot or somethin' and some pore fool sends her a telegram that I'm dead."

"Do you get shot often?" Gayle asked smilingly.

"Yes, ma'am. Reg'lar, once a month. An' I don't mean what you mean. No'm. I never drink likker. Tried it oncet when I was a kid and I been tryin' to figure out ever since why Cayenne pepper an' water wouldn't make just as good a drink and a lot cheaper." He stuffed another sandwich into his mouth. "But I'm ramblin' in the head. Must have a talkin' jag like some of the boys tell about. But how I got it I don't know, unless hard work—"

"That is quite possible," Gayle interrupted. "Don't

you want to sit down and rest while you finish your lunch?"

"Sit down?" Don Coyote glanced at the ground; it looked surprisingly inviting. "Don't mind if I do. Will you keep me company?"

"For just a few minutes, until you finish eating. Then we're going down and get one of the men to take your place."

"Are we?" he smiled, and added almost reverently, "say, now, you're a right thoughtful li'l lady."

They sat down side by side, so close that their shoulders touched. A little thrill coursed down Don Coyote's aching spine and he suddenly became silent. His bantering mood had left him; he no longer felt inclined to joke. He wanted to speak. Yet there was only one thing that he wanted to say, and he dared not say it. He finished eating and laid the tray beside him. Quite by accident his hand came to rest on Gayle's. He started to move it away and found that his power of will had suddenly deserted him.

"Damn!" he said softly.

Gayle looked around at him; in the moonlight he caught the full radiance of her delicate features, winsome and at the same time wistful. He sighed and turned his head away, conscious that she had moved her hand from his and hurt by the action.

"What's the matter, Don Coyote?" she asked very soberly.

"Nothin'. Ain't nothin' the matter. Only—I

reckon I better take a li'l cruise along the ditch. Might have sprung a leak."

He rose hastily and held out his hand to help her to her feet. She took it and he drew her slowly upward. Their gazes met and held. Then he bowed his head, but he did not release her hand.

"Miss Dorrington," he began humbly, and found himself suddenly tongue-tied.

"Yes, Don Coyote."

He took a deep breath. "Would you be awful mad —if I told you—that I loved you?"

She did not answer at once, did not move. Then she smiled gently and pressed his hand. "Mad, Don Coyote? Of course I wouldn't be mad."

He gulped. "Then this is me tellin' you."

"But I am afraid I might not believe you," the girl declared.

"Might not believe me!" Don Coyote looked up in surprise. "Why, if I tell you somethin' is true, I reckon you've *got* to believe me. I ain't used to lyin'. And I don't reckon I ever told a lie to a lady in my life."

"Oh, but you misunderstood me," Gayle told him. "I don't mean that you'd lie to me deliberately. But —well, how many different girls have you declared your love for, Don Coyote?"

Very miserable, he stared at the ground. "Quite a few, I reckon," he answered truthfully.

"There, you see? Surely you couldn't have loved them all."

"I thought I did."

"I know. And probably you think you love me. But you can't—not yet. You haven't known me long enough."

"I've known you long enough," Don Coyote began impetuously, "to know that you're the sweetest, purtiest—"

"Oh, please, please!" Gayle interrupted him gently. "We mustn't stand out here on the hillside talking like this."

Don Coyote glanced up, took in the moon, the great star-pierced bowl of sky, the circling mountains, the winding trail of silver far below. "I don't know of any better place to talk about it," he said simply.

"But don't you see? It's foolish to talk about it at all. And it is foolish for you—even to think about it."

Something in her voice, more than her words, caught him; it was as though an icy hand were suddenly tightening about his heart. There was fear in his voice as he asked: "Why do you say that?"

Did she hang her head or did he only imagine it as she answered: "Because I am going to marry Wilcox Chandler."

The world swayed beneath his feet. Anger, hopelessness, futility—these emotions surged over him in turn, and left him cruelly hurt. He took a deep breath, hoping it would clear his reeling head.

"I am sorry—I spoke," he stammered. "Good night, Miss Dorrington."

She pressed his hand reassuringly. "Good night,

Don Coyote," she smiled gently and started down the hill.  She had gone a few steps when she paused and called over her shoulder: "I am going to wake one of the men and send him up to relieve you."

But Don Coyote did not hear her.  He had already shouldered his shovel and started out along the ditch.  As he walked he muttered to himself, over and over again: "Marry Wilcox Chandler!  Huh!  Over my dead body she will!"  And never once did he realize how theatrical were his words.

# CHAPTER XXIV

DON COYOTE did not get away from the mine until nearly ten o'clock the following morning. He rose late, not because he wanted to sleep so long, but because he did not waken. Even the burly cook failed to call him and, more unusual, failed to upbraid him when he presented himself for breakfast long after the others had finished.

"I'm goin' to ride in," he told Dorrington after he had saddled Cleopatra. "The li'l mare needs the exercise. How'd it be for you to send in one o' the boys with the wagon to haul out the new men? There'll be six of 'em and we ought to have them out here by to-night. From the way that stream is runnin' into the shaft, I wouldn't be surprised to see her filled up by to-morrow morning. If she is, we can start right to work."

Dorrington shook his head and chuckled. "I'm afraid we won't get started to-morrow. Most of the boys aren't able to move to-day."

"What's the matter? Too much work yesterday?"

"No, too much sun. Their backs are all blistered."

Don Coyote laughed heartily. In a way he surprised himself. When he had turned in early that morning he had told himself bitterly that he would never laugh again; the human mind was indeed an adaptable affair, he reflected.

"Where are they?" Lawrence asked after a moment. "I don't see none of 'em around the camp."

"They're all lying down in the river, trying to cool off."

"H-m, reckon I'll go down an' take a look at 'em."

Don Coyote mounted, looked about for one last glimpse of Gayle, failed to see her and rode off down the steep trail which led to the river. Just below the mine there was a small dam, backing up the water for the turbo-generator which supplied the mine with electric current. In the shallow pond created by the dam, Don Coyote found the crew of the Buck-aroo. They were stretched out in the icy water with only their heads showing. He regarded them angrily.

"This is no way to earn your wages," he shouted. "The shaft has filled up. We're ready to drain her an' go to work. On the job now, boys. No more loafin'."

Two score eyes stared at him unblinkingly. Not a man moved.

"Well, how about it?" he demanded. "Do you want to get back to work or do you want to get fired?"

Still no one moved, possibly because the twinkle in Don Coyote's eyes was too readily discernible. He sighed at last, smiling. "Jokin' aside, men. Cold water ain't the best thing in the world for sunburn.

You'd be a lot better off if you bummed a pail o' lard off the cook and smeared it over your backs. No foolin'. I ain't kiddin' yuh."

With that he turned the mare smartly and swung up the trail. He felt immeasurably better. Trouble and unhappiness never rested heavily on the shoulders of Don Coyote, and Gayle was for the time being forgotten. For the time being, yes. But the next time he saw her, the next time he touched her hand, he knew that that overpowering heartache would come back. He knew that it was waiting for him just around the corner. He knew that it would come back, again and again, as long as he was near her—unless—

"Ah, well, it's a pretty fair world after all," he told the mare. "And then again it ain't. Sometimes it's a damned onery world. Now how in the Sam Hill can I convince that li'l lady I know what I'm talking about when I tell her I love her? Answer me that, Cleopatra. How can I make her know I'm tellin' the truth? How can I make her change her mind about marryin' that other feller? She's got to change it. Yes, sir, she's just got to. Because I never killed nobody in my life and I don't want to have to start in on that Chandler cuss, however much he rates it. Cleopatra, answer me."

But Cleopatra answered only by kicking up her heels and racing down the road at a mad gallop.

Don Coyote arrived in Chandler City shortly after noon. He stabled his horse and started down the street to find a restaurant. The business of eating was of more importance just then than the business of hiring miners. He found an eating house, went in, sat down and picked up a menu. He had about decided on his meal when some one whacked him resoundingly on the back. He whirled in his chair to confront a small, thin-chested individual with ratty eyes and a receding chin, a flashily-dressed little person who looked strangely out of place in a town of big men and mud-caked boots and blue overalls.

"How's it, sarg?" the dapper little man grinned elatedly.

"Sufferin' cats!" Don Coyote growled. "For a little shrimp you pack a mean wallop. What's the idea of bustin' me that way?" His voice was gruff, almost angry; but there was a merry twinkle in his gray eyes that took the barb from his words.

"Matter of principle," the little man replied. "Whenever I meet an old sergeant o' mine, I smack him one. Only usually it's in de jaw. You got off easy, big boy. Put her there."

Don Coyote grasped the outthrust hand and wrung it warmly. "Sit down, Soapy. Dinner's on me. I'm right glad to see yuh."

A queer combination, this pair, as far apart in appearance and mode of living as the poles. "Soapy" Gourd—so named by his buddies because of his almost inhuman ability to keep his person clean under conditions where cleanliness was far removed from godliness—drank hard liquor, considered himself above working for a living and broke the law. Don Coyote never touched strong drink, earned his daily bread by hard labor and tried to obey the law. Yet they were bound by a friendship as strong as death, a friendship that had begun in a certain shell hole near St. Mihiel and had been interrupted—not ended—by a piece of shrapnel on the day before the Armistice. Soapy had collected the shrapnel, somewhere in the neighborhood of his right lung, and Don Coyote had helped place him on a stretcher.

So they had parted, Soapy very white and frightened, Don Coyote rather misty-eyed, to meet again in this fly-ridden, odorous eating house in Chandler City.

For an hour or more they discussed other days, wild, exciting, laborious, dangerous days. Don Coyote quite forgot the mission that had brought him to Chandler City until he chanced to glance at his watch. Then he called for the check.

"Enough of old times," he grinned. "Let's move up to the present. What you doin' in Chandler City?"

Soapy tapped his chest and smiled enigmatically. "De old sawbones told me my pipes was on de bum. So I come West fer me health."

In view of the twinkle in Soapy's eyes, the explanation was not entirely satisfactory. "But why'd you pick on Chandler City?" Don Coyote asked.

Soapy expanded visibly, glanced around with a furtive look in his little eyes and lowered his voice. "Got a big job on here. Boid by de name of Chandler. Crib."

"Corn crib?" Don Coyote asked ingeniously.

"Naw, yah dummy! Come in out o' de rain. I ain't got no corns. I'm talkin' about a safe."

"Oh! I reckon I get you now. You're going to crack a safe."

Soapy patted him on the shoulder. "You'll learn, son; you'll learn."

Don Coyote sighed and regarded the little man thoughtfully. "Did you ever try workin' for a livin', Soapy?"

The little man looked frightened. "What? Me? Work fer a livin'? What you tryin' to do, big boy? Kid me?"

"Oh, come, Soapy! Work never killed anybody."

"No? Well, it ain't goin' to get a chance to kill me. I done enough work in de army to last me fer a long time. I take it easy from now on. Work? Not me, baby!"

Don Coyote smiled faintly. "There's a jute mill in San Quentin, Soapy. And a rock pile at Folsom. Maybe you're mistaken about not doin' any more work."

"Huh? Aw, say, big boy, you ain't talkin' to dis baby. I ain't never been in stir yet an' de sawbones says it'd be bad for me pipes. Besides, de bull ain't livin' dat can collar me."

Don Coyote rolled a cigarette and spoke to the

pile of empty dishes in front of him. "Four dollars a day and board. Washin' dishes an' waitin' on table at the Buckaroo mine. You can start to-morrow."

The wild look of a cornered rat came into Soapy's little eyes. "Aw, listen, big boy! I don't wantta go to work. I got dis job all ready to pull. It's a pipe. Nothin' to it. Dis Chandler boid keeps his payroll—"

Don Coyote seemed not to hear him. "Later on, when we get really workin', I may be able to break you in as timekeeper or somethin' like that. I'm superintendent of the Buckaroo an' I'll see that you get ahead. We better get movin' now. I got some more men to hire."

Soapy looked at his old buddy incredulously. "My Gawd, sarg!" he breathed. "You ain't in earnest?"

"Never more in earnest in my life," Don Coyote nodded quietly.

Soapy Gourd sighed volubly. "I thought I was t'rough takin' orders when dey kicked me out o' de army."

"We all make mistakes," Don Coyote grinned. "Let's move."

He rose from his chair and strode to the counter to pay the check. Soapy stared after him for a moment. Then he too rose and followed along, shaking his head disconsolately.

"Oh, what a dumb dora I turned out to be!" he moaned. "How much did yuh say? Four a day and found?"

To all appearances a relatively unimportant event, this meeting and hiring of Soapy Gourd—and yet in certain ways it marked a turning point in the history of the Buckaroo mine and in the lives of the three men and the woman most concerned in its success.

# CHAPTER XXV

At noon the following day the barrier over the tunnel mouth was ripped off and a deluge of muddy water was sent roaring across the clearing and down the canyon to the river. Standing beside his employer, Don Coyote watched it and grinned pridefully.

"Well, we got the fire out in jig time," he remarked. "That's somethin'."

Dorrington nodded abstractedly. "I'm almost afraid to go into the tunnel, afraid of what we'll find there. Fifteen thousand dollars doesn't go very far these days, when you consider the wages we have to pay and the price they're asking for timbers. I doubt if it will be enough."

"Well, let's not worry about it till we find out what the damage is," Don Coyote suggested optimistically.

When the water from the tunnel had diminished to a trickling stream, they started in, picking their way through the débris of mud and rock and charred timbers that all but clogged the passageway. They moved cautiously, inspecting each set of timbers as they went along. For a thousand feet they groped their way through the moist, dripping tunnel. Then they found their path blocked by a cave-in. Dorrington shone his light on the timbers that were exposed.

"It must have started from this point and burned all the way to the shaft and probably further," he remarked lifelessly. "That will mean at least two thousand feet to clear out and re-timber, to say nothing of the damage that may have been done in the air shaft. It's a big task, Lawrence."

"What of it?" Don Coyote came back. "We've both faced bigger ones, ain't we?"

"Yes, but we've so little money," the old man reminded dubiously.

"Well, we'll use what we've got and then we'll go out an' get some more."

"That will be hard to do, if it isn't altogether impossible. The stockholders absolutely will not advance any more money and we can't force them to, because the stock is non-assessable."

"Any stock in the treasury that we could go out an' peddle?"

"Not a share."

"H-m." Don Coyote pursed his lips thoughtfully. He saw very clearly the task that was laid out for him: he was not only to superintend the work at the Buckaroo but he was also to keep up the flagging spirits of its manager and principal stockholder.

"Any more old tailings that we might run through the mill?" he asked.

"Not a pound."

"H-m." He grinned at Dorrington. "Well, we ain't beat yet, are we?"

The younger man's spirit was contagious and Dorrington could not but smile. "No, by the Lord, we're not," he exclaimed. "And we won't be until our last dollar is gone and our last man is heading off down the road to Chandler City."

"Good! Let's get a crew in here an' go to work."

The days passed swiftly, days of feverish toil for every man at the Buckaroo. Dorrington and Lawrence spent nearly all their waking hours in the tunnel, directing, supervising, encouraging. Even Gayle took part in what Don Coyote termed the "big push." She helped the cook at times, she laughed and joked with the men, she did a thousand and one things to make life easier and more pleasant and more livable for them all.

With Don Coyote she was on the most friendly terms, though never again did their conversation become as intimate as on that night when she brought him his lunch on the hill. This, however, was no fault of Lawrence's. A dozen times during the weeks that followed he assured her of his love. And each time she chose smilingly to treat it as a jest.

"You only think you love me, Don Coyote," she would tell him, "just as you've thought you loved dozens of other girls. You mustn't be foolish."

And Don Coyote tried with all his might not to be foolish; and the harder he tried the more foolish he became—if loving Gayle Dorrington were really foolishness. There were times, indeed, when he thought it was and cursed himself for his weakness. But there were other times, and they were far more frequent, when the very sight of her made his heart ache with longing, when the casual touch of her hand set the blood racing through his veins, when even the thought of her made his head reel with an angry, insane jealousy.

Chandler was a frequent visitor at the mine during those weeks. Though occasionally he chose to disguise the real motive for his visits by inspecting the work that was being done, it was plain to those most concerned—Dorrington and Gayle and Don Coyote—that his real purpose was to see the li'l lady of the Buckaroo, as Lawrence had christened Gayle.

At Dorrington's request—though such a request was unnecessary in so far as Don Coyote was concerned—no mention was made to Gayle of their suspicions of Chandler's duplicity. In fairness to the man, and to Gayle, they could not bring up such a matter without some tangible proof. And as yet they had nothing, not a thing in the world save their own suspicions. Besides, though Gayle had vaguely hinted to her father that she intended to marry Chandler, no date had as yet been set for the wedding. Don Coyote was content to bide his time.

Chandler, it also developed, had taken an unusual interest in Ben Burke. The former superintendent had been declared insane by an insanity commission and had been committed to the state hospital in Napa. Here Chandler had stepped in and, offering to defray all the expenses, had succeeded in having Burke sent to a private sanitarium in Sacramento. The meaning of the move was very plain to Don Coyote and he remarked as much to Dorrington.

"Chandler's scared Burke will talk and that somethin' he says will get back to us. Course, nobody's goin' to set much store by the ravings of an insane man. But just the same he might say somethin' that would connect this fight against the Buckaroo with Chandler. An' that's just what Chandler don't want to happen, if I know anything about this situation. So Chandler don't take no chances. He has him sent to a private sanitarium where he'll be safe. Yes, an' where he'll stay for the rest of his life whether he gets his sanity back or not."

"That is a disquieting thought," Dorrington frowned. "Burke was never any particular friend of mine. Personally, I never cared much for the man. But I hate to think of his being cooped up in an asylum if he really should recover his sanity. Do you think there is much chance of it, Lawrence?"

"You can't prove it by me," Don Coyote smiled. "I ain't an expert along them lines. But speakin' off-hand, I'd say he had as good a chance as any other nut. Lots of 'em do snap out of it. Happens every day. But if he does, it won't last long—not if they keep him cooped up in a crazy house with a lot o' lunatics. Maybe a year or two, maybe only a few months, an' he'd be ravin' again."

"It is unpleasant, very unpleasant," Dorrington said quietly, and for the time being the affair was closed.

The task of clearing and re-timbering the Buckaroo

tunnel was not completed until the middle of October. The smaller streams were dry now; the water in the Gila was very low. The aspens were flaming in their new dress of salmon-pink. Laden with pine-nuts, the Indians were returning from their fall pilgrimage to the dry hills east and south of the mine. There was a chill in the night air that gave promise of an early winter.

Don Coyote came out of the tunnel one morning with the jubilant announcement that their long task had been completed. They were at last ready to go ahead with new work.

"First of all," he told Dorrington, "I reckon we better make a new survey of the whole workings. You was tellin' me that you should have hit that old ore chamber long before this. Somethin' must be wrong an' it's up to us to find out what it is."

"I agree with you perfectly, Lawrence," Dorrington nodded, with a slow smile. "Something is wrong and I am quite certain that it is not my surveying. However, it won't do any harm to go over the whole thing again."

They spent two days running their lines. The old shaft, which had been sunk by the original Buckaroo Mining Company in 1869, was the base of their survey. It was caved and could not be entered, but the shafthead was easily discernible, a shallow depression marked by rotting timbers and a heap of rusted hoisting machinery.

Their result, when the survey was completed, was

the same as Dorrington and Burke had arrived at; according to the old map, Dorrington's tunnel had crosscut the ore chamber exactly in the center.

"But we ain't got no more ore chamber than a jackrabbit," Don Coyote mused on the evening they finished the survey. "You've already run the tunnel a hundred feet past where it ought to be. But it ain't there. No use goin' any further."

They were seated in the living room of Dorrington's home. A cheerful fire was blazing on the big hearth. Gayle was idly turning the pages of a magazine, while she listened to the discussion. It was a cozy, home-like scene, a scene that contrasted pointedly with the dread thought of failure that was in the minds of all three.

The old man stared into the fire for a long time, a helpless look in his fine eyes. "But what can I do, Lawrence?" he asked at last. "Every cent I have in the world is tied up here. If I admit failure, if I give up now, it means—well, it means that I shall have to go out and look for a job. I'm not a young man any more, Lawrence. It might be hard for me to find work."

Though the thought was unexpressed, both Gayle and Don Coyote knew what was in the mind of the older man. A man without dependents might live very cheaply; certainly any man with his health would not have a hard time earning his daily bread and keeping a shelter over his head. But a daughter demanded a home, clothes, a thousand and one things that a man might class as luxuries.

"I wouldn't worry, dad," Gayle put in after a moment. "I can always go to work, you know."

It was odd, Don Coyote reflected, that she made no mention of her coming marriage. Had she changed her mind? Had something about which they knew nothing come up between Chandler and Gayle? But his hopes were quickly blasted, for she added, with heightened color:

"Besides, after I am married you will never need to worry again."

Dorrington straightened in his chair. "You must know, Gayle," he replied, "that I shall never accept money nor favors from Wilcox Chandler."

"But why, dad?"

He smiled gently. "I think we've been over that, dear." He turned back to Don Coyote. "Let's come down to cases, Lawrence. As you say, there is no use running that tunnel any further. I have about two thousand dollars left. Shall I spend it in prospecting around, running a few short drifts this way and that? Or shall I give the whole thing up as a bad job, keep my share of the two thousand and call it quits?"

Don Coyote shook his head obdurately. "No, we ain't quittin'. Not yet. From all reports, there's millions o' dollars left in that mine—ore that was too low grade to pay to ship out o' the country in the old days. We're goin' to get that ore, if we have to turn

the whole mountain over to find the ore chamber an'
the ledge it opens up."

"But we can't turn the mountain over without
money. Neither can we open up the old workings and
find it that way. It would take fifty thousand dollars
to clean out that original shaft and tunnel. We haven't
got the money and I don't see where we can get it."

"We might interest other capital," Don Coyote suggested.

Dorrington shook his head. "No, it couldn't be
done. On the strength of the reports I have and that
map, we might do it. I raised a good deal of money
on them when we first incorporated. But we have
proved the map is not authentic. That turns the whole
proposition into an out-and-out wildcat. So there we
are. It looks—like we're beaten."

"No!" Don Coyote's voice rose. "We ain't beaten!
Not much we ain't! Let's see that map."

The map was lying on the table. Dorrington handed
it to him in silence. Lawrence bent over it. For the
space of five, then, fifteen minutes he pored over it.
Dorrington rose from his chair at last and took a few
turns up and down the room. The lines of worry in
his face were graven deeply now; there was a hopeless look in his eyes; his shoulders were bowed as
with a heavy weight. He seemed very old and forlorn
and beaten. Gayle's eyes grew misty as she watched
him.

Don Coyote straightened up at last and laid the map
aside very quietly. "Would you mind walkin' over

to the bunkhouse with me a minute, Mr. Dorrington?"

"Yes, of course."

Don Coyote turned to Gayle and bowed gravely. "Good night, Miss Dorrington. An' don't you worry your li'l self about this thing. I got a mighty strong hunch we're goin' to pull through all right. An' when I get a hunch—well, just lay your money on me. You'll win in the long run."

There was something in his eyes, his voice, his bearing that gave her renewed hope. No one could long remain downcast in the face of the optimism of this smiling, confident young man.

"I'll try not to worry, Don Coyote," she smiled. "Good night."

The two men passed out into the darkness. "Just wanted to ask you a question," Lawrence explained in a low voice. "Didn't care about the li'l lady hearin' me. Has that there map ever been out of your possession?"

Dorrington looked at him quickly. There had been a different quality to his voice but the light was too faint for the old man to see his face.

"Yes," he admitted. "When I was organizing the company I turned it over to Wilcox Chandler. He kept it for me in his safe."

"Long?"

"Several months."

"H-m. That's all I wanted to know. Thanks, Mr. Dorrington."

"Do you think—" Dorrington began.

"No, I ain't thought nothin' yet," Don Coyote cut in.

"I'm goin' to do my thinkin' now. I'll tell yuh about it in the mornin'. Good night, sir."

Puzzled and bewildered the old man muttered "Good night," and watched Lawrence stride off toward the bunkhouse.

# CHAPTER XXVI

Don Coyote went to bed at once, but he did not go to sleep for many hours. It was quite plain to him now why Dorrington had failed to locate the old ore chamber. The map in his possession was not the original. Several things forced him to this conclusion. In the first place, the map was not authentic; distances or directions, one or the other, were incorrect—for if they had not been, the new tunnel would have struck the ore chamber. The map might have been drawn incorrectly in the first place but that was not likely. It was a simple thing technically; even an inexperienced engineer could have prepared it without making any great error.

In the second place, there were several things about the map that, figuratively, did not ring true. The lettering, for instance. Printed in an ornate style long out of date, the characters lacked firmness and confidence, as though the man who had made them were not used to printing that particular type of lettering. In short, they were drawn rather than printed—there is a wide distinction between the two.

In view of these facts Don Coyote came to the inevitable conclusion that the map now in Dorrington's possession was a forgery which had been substituted for the original. The substitution had been made,

naturally, when Chandler had the map in his safe.
Why? Again Don Coyote, like Dorrington, came up
against a stone wall.

Chandler was a stockholder in the company. He had
put up considerable money for the development of the
mine. It was unreasonable to assume that he would go
out of his way to wreck the company. And yet that
was the assumption Don Coyote had made in the beginning and he resolved to stick to it until he found
proof that some one else was guilty. Some day, he
hoped, Chandler's real motive would be brought to
light. In the meantime, the mining magnate either
had destroyed the original map or now had it in his
possession.

How to find out and, if he actually had it, how to get
it. There was the problem. Don Coyote put a great
deal of thought on the question. It was an ethical one
and, despite his apparent wildness, Don Coyote was an
ethical young man. Was burglary, under the circumstances, justified? He rather thought it was. If
Chandler actually had the map, he had gained possession of it by fraudulent means—at least his substitution
of a forged map was fraudulent. Would it, then, be
wrong to burglarize Chandler's home and recover this
document which rightfully belonged to Dorrington?

Don Coyote pondered. It was rather an involved
question of ethics. Two wrongs certainly didn't make
a right. On the other hand, Dorrington's future happiness and the fortunes of the other stockholders in the
Buckaroo depended on the recovery of that map. With-

out it, the mine was worthless. With it, the property might make millions for its owners.

And still Don Coyote pondered.

"Reckon I'd best sleep on it," he decided at last. "That's the best way to figure out a problem. Get all the facts straight in your mind an' then sleep on 'em. The answer'll be waitin' for you in the mornin'. An' it'll be the right answer, too."

Morning found Don Coyote poking his head into the cookhouse. "Soapy, I would palaver with thee," he announced.

Soapy grunted. He was a different man from the one Lawrence had literally dragged out to the Buckaroo three months before. He had lost his cough. The spots of color that had flamed on his high cheekbones had given way to a healthier tinge. He had gained nearly fifteen pounds, not an inconsiderable amount when one considered Soapy's diminutive stature. Yet despite these facts, Soapy had never quite forgiven his former sergeant. Born with the immutable idea that the world owed him a living, the realization that he was actually working for that living was a heavy blow to his pride.

"What yuh want, big boy?" he asked when they had walked out into the clearing.

Don Coyote glanced around, saw that no one was within hearing and said quietly: "You were tellin' me somethin' about robbin' a safe when I met you in town. Fact is, I believe it was Wilcox Chandler's safe you were plannin' to rob. Is that right, Soapy?"

"Yeh, dat's right!" Soapy growled. "An' I'd a done it if it hadn't been fer you. Gee, what a sucker I been. Out here peelin' spuds when I might o' been on easy street. I never knew there was so many spuds in the woild as I've seen right here."

Lawrence smiled. "But ain't it some satisfaction, Soapy, to realize that you're earnin' your own livin'? When yuh get your ol' pay envelope at the end o' the month, don't it kind o' please yuh to think that you earned that money yourself, honestly?"

"Naw! It jus' makes me feel sick fer bein' such a sucker," Soapy grunted. There was a sparkle in his little eyes, however, that told Don Coyote that Soapy wasn't telling the exact truth.

"Listen, Soapy! How long would it take you to cook up some soup out o' dynamite an' get ready to rob that safe?" Lawrence asked casually.

"Huh! Say, what you drivin' at?"

"I'm drivin' at robbin' that safe," Don Coyote answered calmly. "I want you to help me."

Soapy swallowed audibly and looked away. He did not speak at once and Don Coyote became conscious that the little man was trembling.

"Why, Soapy! What's the matter?"

"Aw, shucks! I guess this spud peelin' an' dish washin' has turned me into a yaller dog. I dunno. When I look down th' canyon dere an' breathe dis air an' hear th' boids singin', I—I—aw, damn it, I get to t'inkin' about dem poor suckers cooped up down in San Quentin an' I get cold feet."

Don Coyote caught his breath. Here was a contingency he had overlooked. He wasn't afraid to take a little risk himself. But now that he thought about it, he knew he shouldn't drag Soapy into the affair. Soapy was all right. Given a fair chance he'd go straight. Drag him down to San Quentin and he'd be an enemy of society as long as he lived, which probably wouldn't be long. No! Don Coyote shuddered. If Soapy got caught, was sentenced to prison and died there, he'd feel like a murderer.

"Forget about it, Soapy," he said hastily. "I was just kiddin' you."

Soapy looked him squarely in the eye—rather an unusual phenomenon, for Soapy rarely looked any one in the eye; he'd gotten out of the habit.

"You're lyin'," the little man pronounced. "You wasn't kiddin' me at all. You got somethin' up yer sleeve. Out wit' it, big boy."

Don Coyote fidgeted. Deceit was foreign to his nature; he couldn't lie convincingly, not even to Soapy Gourd. "This feller Chandler has got somethin' we need," he admitted at last. "Leastwise, I think he has. It's a map. He got it from Dorrington by trickery. The old man give him this map to keep for him an' he substituted a phoney one. If we don't get that map back, the old man goes busted. I was thinkin' that you might be able to give me a hand. But, doggone it, Soapy, I ain't goin'—"

"Aw, dry up!" Soapy growled. "What you tryin' to do, show me a good time? Think I'm goin' to lay down on a pal? Not me, big boy! If dere's somethin' in dat safe you want, tell me what it is an' I'll get it for yuh. An' I don't mean maybe."

Don Coyote wavered. "You ain't goin' alone. If you go, I'll go with you. You'll have to have some help. It's a big job to blow a safe, ain't it?"

"What? Dat safe?"

"Well, I've never seen it."

"I have. I got a slant at it t'rough a window. It's an ol' tin can, dat's all it is. I could open dat box wit' my pocketknife. Don't even need dat. Why, dat box is a million years old. Come over on th' ark, dat baby did. I betcha the tumblers click so loud when yuh turn the knob dat you c'n hear 'em all over town. It's a pipe. Nothin' to it. No Jimmy Valentine stuff, no sandpaper, no nothin'. Jest a good ear an' blooey! She's open."

"And you won't have to blow off the door or wreck anything?" Lawrence questioned dubiously.

"Naw! Nothin' like dat!" Soapy scoffed. "It's simple as pullin' de pin out of a hand-grenade."

Don Coyote sighed deeply. "All right, Soapy. Don't say anything about it to anybody. But we'll go to town to-night."

"We! I tell yuh I don't need no help!" Soapy insisted.

"An' I tell you you ain't goin' alone. That's settled."

Soapy shrugged. "Suit yerself, big boy. See you later. I hear that big tub of a cook callin' me. More spuds, damn 'em."

There was an eager light in his pale eyes and a cocky tilt to his shoulders as he hurried off toward the cookhouse. Don Coyote was filled with vague misgivings as he watched him out of sight. His conscience was not entirely clear. It was bad enough to be mixed up in this sort of business himself. But to drag Soapy into it, to let the little man risk his freedom over an affair that was none of his concern—that wasn't exactly right. Still, what could be done about it?"

Don Coyote's heart was heavy as he walked slowly over to the house.

# CHAPTER XXVII

"I GOT somethin' up my sleeve, Mr. Dorrington,"
Don Coyote told his employer a few minutes later. "I
ain't ready yet to say what it is but I think me an'
Soapy Gourd had better take the afternoon off an' go to
Chandler City. Got a li'l business down there I want
to see to."

Dorrington scanned him narrowly and, despite all
efforts to appear casual, Lawrence dropped his eyes.
The old man assented readily enough, however, with
never a question as to the purpose of his trip. Don
Coyote knew that he had the presence of Gayle to thank
for this. Had they been alone, Dorrington might have
made unpleasant inquiries.

"There's enough work to keep the men busy cleanin'
up tag ends," Don Coyote remarked, "and if I was
you, I wouldn't run the tunnel any further till you hear
from me."

Dorrington nodded. "Yes, I guess there isn't much
use running it any further in that direction anyway."

"Aren't you awfully mysterious, Don Coyote?"
Gayle put the question smilingly.

"Me?" Lawrence grinned innocently. "I don't
mean to be. Fact of the matter is, Soapy Gourd has
some business in town an' I want to be there to see

that he does it right. I'm sort of his guardian, don't yuh know?"

"I've noticed that. I don't think he'd have worked here a day if it hadn't been for you. But, by the way, would you be offended if I invited myself to ride in with you this afternoon? I am going to town and I don't care about going alone."

"Offended!" Don Coyote exclaimed. "I'll be tickled to death."

"Then I won't come."

"Won't come! Why not?"

"I don't want to be the cause of your death."

"Now you're kiddin' me again," Don Coyote drawled and started toward the door. "Two o'clock all right with you?"

"Two o'clock will be fine."

Don Coyote was smiling when he walked out of the door, but by the time he gained the foot of the steps he was scowling. He didn't like this business, not even a little bit. He was nervous and fidgety already; he certainly had never been born to be a safe-cracker. He wondered if Dorrington and Gayle had noticed his disconcertion. Was that what had prompted the girl to invite herself to go along with them?

But that was absurd. Gayle could have no suspicions as regarded his mission in Chandler City. She was probably going out with Chandler again. Or possibly going to some party.

Shortly before two o'clock Soapy Gourd edged into the barn where Don Coyote was saddling the horses.

He had changed in the last few hours. The furtive look that had almost gone out of his eyes during his sojourn at the Buckaroo had returned. He spoke out of the side of his mouth as of old. He was once again the law-breaker, the man who lived by his wits, the enemy of society—and Don Coyote was infinitely sorry.

"Got a rod?" Soapy demanded in an abrupt whisper.

"A rod?" Lawrence queried mildly.

"Sure! Don't you know what a rod is?" the little man asked, aghast at the other's ignorance.

"Ah, mebbe you think I don't. A rod is sixteen and a half feet."

Soapy shook his head disgustedly. "Naw! I ain't talkin' about feet. Besides, yuh don't call 'em feet any more. They're dogs. Where was you brung up, big boy?"

"Texas, mostly," Don Coyote admitted.

"Huh! No wonder! Always thought there was somethin' wrong wit' yuh, but I never knew before that you was a foreigner."

"Don't kid me, li'l shrimp," Don Coyote grinned. "Now what for did you ask me did I have a rod?"

"A rod, baby, is a gat, a gun."

Lawrence's grin gave way to a frown; he shook his head. "That's out, Soapy. I ain't got a gun to my name. Ain't got no use for one. What's more, we ain't packin' no guns to-day."

"What? Goin' out on a job wit'out a gun?" Soapy gasped his amazement.

"We're aimin' to open a safe, not kill somebody," Don Coyote returned.

"But suppose some bozo tries to queer our game?"

"Then our game'll be queered. You got a gun, Soapy?"

"I'll say!"

"Gimme it!"

Soapy cursed and spat disgustedly out of the side of his mouth. He knew the futility of arguing with Don Lawrence. He delivered the gun, under protest, and watched Don Coyote hide it under the hay in a manger.

"You can get it when you come back," Lawrence told him with a slow grin.

Soapy shrugged. "What you saddlin' three horses for?" he demanded. "Ain't two enough to carry you an' me?"

"Miss Dorrington is going with us."

"What! On dis job?"

"Naw, yuh foolish li'l shrimp. She's just ridin' in with us. When we hit town she'll go on about her business an' we'll go on about ours."

Soapy shook his head gravely. "The game's queered. I never seen a skoit yet that wasn't a jinx. She'll put the kibosh on us sure's the devil. Better keep away from her. Let her ride in alone."

"I don't believe I'm afraid of her, Soapy. I believe in a hunch now and then but I never set much store by jinxes. You can ride on ahead if you want to. We'll overtake you before we get to town."

It was Soapy's turn to grin. "Yer a wise guy, now

ain't yuh? But dat suits me. Gimme one o' dem nags an' I'll be on my way. See yuh at th' city limits."

Lawrence led one of the horses out of the stable for him and handed him the reins. Soapy approached on the right side and narrowly avoided a healthy kick for his pains.

"Try the other side, Soapy," Lawrence advised. "Horses on the left and cows on the right. That's the rule."

Scowling angrily, the little man edged around to the other side of the animal, mounted without difficulty and rode away, showing blue sky between himself and the saddle at every step.

Don Coyote led the other horses over to the house and called for Gayle, who appeared a moment later in the doorway. "All ready?" she smiled. "Where's your little friend?"

"He went on ahead. Got impatient, I reckon."

As Don Coyote helped her to mount, she asked laughingly: "Are you sure he didn't go on ahead by request?"

"Cross my heart," Don Coyote vowed, as he swung into the saddle. "But now that you bring it up, I'll admit it wasn't a bad idea. Gives me another chance to ask you to marry me."

Gayle did not reply as they started off down the road.

"Ain't you goin' to?" he persisted.

For the first time since that night on the hill she

took his question very soberly. Her grave, wistful eyes met his and there was no smile on her lips.

"I think I could make you love me, Gayle," Don Coyote went on tremulously. "I ain't much for looks, I'll admit. And I reckon I seem kind o' rough an' coarse to you. My grammar ain't what it ought to be, neither. They never taught much grammar in the school I was educated in. Still an' all, I'd be mighty nice to you. They's lots o' worse men in the world than me."

"And mighty few better ones, Don Coyote," Gayle said seriously.

"Aw, there yuh go, kiddin' me again."

"No, I'm not, Don. I mean it. You're a dear and you've got a heart as big as all outdoors. But—I really can't marry you."

Don Coyote smiled at her ruefully. He was persistent, if nothing else. "Course, Wilcox Chandler has got a lot more money than I'll ever have. But when you come right down to it, do you think he'll make any better husband than me?"

The girl must have spoken before she thought, for she said quickly. "I doubt if he'll make as good a husband as you would, Don Coyote."

Lawrence looked at her sharply, through narrowed eyes. "Then maybe you'll tell me why you're goin' to marry him."

She smiled, not without an effort. "Did you ever stop to think that I might love him?"

Don Coyote nodded very gravely. "Yeh, I thought

o' that. But, somehow, I don't believe it. He ain't your kind, Gayle. Not that I am," he disclaimed quickly. "There ain't a man in the world good enough for you. But Chandler ain't—well, he ain't the sort o' man you'd fall in love with. Now is he, Gayle?"

The girl smiled gently into his eyes and looked away. "Don't you think you are acting rather foolishly, arguing with me this way?"

He was instantly and completely repentant. "I'm sorry. Please forgive me, Gayle. Only I love you so blamed much that—aw shucks! I won't bother you no more."

Don Coyote felt the barrier of constraint that his clumsy love-making had raised between them. He did not speak again for several miles. Gayle addressed him now and then, but apparently sensing the feeling that had come over him she said nothing that necessitated a reply. She commented on the changing scenery of the canyon and on her visit to town—Wilcox Chandler was giving a party for a number of his acquaintances. She was going to change to her evening dress at the home of a girl friend and Chandler was going to bring her back to the mine in his car. Her horse would be left in town until the supply wagon went in again.

Don Coyote pricked up his ears at the mention of Chandler's party. That would necessitate a change in their plans. They could hardly rob a safe in a house full of people. Chandler was bringing her back to the mine after the party, though. That was good news. He'd be out of the way, even if his servants weren't.

His thoughts, however, did not remain long on the night's adventure. As always when he was with Gayle, he could think of little else save his love for her. While she conversed casually, Don Coyote held his peace and did some heavy thinking.

They were within a mile of the town and Soapy Gourd had appeared in sight a few hundred yards ahead of them before he spoke again. Then he put his hand on her arm, forced her to meet his gaze.

"If I ask you one question will you answer it for me?"

"Why, I think so," she said, surprised. "What is it?"

"Promise to answer it truthfully?"

"Why, of course. I don't usually lie to you, do I, Don?"

"No, yuh don't. Still—this is kind of an important question."

"I'll answer it—" she caught herself— "if it has nothing to do with love."

"It hasn't—not directly."

"All right, Don. Cross my heart I'll tell you the truth."

"Here it is: If we found that ore body and made a big success of the Buckaroo, would you still insist on marryin' Wilcox Chandler?"

The girl caught her breath; the color faded from her cheeks. "Don! You're not fair. That's not a fair question. I—"

"I'm sorry," he interposed hastily, and the color

went out of his cheeks, too. "You don't need to answer it. We won't say nothin' more about it, Gayle."

And nothing more was said—indeed, there was nothing more that needed to be said. Don Coyote had his answer, as plainly as though she had spoken the words: "No! No! No! It is the failure of the Buckaroo that is forcing me to marry Wilcox Chandler!"

# CHAPTER XXVIII

Don Coyote and Soapy left their horses at the livery stable and had dinner that evening in the same restaurant in which they had met three months before. It was a different Don Coyote, however. His face was leaner. The lines about his mouth had deepened. There was a worried, baffled look in his gray eyes. Not until now, perhaps, did he realize the importance of the battle which engaged him. More important than life itself, it almost seemed, for without Gayle Dorrington the world would be a drear, dead place.

He saw now why she had agreed to marry Wilcox Chandler; he saw, too, why she had postponed the ceremony so long. She probably liked the man but she most certainly did not love him. Nevertheless, she would marry him to spare her father the humiliation of failure and defeat. With Chandler's millions, she would be able to provide for him at a time when he seemed fast losing his powers to provide for himself. Dorrington wasn't old, as men go, but successive defeats had left their indelible mark upon him. He wasn't a quitter, either; he'd fight as hard as the next man. But it is hard for the old to win in a world that is made for the young. Don Coyote knew it and the thought brought realization of the necessity for getting possession of the map. With that map, they would at least have a chance of winning. Without it, they were foredoomed to failure, defeat, heartache, misery.

"You ain't got much to say, big boy," Soapy growled across his soup. "Ain't got cold feet, have yuh?"

"No, Soapy; I'm just thinkin'," Don Coyote answered. "Yuh know, if we don't get this h'yar map to-night we're going' to be in a devil of a mess. Dorrington will have to close down the mine. It's just a waste o' money to do any more development work without knowin' where he's at. If we fail, it will be an awful blow to him. He's got every last red cent he owns tied up in this thing. If it flivvers, it'll about kill the old boy. We just got to get that map."

"We'll get it, don't worry none about that," Soapy returned confidently.

"If it's there," Lawrence reminded. "Yuh got to remember, Soapy, that I'm just playin' a hunch. I ain't nowise sure that Chandler has the map. Besides, it may not be in his safe."

"Where else would it be? There ain't no safe deposit boxes in this town."

"How do yuh know, Soapy?"

The little man grunted. "'Cause it's part o' my business to find out them things. That's why I know."

"Do yuh know where his safe is? What part o' the house it's in?"

"Sure I do. I spent a week gettin' the lay before I met you that day. I know right where it is an' how

to get there.  It's in kind of a study on the second
floor.  We can git in the back door, through a pantry
and up th' back stairs.  It's a pipe."

"Here's another thing, Soapy," Lawrence spoke up,
recalling what Gayle had told him about the party that
night.  "Chandler is putting on a big party to-night.
It will probably last till midnight or later.  We'll have
to lay low till it's over, when he'll pull out to take
Miss Dorrington home."

"Lay low me eye!"  The little man shook his head
hopelessly.  "Big boy, your ignorance gives me a pain
in the neck.  You don't know nuttin' about dis game.
A party is jus' de t'ing.  Makes everyt'ing sweet an'
pretty.  Lots o' people runnin' around, see?  Lots o'
noise, see?  Maybe a little drinkin', see?  All that's so
much the better fer us.  If we stub our toe on the
kitchen steps, nobody hears us.  If we slam a door or
kick somethin' over, nobody'll pay any attention to it.
Get me?"

"Yes-s-s, I reckon there is somethin' to that.  You
think we ought to pull it off when the party's at its
height, huh?"

"Dat's de stuff!"  Soapy applauded.  "You'll learn,
big boy; you'll learn."

Don Coyote smiled grimly.  "I don't know's I want
to learn, Soapy."

When Lawrence walked up to the counter to pay the
check, he observed a tall man with a cadaverous face
and intense dark eyes, who stood idly chatting with
the proprietor.  Don Coyote gave him little heed as

he paid his bill and walked out. It was just dark and there was still considerable time to be killed. Lawrence and Soapy wandered slowly down the street. They passed a cigar store and Don Coyote remembered that he was short of tobacco.

"Wait a minute, Soapy. Got to get some makin's."

He turned around to go back to the tobacco shop, only to collide with the man with the cadaverous face. Don Coyote mumbled an apology and went on into the store. The incident set him to thinking, however, and when he came out his face was grave. He rejoined Soapy and glanced casually up and down the street. The thin man with the intense black eyes and the deathlike face was staring into a nearby shop window. Don Coyote quickened his pace and started across the street.

"Where yuh goin' an' why all th' rush?" Soapy demanded.

"Makin' a test, son. Don't turn around now, but I got a hunch that somebody is trailin' us."

Soapy started and checked an inclination to glance over his shoulder. "What makes yuh think so?" he asked anxiously.

"Tell yuh in a minute. Just keep your shirt on an' follow me. We'll wander around two or three corners and then if this bird is still on our trail, we'll know he's followin' us."

They rounded their two or three corners, walking more slowly now, as though trying to kill time before going somewhere. Then Don Coyote stopped and gazed casually into a window. He waited a few moments and then saw the reflection of a tall, thin man walking slowly along on the opposite side of the street. Soapy, watching his friend's face, read the bad news.

"Yuh don't need to tell me," he muttered. "We're sunk, big boy."

Don Coyote nodded, very thoughtfully.

"Now how in the devil—" Soapy began.

"Plain's the nose on your face," Lawrence said. "Miss Dorrington told Chandler that I rode into town with her. Never thought it would do any harm, I suppose. And Chandler is suspicious of me, has been all along, and puts a shadow on my trail."

Soapy swore manfully. "Oh, you big dub!" he groaned. "Didn't I tell yuh? Didn't I tell yuh dat skoit would be a jinx?"

"Yes, I reckon you did, Sonny," Don Coyote admitted ruefully. "Still, the day ain't lost yet. Chandler hasn't any way of knowing what we're up to. He can't know that we figured out he'd substituted that phoney map for the real one. He's just suspicious of me and is playin' safe by havin' me watched by that long drink o' water over there. Why can't we give that feller the slip an' go ahead like we planned?"

"Fair enough, big boy. It suits me. Only we got to be darned careful about givin' that boid de slip. If he gits wise to de fact that we're tryin' to ditch him, it may gum the whole works."

"Right you are, Soapy. We got to go easy. Just as you say, if we let this skinny feller know we're tryin' to give him the slip, it'll queer things for fair. Chandler'll know for sure that somethin' is up. Let's see what we can do."

"Lemme lead the way," Soapy suggested. "I've had more practice at dis game dan you."

"Shoot, Soapy!" Don Coyote invited.

They walked off. For the next hour they wandered about the town, never once glancing behind. Soapy tried all the tricks he knew, and they were many. They paused in doorways, they doubled back on their trail, they entered stores and left through rear doors, all very casually and innocently. But through it all their shadow kept doggedly on their trail.

"Can't be done!" Soapy said at last; he was perspiring freely now and he was slightly rattled. "I can give him the slip all right. Don't think I can't. But if I do, he'll know we're onto him."

"No, I reckon we can't afford to let him know that," Don Coyote observed. "Suppose we get our horses and ride up the road toward the mine. Just for fun, to see what he'll do."

"Suits me. Let's go."

They returned to the stable, saddled their horses again and rode casually out of town. A mile up the road they rounded a turn and Don Coyote pulled over to one side. There was no moon and the trees at the side of the road could effectually hide a hundred men. Soapy followed in silence.

"We'll wait here an' see what happens," Don Coyote

said.  His voice hardened as he added: "If he's still on our trail, there'll be trouble."

With every passing minute Lawrence realized more keenly the paramount importance of his mission.  He *must* get that map, he told himself over and over again. Nothing must be allowed to stop him; nothing, at least, short of taking a human life.  That was the only thing at which he drew the line.

"Wish I had a rod, damn it," Soapy growled in an undertone.

"An' I'm blamed glad you haven't," Don Coyote answered shortly.

They waited in silence after that, the minutes dragging by slowly.  Had they given the tall man the slip? It began to seem that way.  Don Coyote was about to give the word to start back to town when he heard the swift thud of hoofbeats.  He held his breath, peering down the white stretch of road.  A rider rounded the turn below them.  The light was poor, but Don Coyote instantly recognized the tall form of the man who had been shadowing them.  He cursed softly and with swift fingers untied the lariat from his saddle.

"Enough is enough," he murmured.  "I'll fix that feller so he won't shadow us no more this night."

# CHAPTER XXIX

THE tall man was just abreast of them when Don Coyote's rope flashed across the road and dropped over his shoulders. He screamed wildly once. Then, the breath knocked out of his lungs by the tight loop, he was jerked out of the saddle into the dust of the road. Don Coyote was on his feet the next instant. He leaped across the intervening distance and threw himself on the tall man, holding him to the ground. He realized at once, however, that the form was limp.

"H-m, knocked him out," he told Soapy. "Don't wonder. He shore hit the ground with a bump. Ain't hurt, though. We'll drag him over into the trees and tie him up."

Soapy was already stooping over and going through the tall man's pockets. He straightened up triumphantly. Don Coyote saw something dark and shiny gleaming in his hand.

"Gimme!" he ordered.

Soapy handed over the revolver with a sign. Lawrence tossed it into the brush. Then he bent down, picked up the unconscious man, threw him over his shoulder as though he were a sack of flour and trudged off into the trees. Propping him in a sitting posture against a tree, he bound his hands securely behind him.

"There," he said, straightening up. "That ought to hold you for a while. Come on, Soapy. Let's catch his horse and tie him up, too. Won't do to have him wanderin' back to the stable alone."

They caught the horse without difficulty, tied him to a tree near his erstwhile rider and started back to town. Don Coyote felt immeasurably better. He had met the foe once and beaten him. To be sure, it was only a minor victory and was not greatly to his credit. Any man could have done as much, at least, any man who could handle a lariat. But it was a good omen anyway. And, though Don Coyote had little fear of a jinx, he did have a certain amount of faith in what he considered a good omen. A decided optimist was Don Coyote.

As they neared the town, Lawrence glanced at his watch. "Almost ten o'clock," he told Soapy. "Reckon we might as well proceed to the business at hand. No use waitin' any longer, is there?"

"Nope. Now's as good a time as any."

There was a grove of cottonwoods near the southerly limits of Chandler City and Don Coyote decided to leave the horses there rather than return them to the stable. "Somebody might get suspicious if we went back again now," he explained. "Besides, we'll want to get away in a hurry."

They rode into the grove, dismounted and tied their horses to a tree. "You'd best lead the way now, Soapy," Lawrence suggested. "You know the lay o' the land better'n I do. An' for the love o' heaven go easy. I'll never forgive myself if I get you into trouble."

"Huh! Worry about yourself, big boy! I'm able to take care o' me."

Soapy started off in the lead. He walked silently, cautiously, alert to every sound and shadow. Then, as later in the evening, Don Coyote could not but admire him—as one might admire any person who executes a task with finesse and skill. From beginning to end Soapy made no false moves, wasted no energy, took no more chances than were absolutely necessary.

Chandler's home, fortunately, was on the southern fringe of the town. It was a large house, probably the largest and most pretentious in that section of the state, and was surrounded by spacious gardens that afforded excellent concealment for Lawrence and Soapy. They found it brilliantly alight, every window glowing, and even from the distance they could hear the sound of music and laughter and revelry.

As they slipped over the fence and dodged into a dark mass of shrubbery, Don Coyote felt the first twinges of fear, the first premonition of disaster to come. He didn't like this sort of business. It wasn't his game, this sneaking around like a damned coyote. The thought startled him. Don Coyote! Despite the gravity of the situation, he smiled broadly. Apparently he hadn't been misnamed after all. For the first time in his life he was actually living up to his appellation of Don Coyote. The idea comforted him. Another good omen!

Swinging around to the rear of the house, Soapy stalked it cautiously. There was no one in sight. As they drew closer they even saw that the back door was slightly ajar.

"Dis is goin' to be a pipe," Soapy whispered. "Nuttin' to it. Keep close to papa, big boy."

They worked their way through the garden until only a small open space separated them from the door. But this space was bathed in light from the window and Don Coyote felt extremely dubious about negotiating it. What if some one chanced to glance out of the window just as they started across? He had little opportunity to speculate on this contingency, however.

"Come on," Soapy whispered, and strode boldly out into the light. The little man walked casually, quite as though he had business there and didn't care who knew it. Don Coyote followed, trembling in his boots. They gained the doorway without mishap and slipped into a small hall. Here Soapy paused, listening. He pointed to a closed door on their right.

"Kitchen!" he whispered. Then nodding toward another straight ahead: "That's ours. Come on."

The little man opened it cautiously and peered up a flight of stairs. He found them clear and started to mount them, Don Coyote following close behind him. Before he gained the top, however, Soapy paused several times, listening, watching, every sense alert.

In another part of the house the guests were dancing. Lawrence could hear the scrape of feet and the music of the orchestra. His heart seemed to contract within his breast. But a few feet away, separated from him only by two or three partitions, Gayle Dorrington was an honored guest in this house. While he, Don Coyote Lawrence, who had always tried to play the game squarely, was sneaking through a back hallway bent on burglary.

Don Lawrence felt suddenly faint. He wanted to throw up the whole regrettable business. Chandler could keep the map. The Buckaroo could go to the dogs. Dorrington could fight his own battles. Gayle could marry any one she pleased. Don Coyote though he might be called, he'd be damned if he'd play this sneaking game any longer!"

"Hey, big boy! Goin' to sleep?"

The hoarse whisper startled him. He glanced up at Soapy, saw that the little man was beckoning to him from the top of the stairs. With a sinking heart he realized that he had gone too far to turn back now. He'd have to see it through to the end.

When he gained the hallway at the top of the stairs, he found Soapy kneeling before a door, working at the lock with a slender sliver of steel. "Locked, damn it!" he muttered. "Must be a suspicious cuss to lock his door wit' a whole house full of his friends."

Literally trembling with fear and uncertainty, Don Coyote waited nervously for Soapy to pick the lock. At the front end of the hall was a wide flight of stairs leading down to the main floor. The sound of voices and laughter floated up to them, so distinctly that had Lawrence known them he could have recognized the speakers. Every instant he expected to hear footsteps and see some one appear above the stairs. Ever present was the dread fear of discovery, humiliation, jail—and failure.

Then he saw the door swing open into a lighted room. It was a large room and a single glance assured him that it was not occupied. He leaped into it, so hastily that he almost bowled over the little man ahead of him.

"Take yer time, baby," Soapy grinned, as he softly closed the door. "We got all night. This here's an office, yuh know. An' Chandler ain't monkeyin' around no office to-night."

"But the light!" Don Coyote exclaimed in a whisper.

"Forgot to turn it off. Dese big butter an' egg boys don't care nuttin' about the electric bills, yuh know. An' say, take a slant at dat box, will yuh? Did yuh ever see an' ol' tin can like that baby? You could open that t'ing yerself, wit' a can-opener. Cripes, what a pipe!"

Don Coyote stared at the huge safe that stood in one corner of the office. At that particular moment, however, he could not have discerned the difference between a late model manganese steel vault and a tin strongbox. He was conscious only of the fact that Soapy shoved a slip of paper and the stub of a pencil into his hand and ordered him to write.

The little man knelt in front of the safe and gave the dial an experimental twirl. "Huh!" he grunted disdainfully. "Ought to have a few blankets to muffle dis t'ing. They're liable to hear them tumblers out on the front porch."

Which, of course, was something of an exaggeration. For strain his ears as he would, Don Coyote could not detect the slightest sound as Soapy turned the dial. "Nine," the little man said, and Lawrence wrote it down on the slip of paper. Soapy worked slowly, his ear close to the dial, his sensitive fingers touching it ever so lightly. He showed finesse and experience, did Soapy, and admirable poise.

"Sixteen. . . . Four. . . . Nineteen. . . . Seven. . . . Two." Soapy swung around. "That'll be all of 'em. Gimme that paper."

While Don Coyote marveled, the little burglar twirled the dial dexterously and at last swung the heavy door open. He turned around then, squaring his shoulders and grinning with the pride of a master craftsman. "An' I been peelin' spuds fer t'ree months," he said. "Ain't life hell?"

Don Coyote hastily described the map to his accomplice and the two of them started to search the drawers and compartments of the safe. Then, out of the corner of his eye, Don Coyote saw his little friend reach toward a thick packet of bills which lay in a small drawer. Soapy's hand poised above them, wavered there for a long moment. The hand was half closed, like a talon, and it was trembling. Don Coyote did not speak, did not move, as he realized the silent struggle that was going on within the soul of the little man.

Then the hand snapped the drawer shut, resolutely.

"Good boy, Soapy," Don Coyote breathed.

"Damn fool, **yuh** mean!" Soapy grunted and went on with the search.

They found the map after five minutes of frenzied effort. It was brought to light by Soapy—a roll of yellowed paper tied with a string. On the outside was written in pencil: "Buckaroo."

"Here yuh are, big boy!" the little man announced jubilantly.

Don Coyote's eyes lighted as he grasped the paper. His trembling fingers fumbled with the string. "You shove those drawers back an' close the safe, Soapy. This must be what we been lookin' for."

While Soapy put the safe in order again and swung the heavy door shut, Lawrence ran to the table and spread the map out under the light. His position and its dangers were for the moment forgotten, as he pored over the plan. The rôle of safe robber was cast aside—he was again the mining engineer.

"H-m! Shortened the tunnel eighty feet. Changed its direction from North 2 West to North 47 West. Cut sixteen feet off the shaft, too. The dirty crook! No wonder Dorrington missed that ore chamber. Didn't miss it by much, at that."

He rolled the map up again and thrust it into his hip pocket, under his coat. "Come on, Soapy," he ordered. "Let's clear out o' here pronto. I'm nervous."

They started toward the door together and then drew up sharply. There was some sort of commotion in the hall. Some one was talking angrily. Footsteps were coming toward them. The two men looked at each other. Instinctively each read the meaning of those sounds.

Soapy paled. "My God, big boy!" he groaned. "We're sunk!"

# CHAPTER XXX

Don Coyote's first thought was of Soapy—and his last thought, too. His little friend had proved that he could go straight. More than that, he had proved that he wanted to go straight. Now he would be robbed of the opportunity because Don Coyote had mixed him up in this mess. There would be a trial, certain conviction, a prison term—and Soapy would come out in the world again a vowed and immutable enemy of society.

It was characteristic of Don Coyote that no thought of personal danger entered his head. The map, the Buckaroo, Dorrington, Gayle—everything was forgotten save the fact that Soapy Gourd, his old friend and buddy, was caught in a trap of his making. He'd have to get him clear. And he'd have to work fast. The footsteps were very near now.

"Open that window, Soapy!" Lawrence ordered tersely. "You can lower yourself over the sill and drop to the ground. It ain't far. I'll hold the door till you can get the window open."

"What about you?" Soapy demanded.

"Never mind about me. You get out. One of us has got to hold this door till the other gets the window open. You ain't heavy enough. Hurry, damn yuh! I'll follow you if I can."

Don Coyote hurled his weight against the door just as the knob started to turn. There was no key. Had there been one, he might have turned it and escaped with Soapy before the men in the hallway had time to break down the door.

Soapy was fumbling with the catch on the window now. He was a bit dazed; he wanted to argue with Don Coyote but he knew the futility of any argument. Always in the past he had gone down to defeat before the superior will of his friend. It would be the same now. Besides, he undoubtedly reasoned, there was no reason why both of them should be captured when one might escape.

The catch gave and Soapy hurled the window up. With one leg over the sill he hesitated. "Damn it," he growled. "I never took a run-out powder on a pal yet. I'll be damned if I—"

At that moment some one pounded heavily on the door. An angry voice, Chandler's: "Get away from that door or we'll start shooting."

Soapy winced and began to tremble violently; his face was ashen. And yet he still made no move to drop to the ground. His small eyes met Don Coyote's appealingly. "I ain't no quitter, Don," they seemed to say. "I don't wanta walk out on a pal."

"Get out, you fool!" Lawrence whispered hoarsely.

Soapy stared at his friend reproachfully. Then, without another word, he lowered himself until only his small hands showed on the sill. Don Coyote smiled as they slipped suddenly out of sight. Soapy was all right; he was mighty glad he'd got clear.

He waited a moment or two, paying little heed to the angry voices on the other side of the door. Then he stepped aside. The door swung open and he was suddenly confronted by Chandler. The mining magnate had a pistol in his hand; behind him were the tall fellow with the pale face and two other men, servants most likely.

Don Coyote bowed gravely. "Good evening, Mr. Chandler."

Chandler stared at him for a moment without speaking. Then his eyes darted toward the safe. He saw that the door was closed and an involuntary sigh of relief escaped him.

"So you're a burglar as well as a mining engineer, eh, Lawrence?" he remarked as he strode into the room. "Luckily we got here in time. You're a pretty slick worker, aren't you? You slipped up, though. They always do. You forgot to gag Kennedy, here." He nodded toward the tall man. "A human voice can carry a long way here in the mountains. And by the way, you'd better put up your hands until we can search you."

Don Coyote's heart seemed to stop beating at the words. For the first time he recalled the map that was in his hip pocket. He cursed softly as he raised his hands in the air.

Chandler smiled. "So you have a gun after all.

Lucky you didn't try to use it, Lawrence. I'm a pretty fair shot. Kennedy, search him."

The tall man pocketed his revolver and stepped forward. He found no gun, of course, but his long fingers did bring to light the roll of paper on which hinged the fate of the Buckaroo. He handed it to Chandler in silence. The latter started with surprise. He glanced again at the safe and then back to Lawrence.

"Where did you get this?" he demanded.

Don Coyote nodded toward the safe. "I got it where you left it, o' course," he answered readily. "I didn't pick it up out in the street."

"Oh, didn't you!" Chandler returned sarcastically. "Then maybe you'll tell me how you opened that safe."

Don Coyote shrugged nonchalantly. "Anybody could open an old-timer like that. Nothin' to it. All yuh need is a sensitive finger an' a good ear. It's a cinch. I've opened lots of 'em."

"Have you now! Well, I rather imagine this is the last safe you'll open for some time. Kennedy, get Sheriff Boylston on the 'phone and tell him to come here immediately. Better have him bring a couple of deputies, too."

"Just a minute, Chandler," Don Coyote ordered in a level tone. "I got a few things I want to say to you an' I think you'll want to hear 'em. This ain't nothin' to go off half cocked about."

There was something in the young man's tone that made Chandler pause. He stared at Don Coyote for a long moment. The clear gray eyes held his steadily. At last, with no great decision, Chandler said: "I don't believe there is anything I care to talk over with you, Lawrence. This is a clear case of burglary and I assure you that you will not be able to talk me into letting you off."

"I don't mean to try to talk you into anything," Lawrence asserted coolly. "I only want to remind you how you got that map of the original workings of the Buckaroo. Seems to me a man in your position wouldn't care about havin' a thing like that made public. Course, I may be wrong. Maybe everybody knows you're a blamed crook anyway. Still, I reckon there is one person that'll be sort o' surprised to find it out."

"Damn you!" Chandler snarled, and raised his gun threateningly. "That your game, is it? Going to blackmail me into letting you off, are you? Well, you've got another think coming, Lawrence. There's a mighty easy way of stopping that."

"Yeh? What is it?" Don Coyote's voice was calm and his steady gaze did not waver.

"I can kill you where you stand!" the magnate flamed. "I can get away with it, too. I caught you in the act of robbing my home. I can shoot you down—"

"But you ain't goin' to shoot me down," Don Coyote broke in coolly.

"No?" Chandler demanded angrily. "What makes you think I'm not?"

"You ain't got the nerve."

"Haven't I?"

"No, you ain't. Oh, it's easy enough for you to order somebody else to get me out o' the way, like you did Burke. You're a murderer at heart, all right. I ain't denyin' that. But when it comes to shootin' a feller down in cold blood—" he waved his hand in an expressive gesture—"well, you just ain't got the guts, that's all."

Chandler's gun slowly raised. There was a berserk light in his dark eyes and for a moment Don Coyote thought that he had lost the game. Then Chandler lowered his gun and turned to the men behind him.

"You men stand by outside," he ordered. "I want to talk to Lawrence alone."

Kennedy and the servants departed without a word. Chandler closed the door behind them and motioned Don Coyote to a chair on the other side of the wide table that stood in the center of the room. Don Coyote went around and sat down. He felt strangely exhilarated, for he sensed that he was meeting this man at his own game and beating him. Chandler sat down across the table and rested his gun on it.

"All right, Lawrence," he began. "Have your say and be done with it."

"I reckon I've said about all I got to say," Don Coyote drawled. "I know you been holdin' that map illegally. I know, too, that you been doin' everything you could to bust Dorrington. I don't know why, but that ain't important. The point is this: when I tell

Dorrington what I know about that map, you'll be queered for life with that family."

"Then Dorrington doesn't know you came here tonight," Chandler said.

"No, he don't know it now. But he'll know it blamed quick when I get sent to jail. And he'll know why I came, too."

Chandler considered. He was trapped and he knew it. He realized that it was up to him to make the best of a bad bargain. "What do you want me to do?" he asked at last. "Turn you loose?"

Don Coyote grinned. "Well, I got to admit it wouldn't break my heart none."

"Wouldn't it now?" Chandler came back sarcastically. "All right, suppose I agree to turn you loose. Will you agree to give up your position as superintendent of the Buckaroo immediately? And will you further agree not to mention a word about this map to anybody?"

Don Coyote considered briefly. "Who gets the map?" he asked.

"I do, naturally."

"H-m."

Don Coyote saw the situation very plainly. The price of his freedom was the failure of the Buckaroo, the defeat of Dorrington, the loss of Gayle. A rather heavy price, almost too heavy. And yet, he reasoned, what was there to gain by refusing Chandler's offer? A chance to ruin the man's reputation by telling what he knew. A chance, that was all. It would be Chandler's word against his, and he would be a convicted burglar. And as far as the map went, Chandler might easily deny any knowledge of it.

"Suppose I promise to quit the Buckaroo and not say nothin' to anybody about his business. How do yuh know I'll keep my word?"

Chandler shrugged. "I don't know it. But I do know that if you don't keep it, I shall swear to a warrant for your arrest."

"You won't need to swear to no warrant," Don Coyote came back. "If I give yuh my word, I'll keep it. I never busted my word yet and I ain't startin' in now. My word is as good as your bond."

"I wouldn't be surprised if it were," Chandler admitted, half sneeringly. "Do you agree to my proposition?"

"Yes. I give you my word I'll quit my job at the Buckaroo. I'll promise, too, that I won't say nothin' about this night's business nor about the map."

Chandler rose abruptly. "Very well. You're free."

Don Coyote got to his feet a bit wearily. His mind was not as clear as it might have been; he was assailed by grave doubts. Had he done the right thing? Had he done the fair thing? Frankly, he didn't know. It was a question that would have to be settled with his conscience. And yet it was too late for that. He had given his word. There could be no recrossing of bridges now. The incident was closed.

"Reckon I'll be movin' along," he said, and took a

step toward the door. He paused as a knock sounded on it.

"Come in," Chandler ordered.

The door opened slowly and Don Coyote's face blanched as he saw the visitor. It was Gayle Dorrington, resplendent in an American beauty evening dress, shining, radiant, adorable. She did not see him at once.

"The Penningtons are leaving, Wilcox," she said quietly. "Don't you think you'd better come down and bid them good-by? I knew you were up here and I thought—"

Then she caught sight of Don Coyote and her eyes widened. "Mr. Lawrence! I didn't expect—"

"Mr. Lawrence and I have just been talking," Chandler interrupted her with an easy smile. "I caught him in the pleasant occupation of robbing my safe."

"Robbing—your safe!" Gayle exclaimed.

"Yes. But he took nothing, Gayle, so I am going to let him go. He has been a great deal of help to your father out at the Buckaroo and I am going to repay him by giving him his freedom. Of course, he will resign his position immediately. I know your father wouldn't care to have—"

But Gayle was not looking at him. Her eyes were on Lawrence, questioning, searching.

"It's not true!" she cried at last. "Don Coyote! Tell me it isn't true!"

Don Coyote smiled gently and slowly shook his head. "No, it's true enough. He caught me with the goods."

His smile faded as his eyes met hers. He gazed at her appealingly for a moment and then took an unsteady step toward her. He checked himself, looked away and edged toward the door.

"Reckon I'll be movin' along. Good night, folks."

He passed so close to her that his hand brushed her dress. For an instant he was minded to throw up the whole thing, to break his word, to tell Gayle the truth. He knew instinctively, however, that that would be the wrong play. His mind was already busy making new plans for the future. He dared not disrupt them by any foolish display of emotion. Besides, he had given his word to say nothing.

He passed on into the hall, moving slowly toward the stairs. Very faintly he heard the girl's voice behind him.

"Wilcox, if you'll take me downstairs, you may announce our engagement to your friends."

Crushed, Don Coyote groped his way down the stairs and out into the friendly darkness.

# CHAPTER XXXI

In the cottonwood grove where they had left their horses, Don Coyote found Soapy. The little man was pacing back and forth, puffing furiously on a cigarette and cursing softly from time to time. Lawrence's footsteps made no sound on the soft turf and Soapy did not see him until he was but a few feet away.

"Cripes!" Soapy burst out. "Are you you, or are you a ghost?"

"I'm me, all right, Soapy," Lawrence answered with a slow smile.

"Then put her there, big boy!" The other thrust out his hand and started to pump Lawrence's. "If you got out o' that mess wit'out bracelets on yer wrists, I'm for yuh. How'd yuh do it?"

Don Coyote explained the bargain that he and Chandler had made. "In some ways," he ended, "we're right where we was when we started out. And in others, we ain't. For one thing, Chandler knows we're onto him. That's against us. On the other hand, I got that map pretty well in my head. Still, I'm honor bound not to mention the map to Dorrington nor anybody else."

"Rats!" Soapy scoffed. "Honor bound, me eye! Ferget about this honor business. Go on back to the

mine an' tell Dorrington the whole lay. Come clean
wit' him."

"No, I can't do that," Don Coyote shook his head
slowly. "I gave my word I wouldn't mention it."

"Aw, git on de boat! You gimme a pain. What
d'yuh t'ink yuh are? A Sunday school teacher?"

"No, I ain't a Sunday school teacher, Soapy. I ain't
never been in a Sunday school in my life. But I keep
my word. Besides, if I spilled the beans to Dorrington,
Chandler would find out about it and have me pinched."

"Git out o' the country, then," Soapy suggested.

"No, I don't want to get out of the country. I like
it too well."

Soapy grinned wisely. "Don't kid me, big boy! It
ain't the country dat's holdin' you here. It's dat
country skoit."

"Well, possibly," Don Coyote admitted. He started
toward the horses. "Let's get back to the mine, Soapy.
We ought to get some sleep to-night."

"Hey! Wait a minute!" The little man pulled at
his sleeve. "What's the matter wit' me spillin' the
beans to Dorrington. I ain't made no promises an'
Chandler don't even know I was in on the job. I
could tell what I know an' Chandler couldn't say a
woid."

"But you don't understand, Soapy!" Don pointed
out. "If you told what you knew, it would be just the
same as me tellin' it. Dorrington would tell his daughter. She'd give Chandler the go-by and Chandler'd
know the reason she done it. He'd blame me, see?

He'd figure that his reputation was ruined and that he'd
lost the girl.   So then he'd prefer charges against me an'
either throw me in jail or run me out o' the country.
No, Soapy.   We both got to keep our mouths shut, and
shut tight.   It's the only way.   Understand?"

Soapy nodded dubiously.   "Yeh, I guess yer right.
S'tough situation.   I don't know but what I ought to
go back there an' bump off that Chandler boid."

"Now you just keep your shirt on, Soapy," Lawrence
ordered sharply.   "You ain't bumpin' off anybody.
Leave this thing to me.   I'll work it out some way.
An' when I get through with Chandler, he'll feel like
bumpin' himself off."

"Suit yerself," Soapy grunted.   "Which side did yuh
say yuh get on these darned nags?"

"The left, Soapy.   Always the left."

They rode back to the mine in silence, Soapy infinitely disgusted with the way the night's adventure
had turned out, Don Coyote busy with his thoughts and
plans for the future.   The days ahead looked dark,
he was forced to admit.   Chandler had the upper hand
and there was no denying it.   But the situation wasn't
wholly hopeless.   Don Coyote had been in tighter
places and come out on top.   He could come out on
top again.

Only one thing really worried him.   That was the
hurt, reproachful look that had come into Gayle Dorrington's eyes when she had confronted him in Chandler's office.   He shuddered a little when he thought of
that.   It was not a pleasant memory.

They arrived at the mine and stabled their horses. The house was dark. Gayle had not yet returned from town and Dorrington had apparently gone to bed. "Reckon I won't wake the old man up," Don Coyote decided. "Time enough to tell him I'm quittin' in the mornin'."

"We're quittin', yuh mean," Soapy told him.

"Wrong again, Soapy. I want you to stay here. Might need you in my plans."

"What plans?"

"Plans for beatin' Chandler an' runnin' him out o' the country."

"Huh! you don't hate yerself much, do yuh?" Soapy laughed. "That boid has got millions, big boy. When yuh tackle him, yer tacklin' somethin'."

"The bigger they are, the harder they fall, you must remember, Soapy."

"Huh! You mean the littler they are, the further they get knocked."

"Well, we'll see. In the meantime let's hit the hay. I'm powerful tired."

"I ain't tired. I'm just dead. See yuh in the mornin', big boy. Call me early, mother darling, for I'm to be queen of the May."

"Tra-la, tra-la!" Don Coyote added with a grin as they strode into the snoring bunkhouse.

Lawrence rose early the following morning, gathered up his few belongings, saddled the mare and had breakfast. His last morning at the Buckaroo! The thought depressed him immeasurably. Promise or no promise, he knew that it would require all his will power to tear himself away. The world beyond held no interest for him. His life had become wrapped up in the Buckaroo and Dorrington and Gayle.

His face was long when he rose from the breakfast table. He paused a moment in the doorway of the dining room, looking out over the canyon to the west and south. Which way? He shrugged. It didn't make much difference which way he went, so long as he did not go far. He walked thoughtfully out into the cookhouse. The beefy cook was deftly flipping hotcakes which were spread out on the black shining surface of the big range.

"Slim, who's this h'yar cabin about a quarter of a mile up the canyon belong to?" he asked casually.

"Don't belong to nobody," the cook answered. "Some prospector built it years ago. Had a little claim across the river." His round eyes scanned Lawrence narrowly. "What you figurin' on doin'? Goin' to change your residence?"

Don Coyote sighed, though the cook's words had brought a new light into his eyes. "Wouldn't be surprised," he answered cryptically and passed on out into the clearing.

He crossed to Dorrington's home with lagging footsteps, dreading the meeting that must ensue. There would be explanations demanded—and he could make none. He could not open his mouth about the events of the night before. No, that wasn't exactly true. There was one thing he could reveal and still not break his promise. It was important, too, a hundred times more important than his personal affairs.

He knocked gingerly on the door, praying that he would not have to bear the ordeal of meeting Gayle. His prayers were not answered, however, for the girl herself answered his summons. She stared at him a moment and, oddly, there was little of reproachfulness in her eyes. They were faintly questioning, neither openly friendly nor patently distant.

"Your dad," Don Coyote began miserably, "is he in?"

"He is dressing. Won't you come in, Mr. Lawrence?"

Though her voice was not cold, the form of address cut him deeply. He sighed, averting his eyes.

"Thanks, I'll wait for him if you don't mind."

Don Coyote walked into the big room, took the chair she offered and sat down. He rolled a cigarette and lit it with unsteady fingers, tossing the match into the dead ashes of the fireplace. The girl hovered near the window, staring with unseeing eyes out over the canyon. Plainly she was troubled, as much so as Don Coyote. For some moments she said nothing. Then she swung about suddenly, fastening her blue eyes on the dejected figure by the table.

"Don Coyote!" Her voice was low, a bit strained by emotion. "Why did you do it?"

Lawrence started, looked at her quickly and then glanced away. "I'm sorry, Miss Dorrington. I ain't got nothin' to say, no excuses to offer. I went up there to rob that safe. I got caught. That's all there is to it. I'm guilty as the devil."

A deep inhalation that was half a gasp and half a sigh was her only answer as she turned back to the window. Don Coyote watched her for several moments. His face was set. His pulse was beating wildly. If only he could make a clean breast of the thing! But to do so would be to break his word. That, in itself, wasn't so much, he realized now. But there were other things at stake. His own freedom. The success of the Buckaroo.

The former did not mean so much. The latter meant everything. As things stood now, Chandler would not be likely to take any further measures toward crippling the mine. Dorrington was to all intents and purposes defeated. But if Don Coyote told what he knew, with no positive proof save his and Soapy's word to back up the assertion, Chandler might take further steps to wreck the Buckaroo.

Yes, Don Coyote told himself bitterly, until he had some tangible proof, he'd have to hold his peace. Yet the thought that Gayle was misjudging him rankled deeply. He rose at last, his face set with determination, and went to her side. Brazenly he took her hand, drew her around until he forced her to meet his eyes.

"Ma'am, I got somethin' I want to remind you of," he began. "You remember the night I come here?"

"Yes, Don Coyote," she said unsteadily.

"You remember me tellin' you all the hell I went through bringin' that bullion back to you?"

"Yes-s-s."

He dropped her hand and turned away. "Think it over," he urged quietly. "Remember when you get to condemnin' me that I went through a lot o' hell to return fifteen thousand dollars in gold bullion to somebody I didn't even know. Somehow I don't reckon that a crook, a real crook, would do a trick like that. Do you?"

"And that is just what I can't understand, Don Coyote," the girl burst out passionately. "Why did you do it? Why?"

The young man smiled wearily as he heard the sound of approaching footsteps. "That's somethin' that I can't tell you—now. There is somethin' else that I can tell you, though. And that is that I love you. I've always loved you ever since I first saw you. And I reckon I'm goin' to keep on lovin' you, though from the way things size up now it ain't goin' to do me a lot o' good."

A door opened and as Don Coyote turned to face his employer, Gayle passed silently from the room. Though Lawrence could not see them, her blue eyes were misty with tears.

# CHAPTER XXXII

DORRINGTON'S face was gray with weariness and defeat. His step was dead, heavy. It was as though he were tired with life, with the world and with Dame Fortune, who had dealt so unkindly with him. The work in the mine was at an impasse; though his every dollar was tied up in it, he did not know which way to turn. The affair of the night before must also have added another burden to his already drooping shoulders.

He nodded, not unpleasantly, and at the same time not too friendly; it was as though he were withholding judgment. "Good morning, Lawrence."

Don Coyote met him with squared shoulders and resolutely tilted chin. "Good mornin', sir. I reckon you've heard what happened last night."

"Yes. Chandler 'phoned this morning. Gayle, too, told me what she knew of the incident."

Lawrence nodded. "I reckon you got my pay check made out."

"No, I haven't. You are not discharged, Lawrence. Not, at least, until I hear the facts of this affair."

"That's nice of you, sir," Don Coyote acknowledged gratefully. "But the fact is, I'm quittin' this morning."

Dorrington met his gaze squarely. "I hate to lose you, Lawrence."

"You don't hate to lose me half as much as I hate to go," the other grinned. "I don't need to tell you that I been sort o' interested in this mine right from the beginning. It's meant a lot to me, workin' here with you an' fightin' for you. But—I reckon I got to go."

Dorrington shook his head firmly. "No, you don't have to go, Lawrence," he contradicted. "I want to keep you just as badly as you want to stay. A word of explanation—"

"I'm sorry, sir. I can't give it."

The old man suddenly rapped the table with his fist. "Lawrence, enough of this beating around the bush and evading. I know that there was something behind this business down at Chandler's home last night. I know that you didn't go there to rob his safe—not of money, anyway. It was something else. Something that concerns this mine and me. Wasn't it now?"

"I ain't at liberty to say, Mr. Dorrington."

"Why aren't you at liberty to say?" Dorrington demanded heatedly. "Has Chandler bound you to secrecy? Has he ordered you to keep silent under threat of sending you to jail?"

Don Coyote's gaze fell. Surprised though he was at the ease with which Dorrington had hit the nail on the head, he did his best to hide his feelings. "I'm afraid there ain't no use talkin' about it, Mr. Dorrington. I'm quittin' this morning. I'm doin' it not only for my own good but for your good as well. I may be doin' wrong. I don't know. But I'm playin' the cards as they're dealt to me an' I think I'm playin' 'em wisely. If you'll give me my pay check I'll clear out."

For a long tense moment Dorrington stared at him. Then he walked silently to a small desk which stood in one corner of the room, sat down and pulled a check book out of the drawer.

Don Coyote sat down at the table and took a pencil from his pocket. A tablet lay on the table. He took it up and carefully drew several lines on it. "Shortened tunnel eighty feet. Changed direction from 42 to 47. Cut sixteen feet off shaft." These thoughts went methodically through his mind, over and over again, as he drew more lines and made several short computations. At last he rose to his feet, tore the sheet of paper out of the tablet and threw it into the fireplace, just as Dorrington crossed the room with his pay check. Don Coyote accepted it, thanked him and clasped his outstretched hand warmly.

"Mighty sorry to see you go, Lawrence," the old man murmured.

"It may not be for long, sir," Don Coyote answered with a smile. "And anyway I won't be far away. I'm goin' to move into that little cabin up the canyon for a spell. I'll be there if you need me, but I don't reckon it'll be best for me to see much of you. Now there's one thing more before I go.

"As things stand, you're in a pretty bad way here at the Buckaroo. Don't seem to be much use of drivin' that tunnel any further, does it? You're already a hundred feet past where the ore chamber should have been. What are you goin' to do?"

Dorrington shrugged wearily. "I guess I'll have to

close down, Lawrence. There doesn't seem to be anything else to do."

"Don't do it," Don Coyote advised quietly. "Tell your stockholders, those who are in town, that you're goin' to keep runnin' that tunnel straight ahead till your money's gone. But don't do it."

"No?" Dorrington's eyes had lightened as he sensed the import of Lawrence's words.

"No. Don't run straight ahead. Turn due south from the face and run forty feet. Then rise sixteen feet. Got it?"

"Due south forty feet and rise sixteen," Dorrington repeated.

"That's the stuff. But for heaven's sake, keep it quiet. Don't tell a soul, not even your daughter. If I was you, I'd fire half the crew. Keep just those you're sure you can trust. And don't let nobody into the tunnel that ain't got business there. Got that?"

"I think I have, Lawrence. And I'm mighty grateful, my boy."

"Don't mention it," Don Coyote grinned. "So long."

"So long, Lawrence. When you want to go back to work for the Buckaroo, you'll find your job waiting for you."

Don Coyote passed out of the house. Without a backward glance, he crossed the clearing to the corral, mounted his mare and rode up the canyon. Though his heart was heavy, there was a twinkle in his eye and a smile on his lips.

"I reckon I kept my word," he mused. "I never mentioned the map. And I quit my job. That's all there was to the agreement."

The cabin was a little clapboard affair of one room, furnished with a table, a chair, a bunk and a rusty stove. Don Coyote surveyed it from the doorway. It was indescribably dirty and he strongly suspected that the roof leaked. He had slept in worse, however, and he had no compunctions about taking up his abode in this one.

"Ought to be cleaned up," he remarked to the mare. "But I reckon that'll have to wait, Cleopatra. More important to get in some grub."

Untying his scant belongings from behind his saddle, he tossed them through the doorway without dismounting and turned the mare down the canyon toward Chandler City.

It was dusk when he returned. He dismounted, unsaddled the mare and turned her loose, and with his arms full of packages turned toward the door of the cabin. It was closed.

"H-m. That's funny," he mused. "I'd swear I left that door open. Oh, well, wind might have blowed it closed."

But the wind hadn't closed it. He knew that as soon as he poked his head into the cabin. It was clean, shining, as spotless as an old shanty could be made. His clothes hung on nails on the wall. There was a mattress on the bunk, and clean blankets. The stove was polished. Clean cooking utensils replaced the rusty ones that had been on. A miracle had been performed during his absence and his eyes shone mistily as he realized who must have been responsible.

"That darling li'l lady! That darling li'l lady! Some day—some day—" He broke off, scowling. "Oh, well, got to forget about her now. Other things more important. But some day I'm goin' to marry that li'l lady."

In a warm glow of happiness he cooked his supper and ate it in the dim light of the kerosene lamp. Then he blew out the lamp, moved his chair outside the door and sat down. He rolled a cigarette slowly, lit it and gazed thoughtfully out across the canyon. Below, the river ran cool and roaring faintly. A colony of frogs somewhere down near the dam set up a sudden chorus, loud and clamorous; it died away, rose, fell. The leaves of the cottonwoods, dry now, rustled faintly in the night breeze. From the hillside came the drowsy murmur of the pines.

Don Coyote rested, leaning back in his chair, inhaling gratefully. He loved this peaceful scene. He loved these familiar sounds that were as old as time and yet as new as an unwritten symphony. The croak of the frogs, the sigh of the wind, the rush of the river. These had always been and always would be sheer music to his ears. Unutterably peaceful it was, so free from the strife and bickering and bitterness of the world of man.

He rested, wholly content.

Then another sound broke the stillness. The thump-

thump-thump of a laden ore car banging on the rail joints. The harshly clashing roar of muck rolling down the dump.

Don Coyote straightened in his chair. Thoughts of peace gave way to thoughts of war.

He had returned from Chandler City that evening with something more than a few pounds of grub. Casual inquiry in town had elicited certain information that Don Coyote believed was destined to prove of great importance.

Ben Burke, the former superintendent of the Buckaroo, was still hopelessly insane and was confined in the Las Palmas Sanatorium in Sacramento. Wilcox Chandler—who had never acquired any great reputation for philanthropy—was still footing the bill.

"Nothin' very startlin' about them facts, when yuh take 'em by themselves," Don Coyote told himself. "And yet, when yuh come to analyze 'em, yuh begin to get suspicious. That Las Palmas Sanatorium is a private bug-house. It costs somethin' to keep a man there. Yes, sir, it prob'ly costs plenty. Now why should Wilcox Chandler be puttin' out the cash to keep Ben Burke in that bug-house?

"Because he's afraid to have him sent to a state asylum, that's why. He's afraid Burke ain't as crazy as he was. He's afraid that if the state authorities got hold of Burke they'd turn him loose. An' Chandler don't want Ben Burke turned loose. Not much. The big feller knows too blamed much. Yes, ma'am. He knows too blamed much. Chandler figures to keep him penned up with them lunatics till he goes bugs for good and all. He'll do it, too, in time. Takes a man with a mighty level head to keep his wits when he's cooped up with a lot o' nuts all the time. Yes, ma'am."

For several hours Don Coyote brooded on the subject, going over this line of reasoning again and again. There seemed to be no loopholes in it, no flaw in his logic. The conclusion he drew was inevitable: Burke was being held a virtual prisoner because he knew too much.

It was nearly ten o'clock when Don Coyote at last got to his feet and started around the shoulder of the ridge which separated him from the Buckaroo. He had come to a definite decision. Sensing vaguely that Burke in some way held the key to the success of the Buckaroo and the end of Chandler's reign of power in that section of the country, he was determined to follow up his lead immediately.

"This mine an' that li'l lady ain't safe till Wilcox Chandler is put in his place. That place is a long way from here an' a whole lot lower down. I'm goin' to put him there if it's the last act of my life."

Don Coyote meant well. His reasoning was flawless. Left to his own devices he would have worked out the salvation of the Buckaroo and accomplished the defeat of Wilcox Chandler without undue difficulty. But other influences were about to take a hand in the proceedings. One of them was a girl, a girl who sought to aid by giving her all and thereby blundering grievously. And the other was Wilcox Chandler himself.

## CHAPTER XXXIII

Don Coyote gained the clearing before the Buckaroo and entered the bunkhouse. He found Soapy Gourd engaged in a heated poker game. He tapped him on the shoulder and nodded significantly toward the door. Soapy turned to one of the onlookers.

"Take my hand, will yuh, Joe?"

"Better cash in," Don Coyote advised.

Soapy, he who hated the taking of an order above all else, nodded obediently and shoved his chips over to the banker. He pocketed the money he had coming, shoved back his chair with a sigh and joined Don Coyote at the door of the bunkhouse.

"Want to take a walk, Soapy?" Lawrence suggested.

"Right-o!" the little man responded readily, though walking was far from his idea of a good time.

They strolled out across the clearing and up the canyon to Don Coyote's new home. The evening was chill and Lawrence built up the fire in the old stove before he opened the conversation. Then, with Soapy sprawled comfortably on the bed and Don Coyote leaning back in the one chair, the latter stated his plans.

"Soapy, I got a job for yuh," he began.

" 'Nother crib?" the little man asked eagerly.

"No, not this time," Don Coyote laughed. "On the contrary, I want to try you out as a detective."

"What? Me? A dick? Aw, listen, big boy! Listen!"

"That's just what I want you to do," Lawrence smiled. "Listen. You've heard the boys talk about Ben Burke, who used to be superintendent here. You've heard how he went loco the night of the fire, when Dorrington made him go into the tunnel after me."

"Yeh, I heard all about dat," Soapy nodded.

"Now Dorrington and I know pretty well that Ben Burke set that fire and that he tried to bump me off an' wreck the Buckaroo at the same time. Burke just the same as admitted it. O' course, he didn't have anything partic'lar against me nor against the Buckaroo—not enough, anyway, to make him pull a trick like that. Dorrington an' I figure that he was workin' for Chandler. Understand?"

"Yeh! I got yuh!"

"Now Burke is in a private bug-house down in Sacramento. Chandler put him there an' Chandler is payin' the bill. Now this bird Chandler ain't any philanthropist. Not him. If he's payin' the bill, he's got a blamed good reason for doin' it. What do you make of it, Soapy?"

The little man lit a cigar and blew a smoke ring toward the ceiling. "Ask me somethin' hard," he grunted. "Chandler's leery dat dis Burke'll get out an' shoot off his mout'."

Don Coyote eyed him narrowly; very casually he

put the question: "But why should anybody be afraid o' what a crazy man says?"

Soapy blew another ring and answered calmly: "Maybe dis Burke ain't loco no more."

Don Coyote leaped to his feet. "That's just the way I doped it out, Soapy," he declared triumphantly. "If Burke was still loco, if he was hopelessly off his nut, Chandler would turn him over to the state to take care of. The fact that he's payin' for keepin' him penned up shows that he's afraid Burke is sane again. Don't that follow?"

"Like a tender follows an engine," Soapy nodded. "Now where do I come in?"

"You're going to find out if this Burke is still cracked," Don Coyote told him. "You're goin' down to Sacramento to-morrow mornin'. Burke is in a sanatorium by the name of Las Palmas. It's up to you to get to him some way. It ought to be a lot easier to get into one o' them joints than out of it. Any way, that's your business, breakin' into places. Talk to him if yuh can an' find out if he's still nuts. Think you can do it?"

"Huh!" Soapy grunted with great disgust. "Think I can do it! Say, can a family o' cooties make a guy scratch? Not much! If I can't do that, I'll promise to buckle down an' peel spuds fer the rest o' my life."

"Fair enough! You borrow a horse from Dorrington in the mornin' and catch the noon train out o' Chandler City. I'd go with yuh, only I think I better stay here an' sort o' keep my eye on things. No knowin' what Chandler will try to pull next an' I reckon I ought to be on hand in case the old man gets into trouble. Soon as you find out anything, gimme a ring at the Buckaroo. Dorrington'll call me."

"Suppose dis bird ain't cracked no more," Soapy suggested.

"Then I'll grab a train and come down to Sacramento. Between the two of us, we'll get him out an' drag him up here. I think he could tell us a lot of interestin' stuff about Chandler. He not only *could* tell us, but I think he *would*. Him an' Chandler have busted up, for some reason that I don't know yet. Burke is willin' to talk, otherwise Chandler wouldn't be so blamed skeered of him gettin' out. See?"

"Yeh, I see."

"O' course, this whole blamed business is just a hunch. I may be off on the wrong foot right from the beginnin'. Burke may still be crazy as a bedbug an' Chandler may be as big-hearted as a Salvation Army lass."

"Yeh, an' the moon may be made o' green cheese," Soapy scoffed.

Don Coyote opened his wallet and handed his little friend a hundred dollars in bills. "That ought to see you through. If it don't, wire me an' I'll send you some more. You got everything now, have yuh?"

"Right-o! Las Palmas Sanatorium. Ben Burke. Find out if he's still cracked an' let you know."

"That's the dope, Soapy. Now clear out an' get to bed. You got a hard day to-morrow."

"I'm on my way. So long, big boy."

"So long, Soapy. An' good luck."

Don Coyote watched the little figure out of sight over the brow of the ridge. Then, for some time, he stood looking out over the dark depths of the canyon, drinking in the crisp air. His old confidence had returned. He felt almost light-hearted. Give him a week, just one week, unmolested, and he'd remove the menace that hung over the Buckaroo—the menace that, too, hung over Gayle Dorrington.

During the three days that followed, Don Coyote kept very much to himself. He loafed, for the first time in many months, and found it to his liking. He fished, and learned that he had not lost the knack of casting a fly. He sat before his little cabin and smoked, and watched the changing colors in the canyon. It was pleasant there on the steep hillside. Many times he told himself that when the trouble was all over, when the Buckaroo was safe and taking out the pay, when he was again installed as superintendent, when the threat of Wilcox Chandler had been removed, he'd build a little home on that very spot for himself and Gayle.

And, strangely, the day did not seem so far distant, the path ahead seemed straight and sure and safe— for he had reckoned without Wilcox Chandler and without Gayle.

On the morning of the fourth day after Soapy's departure, Don Coyote was washing up his breakfast dishes when he heard a knock on the door of the cabin. It was Gayle.

"Good mornin', ma'am," he greeted her airily. "Won't you come in?"

"No, thanks. I just came over to tell you that you are wanted on the telephone.

Don Coyote's pulse leaped. It would be Soapy, of course. No one else would be calling him. He jammed on his hat and hurried out of the cabin, taking Gayle's arm as they started back to the mine.

"I got somethin' I want to tell you, Gayle," he remarked when they had taken a half dozen paces.

She glanced up at him quickly. "Please don't!" she said.

Don Coyote chuckled softly. "Oh, it ain't that. I ain't goin' to say a word about lovin' you. O' course I still do. I love you like the very— But there I go again. I said I wouldn't say no more about lovin' you, didn't I? An' I won't. Still, I do love—"

"Don! Please!"

"I'm squelched," he said hastily. "What I was goin' to say was how much I appreciate you fixin' up my cabin for me. It was turrible dirty, too. Awful mess. It was mighty nice of you. Fact is, it was damned nice!"

The girl looked up at him and then glanced away, a slow smile twisting the corners of her mouth. "I'm afraid you have jumped at conclusions, Don Coyote. I rather suspect that it was Soapy who cleaned up your cabin."

"Soapy!" Don Coyote sighed. " 'Nother fond dream gone up in smoke! Might have knowed it, too. Just like the little rat." He halted, his grip on her arm tightening. "Ma'am, I don't like to contradict anybody, much less a lady. But Soapy never knew I was goin' to move into that cabin. When I spoke to the cook about it the mornin' I quit, Soapy was out in the storehouse."

"Maybe the cook told him," Gayle suggested innocently.

"Maybe he did," Don Coyote laughed softly.

They were before the house now, but Lawrence did not realize it. He had eyes for nothing but Gayle, ears for nothing but her words.

"Soapy might have cleaned up that shack an' he might not," he went on. "It's my own personal opinion that he didn't. The work had—well, yuh might call it a woman's touch. An' I think it was done by them two little hands right there."

He took the two little hands in his own large ones. Bending low, he kissed them, tenderly, reverently. Then he straightened up and met her eyes. He saw, with an odd flutter of his heart, that they were wide and staring. Her face had gone white. Slowly he turned around.

Leaning casually against the door of his automobile was Wilcox Chandler. He was smiling faintly, a smile made sinister by its nonchalance.

# CHAPTER XXXIV

For several seconds the gazes of the two men clashed —Chandler smiling at ease, perfectly poised; Don Coyote startled and angry. It was chagrin, more than anger, perhaps. He felt like a child caught with his hand in the cookie can. And it maddened him. For a moment he saw red. The distance between the two men was a dozen feet. Don Coyote cut it in half with one step. He opened his mouth to speak and realized he had nothing to say. He paused, inarticulate, writhing with fury. Then he whirled on his heel and mounted the steps of the house.

He found the telephone behind the door and dazedly told the operator who he was. "Reckon there's a call for me from Sacramento," he said.

"Just a moment, please."

The moment lengthened into minutes, while Don Coyote shifted his feet nervously and grew hot and cold by turns. Of all the fools! Of all the addle-pated, brainless fools, he had won the prize! Why couldn't he have used his eyes before pulling a stunt like that? Now he'd probably spilled the beans for fair. Chandler had thought he'd cleared out. He'd shown him he hadn't. He not only hadn't cleared out, but he was hanging around Chandler's intended wife— and kissing her hands!

Don Coyote shuddered at the memory. They had been nice hands. He'd wanted to kiss them. He'd like to kiss them again, for that matter. But in front of Wilcox Chandler—

"Here's your party." Then Soapy's familiar voice, cheerful, characteristic. "Dat you, big boy?"

"Yes, this is me, Soapy," Lawrence answered wearily. "Only I ain't so big no more. I feel smaller than a nickel."

"What's dat? What you talkin' about?"

"Nothing, Soapy. What did yuh find out?"

"I found out dat you're the best little fortune teller west of N' York."

"Did I have it doped right?"

"I'll say!"

"How is he?"

"Sore as hell, an' rarin' to go."

"Good! Where are yuh?"

"Taylor Hotel."

"I'll catch the noon train or break a leg tryin'. See you about midnight to-night. G'bye."

Don Coyote snapped the receiver on the hook and dashed out of the house. His embarrassing encounter with Chandler was forgotten as new plans surged through his head like water through a mill race. Indeed, he was only vaguely conscious that Chandler still stood by his car and that he was talking casually with Gayle. Racing around the brow of the hill to his cabin, he burst in the door and started to change into his most presentable clothes.

Five minutes later he was riding across the clearing in front of the mine. Chandler's car was still standing before the house, but the mining magnate and Gayle had disappeared. Don Coyote gave the machine hardly a glance as he headed down the road toward town. He rode swiftly, busy with his plans for freeing Burke and bringing him back to confront Wilcox Chandler.

A half mile from the town he glanced at his watch. It was half after eleven—he'd have plenty of time to stable Cleopatra and catch the train. He slowed the mare to a walk and noted casually that a car was approaching him from town. He pulled over to one side of the road to allow it to pass. Instead of passing, it slowed and came to a stop in front of him. There were two men in the front seat. Don Coyote's heart sank as he scanned them. They wore no stars; there were no guns visible. But he knew the type. He recognized the lean, sun-browned faces and the steady, alert eyes of the man-hunter.

Double-crossed! Chandler had 'phoned in from the mine! Don Coyote cursed softly.

"You Don Lawrence?" the driver of the car asked casually.

Don Coyote nodded. "That's me, I reckon. What's the charge?"

"Burglary. We've had the warrant for three days, but we didn't get orders to serve it till just now. Better hop in here with me and let my deputy take your horse in."

Don Coyote slowly dismounted. The world was whirling about his head. The ground seemed to roll beneath his feet. Plans! Plans! What a fool he'd been! What use would his precious plans be now? Chandler had the goods on him. Witnesses, too. The sky darkened.

Lawrence stumbled over to the car and climbed into the seat vacated by the deputy, a tall, gangling individual who seemed all arms and legs.

"Haven't got a gun, have you?" the driver asked.

"No. Never carried one in my life."

"All right. Take your word for it. You don't look like a gunman. Want to see the warrant? I'm Sheriff Boylston."

Don Coyote grinned sheepishly. "I don't mind tellin' you that I *ain't* glad to meet you, sheriff. And the warrant can go to blazes. Let's get to town. I got some tall thinkin' to do."

The sheriff, a heavy-set man with piercing brown eyes that were friendly for all their intentness, swung the car around and started back to town. Don Coyote carried away only one pleasant memory of the incident of his arrest. It was the sight of the lanky deputy, a whirling mass of arms and legs, thrown high into the air by Cleopatra.

He found the Chandler City jail old-fashioned and obsolete, but fairly comfortable. He found the sheriff unusually considerate, for a sheriff, and unwontedly friendly. Under other circumstances he felt that he would like to know the man; he seemed like a regular fellow, a man one would be proud to call a friend.

"Aren't you the hombre who recovered old man Dorrington's bullion?" Boylston asked as he unlocked a cell and nodded Lawrence into it.

"Yes, I reckon I am," the prisoner answered a bit wearily.

"Didn't you used to hang out down it Goldfield? And aren't you known down there as Don Coyote?"

"Yeh, reckon I'm the feller. Only I ain't so proud of it now as I used to be."

The sheriff lounged against the door and scanned him critically. "H-m. This is a funny proposition. You aren't any burglar."

Don Coyote smiled as he dropped onto the cot, the only article of furniture in the cell. "That's what they got me charged with," he reminded. "Wouldn't be surprised if I'd plead guilty, too. Might as well. They got the goods on me."

The sheriff grunted, his brown eyes very thoughtful. He did not speak for some time. At last he glanced around the corridor, saw that no one was within hearing, and moved a step into the cell.

"Listen, feller!" he began. "I can smell a rat as far as the next man. And when the rat happens to be Wilcox Chandler I can smell him a lot further. I'm not stringing you now. I'm not trying to talk you into convicting yourself. Whatever you say *won't* be used against you. I may be a sheriff but I'm also a white man. And I know another white man when I see one. Give me the low-down on this thing and I'll do all I can to help you. That's straight."

Don Coyote looked at him, met his brown eyes for a brief instant and believed him. Forthwith, with as much confidence as though he were telling it to his own mother, he narrated the whole story of the Buckaroo. He told of his suspicions of Chandler, the burning of the mine, the insanity of Burke, the attempted recovery of the map, his agreement with Chandler and his mission to Sacramento.

The sheriff listened to it all with furrowed brow. "It isn't the first time Wilcox Chandler has played a game like that," the sheriff told him when he had finished his tale. "Though what his game is in this case is more than I can see."

"I've got a hunch," Don Coyote said, "but it's kind of a personal matter an' I don't like to say anything about it."

"I get you," the sheriff nodded. "It isn't important anyway. The fact of the matter is, he appears to have the goods on you. But when he tries to get a conviction it may be a different matter. It may prove pretty hard to get a jury that will convict you, considering everything. You broke the law, but on the other hand there were extenuating circumstances. Chandler was holding certain property illegally and there was no other way to get it except to go and take it. Then again, it may prove difficult to get that angle of it admitted as evidence. It will take a clever lawyer."

"But I don't know any lawyers, clever or otherwise," Don Coyote put in.

"There's none around here good enough for this kind of a case. I have a friend up in Reno, however, who is as good as they make 'em. Want me to drop him a line, state the case and ask him if he'll take it?"

"Say, now, that would be right fine of you if you would."

"Be glad to. In the meantime, sit tight. If the district attorney tries to draw you out, keep mum. Don't tell him anything. He's a good gun and he don't like Chandler—but he's a conscientious sort of a duck and he's working for reëlection. So keep clear of him."

"And how long will it be before my case will come up?" Lawrence asked anxiously.

"Oh, a month or two. Maybe longer."

"What'll my bail be?"

"Ten thousand, probably."

Don Coyote winced. "Too much. I'll never raise it. And yet I can't stay here. There's no tellin' what that skunk will do to old Dorrington in a month or two. The old man's on the right track now. He ought to open up that ore body in no time. Still, he's too old to have to buck a crook like Chandler. And then there's Soapy Gourd waitin' for me down in Sacramento. Lord! I gotta get out o' here."

"I'll telephone your friend Gourd and tell him what has happened if you want me to," the sheriff offered.

"I wish you would."

"I'll do it right away. In the meantime, sit tight.

Chandler may decide not to press the charge, you can't tell. Just sit tight for a few days and see what happens. I'll keep it dark about the arrest, too. None of the newspaper boys have seen you and I won't tell anybody outside of Gourd. No use giving you a black eye. Sit tight, keep your mouth shut, and we'll get you out of this."

"By the Gods!" Don Coyote exclaimed gratefully. "You're the whitest sheriff I ever met in my life."

Boylston chuckled. "Just because a man is elected to the office of sheriff doesn't mean that he has to turn into a yellow dog."

Don Coyote nodded slowly. "Never thought o' that. Reckon you're right."

The sheriff walked out and the steel door clanged behind him. Don Coyote shuddered. With Boylston, a sure-enough white man, in his cell, it hadn't seemed so bad. Now, alone, penned in by concrete walls and barred door and window, Don Coyote came to his first acute realization of what it meant to be in jail. It was not a pleasant sensation.

# CHAPTER XXXV

Don Coyote's first visitor came the following afternoon. It was Soapy Gourd, a furtive, half-frightened little creature who showed plainly his horror of jails.

"Cripes!" he grunted, when a deputy had thrown open the door of Lawrence's cell. "What's the lay, big boy?"

"He double-crossed me, Soapy. Had the warrant waitin' all the time. Had the sheriff pick me up when I was coming into town yesterday."

"Cheese an' crackers! What we goin' to do about it?"

"Nothing much right now. The sheriff is going to get me an attorney from Reno. He says he may get me off if we can get the whole story admitted as evidence."

"Huh! I ain't got much faith in sheriffs, big boy," Soapy growled.

"But this one's different, Soapy," Lawrence defended with enthusiasm. "He's a regular guy, an' no mistake. Don't like Chandler any too well either. I'd trust him with my eye teeth."

"But we gotta get you out o' here. There ain't no time to lose. Dis guy Burke is goin' nuts. He's almost bugs, I tell yuh!"

"Did you talk to him?" Don Coyote asked eagerly.

"Sure I did. T'rough a window couple o' nights ago."

"Did he seem sane?"

"Sure. Sane as you an' me. He says he was only out of his head for a couple o' days. Thinks it was the gas that got him. Didn't remember nothin' after goin' into the tunnel till he woke up here in the hospital. Him an' Chandler had it out. He didn't tell me de details. An' Chandler railroaded him to get him out of the way. An' he's sore, what I mean!"

"Then he wasn't insane at all?"

"I dunno. Temporary, maybe. Or maybe it was de gas. I dunno much about dem t'ings. But he's sure goin' loco now, cooped up in dat bug-house wid all the nuts. Whew! It gimme the willies just to hang aroun' there an' hear 'em yellin' an' moanin' an' screamin'. Cripes! Terrible place! We gotta get him out an' I gotta have you to help me."

"I—I don't know, Soapy," Don Coyote hesitated. "I don't quite see how I'm goin' to get out very soon."

"How about bail?"

"Ten thousand. Too much. Dorrington would help. But he hasn't got that much an' I'm blamed sure he couldn't raise it."

"Does he know you're in de jug?"

"No, I don't think so. Not unless Chandler told him. The sheriff agreed to keep quiet about it and I didn't see no use in worryin' the old man. He's on the track o' that ore chamber now an' I want to leave him alone till he gets it."

"Huh!" Soapy grunted and glanced around. He looked hard at the lock on the cell door, cocking his head thoughtfully to one side. "Caledonian," he mused. "No tumblers. It's a cinch!"

"What was that, Soapy?" Don Coyote asked suspiciously.

"I was just sayin' me prayers. Keep yer shirt on an' yer mouth shut, will yuh?" He lowered his voice. "You sleep in your clothes to-night. Get me?"

"But, Soapy—"

"Dry up!" He rattled the cell door sharply; a deputy appeared and threw it open. "See you in church, big boy." And Soapy was gone.

Don Coyote thoughtfuly rolled a cigarette. Soapy's inference had been plain. He meant to get him out of jail, by just what means he did not know. But he did know Soapy. He had known him long and under far more trying circumstances than the present. He had never known him to fall down on any kind of a job, whether it was bombing a machine gun nest or peeling a sack of spuds. Soapy was little and he looked like a rat. But he had brains, Soapy had, and he had courage and resourcefulness. What more was needed to get a man out of jail?

The ethics of the matter were open to question, of course. The Sheriff had treated Don Coyote mighty fine and it wasn't exactly right for him to escape from his jail. On the other hand, he had a hunch that the sheriff wouldn't care greatly if he did. He was a white man, that sheriff was, and if he hadn't been an officer of the law he might even have helped the escape himself. As he had said, the circumstances were extenuating. He didn't belong there in the first place, and in the second place somebody had to get Ben Burke out of that bug-house before he went nutty for good and all.

Don Coyote made up his mind. If some one came, and opened the door of his cell, and said he was free, and told him to get out as quickly as possible, he'd get out. Who wouldn't? He could make explanations to the sheriff afterward.

And Soapy Gourd came. It was nearly four o'clock in the morning and Don Coyote had about given him up. He came so silently, too, that he was in the cell and had his hand on Lawrence's shoulder before the latter knew the door was open.

"Quiet, big boy!" Soapy cautioned. "The deputy's asleep in the outer office, but we ain't takin' no chances. Follow me."

Don Coyote followed, out the door, along the corridor and through another door into the sheriff's office. Here they found the lanky deputy whom Don Coyote had seen when the sheriff had arrested him. He was breathing heavily, his feet propped up on the desk, a dead cigar clasped tightly between his lips. Don Coyote noticed that his nose was skinned and felt immediately repentant. If this skinny feller was anything like the sheriff, he wasn't a bad sort. Should have warned him that Cleopatra didn't take kindly to strangers.

Soapy's hand was on the knob of the outer door when Don Coyote was struck with an idea. Crossing to the desk on tip-toe, he picked up a pencil. Though he saw out of the corner of his eye that Soapy was motioning to him frantically, he calmly wrote on the desk blotter:

"Sorry I had to leave you. Don't bother to look for me. I'll be back—Lawrence."

Then he was at Soapy's heels. The door opened softly and was as softly closed, and they were on the deserted street. Don Coyote took a deep breath of the cold night air. "How'd you do it, Soapy?"

"Cinch! Watched through the window till he went to sleep. Knew he would. They always do, long about four. Dat's when the sawbones say the ol' vitality is lowest. Soon as he was asleep, I picked the lock of the outer office, walked t'rough into the corridor and picked the lock o' your cell. Cinch! Nothin' to it!"

Don Coyote shook his head; he did not understand this business of picking locks. It was all a mystery to him. But he was thoroughly alive to the results of Soapy's efforts and he was grateful.

"Soapy, when I'm back at the Buckaroo again, you're goin' to get the best job I can give yuh—and at the highest salary I can make the old man pay. I won't forget all you've done for us and he won't either."

"Aw, dry up, will yuh?" Soapy answered characteristically. "We got a long ride ahead of us. We're goin' to Sacramento to-night."

"To-night!"

"Yeh! Yuh don't t'ink we're goin' to sit down on the curb in front o' the sheriff's office till mornin', do yuh? Dat sheriff may be a good gun, but if he sees yuh hangin' 'round outside when yuh ought to be inside, he might get sore."

The little man led the way down two blocks and around a corner. They came upon a heavy touring car parked at the curb, a driver slumped behind the wheel.

"Wake up, Slats!" Soapy cried, thumping the driver over the shoulders. "We're makin' tracks in a hurry." The man roused, blinking. "Slats, shake hands wid Don Lawrence, de only sergeant I ever knew that I didn't want to stick out my tongue at. Big boy, dis is Slats Monohan, the best little stick-up man dat ever pulled a rod. Met him down in Sac, where he's tryin' to go straight by gypin' the public in de garage game."

Don Coyote shook hands with mingled feelings; he didn't know exactly whether he should feel flattered or otherwise at meeting the "best little stick-up man dat ever pulled a rod." He had a hunch, however, that he should feel very grateful. The circumstances, as has been said before, were extenuating.

The three men arrived in Sacramento shortly before noon and went to bed immediately. They were all dead tired and there was nothing that could be done until dark. Don Coyote had at first been in favor of appealing to the authorities in an effort to effect Burke's release. Soapy, however, would have none of it. The man had been declared insane by a supposedly competent commission, he pointed out. To get him declared sane again, to run through the reams of legal red tape that such a course would necessitate, would probably take months. And for more than one reason there was no time to be lost.

"You lemme do this my way, big boy," Soapy advised. "If I don't get him out, then you can try."

Don Coyote nodded, somewhat dubiously as was usually the case where ethics were involved, and they went to sleep.

Around ten o'clock that evening, with their car parked a short distance from the Las Palmas Sanatorium, Soapy narrated his plans.

"Here's de lay. Dis place is just like a prison, see? Guards an' cells an' bars an' everyt'ing. At night there's two men on guard in the office. The rest o' the gang is asleep. Dese two birds have got the keys to all de cells, see? Aw right. Slats, here, stays in de car. Me an' big boy, here, goes up an' rings de bell. We stick up dese two guards wid our rods an' take their keys. Big boy keeps guard over 'em when I sneak down the hall an' let Burke out. Then we all make our get-away in the car. Got dat?"

Slats and Don Coyote nodded.

"Got a rod, big boy?" Soapy demanded.

"No."

"Giv' um yours, Slats, an' we'll get movin'."

Don Coyote felt the gun thrust into his hand. Every nerve on edge, he followed along behind the slouching, stealthy form of his little friend.

# CHAPTER XXXVI

CROSSING the darkened grounds which surrounded the sanatorium, Soapy boldly mounted the steps, pausing before the door. "All set?" he asked.

Don Coyote nodded, clutching his gun. He wished it weren't loaded; he certainly had no intention of using it, save as a threat. And if some one called his bluff—well, he'd learn what the inside of another jail looked like.

Soapy rang the bell and after a wait that seemed interminable, the door was opened by a white-coated attendant. "Put 'em up!" Soapy ordered, thrusting his gun into the man's ribs. "Let out a peep an' I'll put daylight t'rough yuh!"

The attendant took him at his word. The color drained suddenly out of his face and he raised his hands hastily. Soapy shoved him back through the door, along the wide hall and into the office. Here another man, receiving the same order, likewise raised his hands.

"Now gimme yer keys," Soapy commanded.

One of the men motioned to a heavy ring attached to his belt. Soapy took it. "Which one opens Burke's room?"

"Number four."

"Good! Keep 'em covered, big boy. I'll be back in a minute." Don thrust out his gun and tried to look business-like. He hoped they wouldn't see that he was a rank amateur at this game. The thought worried him. Anybody with half an eye, he reflected, ought to be able to perceive that he was masquerading under false colors. He put on his fiercest mien, scowling angrily. And one of the attendants laughed!

"Put away your gun, pardner. You wouldn't shoot anyway."

Don Coyote started. He didn't quite know whether to make a dash for the door or to shoot a hole in the ceiling, just to show 'em.

"It's no skin off our teeth what you do with Burke," the attendant went on, casually lowering his hands and thrusting them into his pockets. "Of course, we got our orders and we got to obey 'em or lose our jobs. But to be frank with you, I'm glad to see you get Burke out of here. He's not insane, but he will be if he stays here much longer."

Don Coyote sheepishly pocketed his gun. "You're the second white man I've met in as many days," he said. "Sorry we had to bother yuh. But we just had to get Burke out o' here. It ain't only for himself. There's others mixed up. White men, too."

"I know. Something about a mine, isn't it? He's told me. Seems as though he got mixed up in a crooked deal and got in so deep he couldn't get out. Got railroaded to this joint. Oh, I know what you're thinking, pardner. But," he shrugged, "a man has to make a living, hasn't he? I got a family and I can't afford to mix up—"

"Cripes!" It was Soapy, standing aghast in the doorway. Behind him loomed the huge form of Ben Burke.

"It's all right, Soapy," Don Coyote assured him with a grin. "These boys are regular fellers, same's you an' me. But I reckon we don't want to stretch 'em too far. Let's get out o' here."

The attendant who had talked to Lawrence walked with them to the door. "I'll give you five minutes before I give the alarm," he said.

"Thanks," Don Coyote answered, and surprised himself by thrusting a fifty-dollar bill into the man's hand.

"Wait a minute. I don't want—" the attendant began.

But Don Coyote and his two companions were already speeding down the path to the street. They did not speak until they were in the car and rolling through town toward the open highway.

"Well, we done it," Soapy grinned over his shoulder to Lawrence and Burke, who were in the back seat.

And, oddly, Don Coyote felt a certain pride at the use of the inclusive pronoun.

Burke did not speak. Thin, wasted, a shadow of his former self, he sat in the corner of the tonneau in a dark silence. From time to time Don Coyote stole a furtive glance at him. He didn't know exactly whether to hate him or pity him. The man had tried to murder him; he had almost succeeded in wrecking the Buckaroo. And still, he had had a pretty rotten deal. All in all, Don Coyote felt sorry for him.

Sacramento was far behind them, Soapy was sound asleep in the front seat and the powerful car was roaring into the foothills when Burke broke the silence of an hour or more.

"I guess it won't do any good to apologize, Lawrence," he said suddenly.

Don Coyote considered. Burke was humility itself; his voice showed that. "Hell! Forget about it, Burke," Lawrence answered. "I reckon we all make mistakes. It ain't what you've done in the past that counts so much, it's what you're goin' to do in the future."

"I know! I know!" the big man groaned. "I'm not a murderer at heart. I'm not a crook at heart. That's why I went batty for a while. Of course, the gas had something to do with it. I was in the Bellingham mine disaster nine years ago and I'm scared to death of that damned white damp. But that wasn't all. It was the thought that I'd tried to kill a man. That's what got me."

Quietly Don Coyote asked: "Why did you do it, Burke?"

"It was that or jail. Chandler has the goods on me. A high-grading job in the Lady Ann, where I was shift boss for a couple of years. He found out about it. Put me into the Buckaroo as super. He wanted to wreck Dorrington and he made me help him. That's all."

"But why did he want to wreck Dorrington?"

"Haven't you guessed?"

"I have a hunch. Was it the girl?"

"Sure. Of course, at the beginning I think he had some plan up his sleeve for bustin' the company. That'd give him a chance to buy in the property for nothin', you might say, and go ahead and develop it. It's sure to be a rich mine, if they can ever find that ore chamber. They tell me that the original company left thousands of tons of high-grade ore untouched. Stuff that'd run a hundred or two hundred dollars a ton but wouldn't pay to ship all the way to England to smelt. If Dorrington can find that ore chamber, he'll be a rich man.

"And that was what Chandler wanted to keep him from doin'. At first, like I said, he wanted to get hold of the mine. But later it was just the girl that was botherin' him. You see, Dorrington is a pretty old man. If that mine flivvered, he'd be in a bad way to make a living for himself and the girl. Knowing the kind of stuff Miss Dorrington is made of, Chandler knew that she'd marry him before she'd let her father go out workin' at day labor. I ain't sayin' that she didn't like Chandler, neither. But she'd never marry him if it wasn't to help out her dad. I know that an' Chandler knows it. That was what was behind the whole damn' business."

Don Coyote considered for a moment. "You know, don't you," he said at last, "that both you an' Chandler are open to charges of attempted murder?"

"Sure we are! Murder an' arson, both of 'em. Don't I know it? Ain't that what caused the trouble between me and Chandler? When I was in the hospital after the fire, I was pretty shaky in the head. Guess you knew that. But I wasn't so shaky that I didn't know I was through with Chandler an' all his dirty work. I told him so when he come to see me. He argued for a while an' then he beat it. Then the first thing I knew they had me up before some kind of a commission. Before I realized what'd happened, they had me declared insane and railroaded to that private asylum. God! Another month or two in that place and I'd have been crazy for keeps."

"Are you willin' to come clean now an' do what you can to square accounts?" Don Coyote asked.

"With Chandler, you mean?" Burke asked angrily.

"With everybody!"

"Blamed right I am! You tell me what to do an' I'll do it, if they send me to jail for life. The worst jail in the country would be better than that crazy house. Lord, I can hear 'em screamin' yet. Long about five in the evening was the worst. One of 'em would start to howl an' then another'd take it up. It got so—"

"I'll see what I can do for you," Don Coyote interrupted quietly. "The sheriff is a pretty good friend o' mine, or was. They say the district attorney is a good gun, too. You and I know that Dorrington and the Buckaroo ain't safe as long as Chandler is in the country. Even if Dorrington strikes that ore body,

Chandler will be so sore that he's liable to make it hot for him. But if you'll come clean, we may be able to run the damn' skunk out o' the country. Are you game?"

"I'm game for anything that'll square my account with Chandler," Burke said firmly.

"Good! Now let's pull these h'yar robes over us an' get some sleep."

# CHAPTER XXXVII

At eight o'clock the following morning, Don Coyote presented himself at the sheriff's office. Boylston had just arrived and was busy at his desk. Lawrence entered without knocking. The sheriff did not glance up at once.

"Sheriff, I'm back," Don Coyote announced a bit sheepishly.

Boylston started but did not turn around. "Your room is ready for you, Lawrence. You can go right on in."

The other's shoulders drooped. "Aw, listen, sheriff! I got somethin' to talk over with yuh. It's important as the devil. I'm sorry I pulled out on yuh. But I just had to do it. If you'll listen to me a minute—"

The sheriff whirled around in his chair. "Lawrence, if you'll tell me how you got out of that cell, I'll listen to you till doomsday."

"Aw, that was a cinch," Don Coyote answered, mimicking Soapy. "Caledonian lock. No tumblers. A cinch."

"Cinch my eye!" Boylston came back. "If you can pick an outside lock from the inside of a cell, you're doing something that I never heard of being done before."

"Who said anything about me pickin' it?" Don Coyote parried.

"Oh! An outside job, eh?"

"Right！"

"My apologies. You're not as clever as I thought you were, Don Coyote. You've taken a load off my mind, anyway. So I'll take a load off yours. Out with it."

"I got Ben Burke outside. He's as sane as you are. He's willin' to make a confession. He's got the goods on Wilcox Chandler. Attempted murder an' arson. We can get him right. Are you with me or agin me?"

"I'm with you, of course. You say Burke is willing to turn state's evidence if we'll grant him immunity?"

"There ain't nothin' been said about immunity. Burke is willin' to take his medicine if he can see Chandler take it too."

"Fair enough! Drag him in. Only I warn you, Lawrence, that you'll have a mighty slim chance of convicting Chandler on the testimony of Burke. Burke has been adjudged insane and though he may be sane enough now, it would go against him with a jury, particularly if he was the only witness against Chandler. However, arrest and a trial of any kind would ruin Wilcox Chandler. He's not the kind who could stand a thing like that, even if he came off clear. It would break him, ruin him, virtually run him out of the country."

Don Coyote laughed without humor. "Aw right, run him out o' the country an' see if it breaks my heart." He started toward the door. "I'll get Burke now."

"And I'll get the district attorney," the sheriff said, reaching for the telephone.

The consultation that followed was long, lasting well into the afternoon. It was held behind closed doors, with only the district attorney, Sheriff Boylston, Burke and Lawrence in attendance. There were many angles to be considered, many points to be settled. Burke came clean, as he had said he would, and told the whole story of the part he and Chandler had played in the fight against the Buckaroo.

The conference had three results. First, Burke was lodged in a cell until Dorrington could be notified and come to a decision about swearing to a charge of arson —this despite the fact that Don Coyote refused to swear to such a charge and was of the opinion that Dorrington would not do so. "Burke wasn't himself when he pulled that job," Lawrence explained his stand, "and I ain't the man to hit a feller when he's down. Personally, I think three months in that bughouse was enough punishment for him an' I reckon Dorrington will think the same. However, o' course you got to hold him."

Second, Lawrence swore to a complaint against Wilcox Chandler, charging conspiracy, arson and attempted murder. "Sounds pretty bad," he grinned, "but I reckon it won't mean much if he ever comes to trial." A justice of the peace was called in and a warrant for the arrest of Chandler was issued.

Finally, the same justice of the peace reduced Don Coyote's bail to one hundred dollars on the burglary charge and the district attorney assured him that if Chandler did not press the charge, the county authorities would not do so. The sheriff, being a white man and also having a strong inclination toward running his office as he saw fit, refused to press any charge of jail-breaking against Lawrence.

"After all," the sheriff smiled, "I guess it isn't such a terrible crime to walk out of a jail if somebody comes along and opens the door for you. And as for this Soapy friend of yours, the little fellow with the rat-face and the close-set eyes—well—" he chuckled softly, his eyes twinkling—"I don't know his name, I don't know what he looks like or anything about him. So how can I go out and arrest him? Only get this straight, Lawrence." The twinkle went out of his eyes and he was again an officer of the law. "If he strays from the straight and narrow again I'll lock him up and throw the key away."

Don Coyote laughed happily. "He's cured, sheriff. I give yuh my word for that." He reached into his pocket, drew out his wallet and handed the sheriff a hundred dollars. "Now I'm free, ain't I?"

Boylston shook his head. "No, you are out on bail. If Chandler insists on pressing that charge, you'll have to go to trial."

"I got a hunch I can take care o' Chandler, provided I can have a free rein for a while. Will you give it to me?"

"Just what do you mean, Lawrence?"

"Here's the dope. If you arrest Chandler, you'll cost the state a lot o' money bringin' him to trial and the chances are ten to one that you won't get a conviction. You'll disgrace him, o' course, but that ain't no money in the taxpayers' pockets."

"I'm beginning to get you," the sheriff nodded.

"Suppose you hold off serving that warrant for a day. Gimme a chance to make a dicker with him."

"What kind of a dicker?"

"I'll offer to withdraw the charge I've sworn against him if he'll do the same for me an' clear out of this part of the country."

"You're generous, Lawrence," the sheriff grinned.

"Generous be darned!" Don Coyote stormed. "That crook was generous to old man Dorrington, wasn't he? He was generous to me, double-crossin' me and sending me to jail, wasn't he? Generosity be damned! I got him over a barrel and I'm goin' to squeeze him so tight that he'll slide into the bung-hole."

"Will he leave?"

"That's up to him. If he wants to go to trial, have the whole story come out, and be disgraced, he can stay. If he wants to save his face an' start over again in some other place with a half-way decent reputation, he'll go. Personally, I'm inclined to think he'll go."

Boylston nodded quietly. "I won't be at all surprised if he does."

"Now gimme a telephone," Don Coyote demanded eagerly. "I got some heavy telephonin' to do."

The sheriff motioned to the instrument on his desk. Don Coyote took up the receiver and gave the number of the Buckaroo. While he was waiting he asked over his shoulder:

"Does Dorrington know that I been arrested?"

"Not unless Chandler has told him. I kept it pretty quiet."

"Does he know anything about this business of gettin' Burke out and gettin' the goods on Chandler?"

"Not so far as I know," the sheriff answered.

Then Don Coyote heard Dorrington's familiar voice. "This is Don Lawrence, Mr. Dorrington," he began.

"Yes, Lawrence."

There was something in the old man's voice that startled Don Coyote. Something was wrong at the mine—or—he had at last made the big strike.

"You've made it!" the younger man exclaimed. "You've hit the old ore chamber. I can tell by the way you talk."

"Yes. About an hour ago."

"And it's rich!"

"Millions, Lawrence, millions!"

Words of enthusiasm, they were, words that would ordinarily have set Don Coyote's pulse to racing and his eyes to shining. But they did neither. Instead his lips tightened and his firm jaw hardened. For those words of victory and triumph and success had been uttered in the lifeless tone of a beaten man.

"Mr. Dorrington! Something's gone wrong. Tell me!"

"It's Gayle. She's gone!"

"Gone!"

"Yes. With Chandler." Dead and lifeless were the words.

# CHAPTER XXXVIII

WHITE of face though he was, Don Coyote recovered quickly. "What happened?" he demanded. "Tell me about it."

"There is nothing much to tell. I came out of the tunnel just a few minutes ago. I found a note, saying she was going away to marry Chandler."

"But she doesn't love that scoundrel!" Lawrence objected heatedly.

"I know. That's what hurts so much. She did it for me. She has never said anything much, but I know she has been worrying. She has hated to see me working so hard and having so much trouble. She thought I was going broke. I never told her about the new drift in the tunnel. She had no idea we were so near the ore chamber. She had lost heart, that's all; lost faith in the mine. She was afraid I'd be beaten and have to go to work at day labor to support her. So she did this—for me, never dreaming that I knew why she did it, never dreaming that it will—break—my heart!"

Don Coyote groaned.

"Chandler came this afternoon while I was in the tunnel," Dorrington went on. "They had a long talk together. The cook told me. Then they drove off in Chandler's car. It was—just about the time—we were breaking through into that ore chamber."

"But where did they go?" Don Coyote demanded.

"To Carson, Gayle said in her note. They're to be married there."

"The devil they are!" Don Coyote shouted. "You sit tight, Mr. Dorrington. I'll knock that marriage higher'n a kite. I'm off."

He snapped the received onto the hook and, unmindful of the questioning stare of the sheriff, rushed out of the office. In a hotel a block away were Slats Monohan and Soapy, resting up after the long trip of the night before. Don Coyote covered the distance in nothing flat, bounded up the stairs, dashed into the room. He found the two men lounging on the bed, smoking.

"What's up, big boy?" Soapy demanded.

"Everything! The devil's to pay!"

"Let's pay him, then!" Soapy grinned, jumping to his feet. "Where to?"

"Come on! The car! Carson! Tell yuh later!"

Don Coyote's voice and actions were enough. Slats and Soapy followed him down the stairs two at a time. They leaped into the car, the powerful motor purred, Slats threw in the clutch and they were off. Slats Monohan might not be called a model driver. When he was in a hurry he took the right of way over one and all and he knew now that haste was required of him. Neither Don Coyote nor Soapy took a deep breath until they were clear of the town's traffic and roaring over the rutted highway that led in a winding white ribbon to the north. Then Soapy turned around in his seat and faced Lawrence, who was in the tonneau.

"What happened, big boy?" he grinned. "Are de dicks on our trail?"

"No, nothing like that. Everything is squared. We're after Chandler. He's got—well, damn him, he's got my li'l lady!"

Soapy's eyebrows raised. "An' we're goin' to get him?" he queried.

"Right!"

Monohan did not spare his car nor his passengers. He knew that he would be paid and paid well. Besides, the spirit of the chase was on him. He opened the throttle and held it open, ruts, chuckholes, deep sand and jagged rocks notwithstanding. Don Coyote's heart was in his throat. But he said not a word. And had he spoken, it would have been only to urge greater speed.

It was some sixty miles from Chandler City to Carson, sixty miles of poor road, a part of it over heavy grades. Ordinarily it would take a car three hours or more to make the trip. At the speed Slats Monohan was traveling, he would make it in an hour and a half—if they had good luck and no blow-outs or breakdown.

"If he's got an hour and a half start on us, we'll still be able to catch him," Lawrence told himself. "Maybe if he's got two hours' start, 'cause it'll take him some time to get a license and get married. Now what time did they leave the Buckaroo? Dorrington never told me. Prob'ly didn't know, anyway. But we ought to get 'em. We got to get 'em!"

Then a disquieting thought. Suppose they had changed their plans? Suppose they had decided to go to some other town? Or even get married in Chandler City? There was no law against that. People got married in their home towns same's any other place. Course, when they eloped they usually went some place else. Why, Don Coyote didn't know. People did it, that was all. And the thought comforted him.

The miles reeled by. An hour passed. Don Coyote caught a glimpse of a sign: Carson 19 miles. They overhauled half a dozen cars. Each time they sighted one, Don Coyote rose in his seat, peering ahead eagerly, only to drop back again as they drew closer. His pulse was racing with the agony of suspense. The perspiration stood out in beads on his forehead. Had they played the wrong hunch? Had Chandler and Gayle been quietly married in Chandler City while they tore off over the country on this wild goose chase?

Then, just as they started up a long grade, Don Coyote caught sight of a big car ahead of them. He knew it instantly, beyond all possibility of error.

"That's it!" he cried triumphantly, standing up in the tonneau. "Catch it, Slats! Give her the gun!"

The car leaped forward and Don Coyote sat down abruptly. He rose again at once, clinging to the back of the front seat, his heart singing, his tanned face beaming happily.

Chandler's car was less than a quarter of a mile ahead of them, traveling along at a leisurely speed. Though it threw up a heavy cloud of dust, Don Coyote was certain that he could see two figures in the tonneau and a man at the wheel. The distance between the two cars shortened swiftly as Slats held the throttle open and raced up the long hill. Two hundred yards, a hundred, fifty.

Don Coyote was trembling with suspense. Though still uncertain as to the occupants of the car, due to the great clouds of dust it left behind, he could wait no longer. When they were within fifty feet of the machine ahead, he shouted to Monohan.

"Give him the horn, Slats! Pass him and block the road."

Obediently Slats blew the horn. Almost before the echo came back from the opposite hillside, Don Coyote knew that he had blundered. The big car ahead speeded up. Valiantly Slats sought to catch up to it, to pass it. His efforts were in vain. Chandler's car held its own, indeed it began slowly to draw ahead. Slats blew his horn again, insistently. The machine ahead showed no intention of slowing down.

Don Coyote sighed and sat down. They'd have to wait till they got to Carson now. The big car ahead might beat them in, but not by more than a minute or two. No harm had been done by his false move. He had only delayed matters.

Then he saw something that chilled his heart. Very vaguely through the dust, like some phantom, he saw the man in the rear seat of Chandler's car swing around. Though he heard nothing above the roaring exhaust, he saw a red dagger of flame leap through the clouds of dust.

"The dirty skunk!" Don .Coyote cried. "He's shootin' at us."

He could distinguish no features through the pall of flying particles, but he knew instinctively that the man was Chandler. Vaguely he realized that Soapy had drawn his gun.

"Let him have it, Soapy!" Lawrence shouted. Then, as Soapy eagerly trained his gun around the windshield, "No! No! You can't shoot! You might hit Gayle. Wait! Let him go. We can catch him in Carson. Take it easy, Slats. No use takin' chances."

Soapy lowered his gun reluctantly. "I could pick dat bird off like nuttin'!" he growled. "Cinch! Nuttin' to it!"

"No, you can't do that, Soapy," Don Coyote's anger was dying fast. "You can't blame him for shootin' at us. He prob'ly thinks we're bandits, tryin' to hold him up. He can't see us through the dust, not enough to recognize us."

"Huh! He'd prob'ly shoot all the more if he recognized us," the little man grunted.

"Well, maybe he would. But it's ten to one he don't know who we are. I hardly know him, the dust is flyin' so bad. Let him get ahead, Slats. No use takin' chances o' gettin' shot."

There was a low, hissing sound, as of boiling water poured on hot metal. Monohan cursed sharply. "Damn him, he's plugged my radiator. We won't be able to go five miles with a dry radiator."

Don Coyote gasped. "What—what was that, Slats?"

"He drilled my radiator. Motor will freeze up without water. We're sunk!"

Still the import of their predicament failed to dawn on Don Coyote. They could get into Carson some way, if they had to walk. And after what had happened Gayle would never marry—

Then it dawned on him. It came like a crushing blow, overwhelming, stupefying. Gayle did not know who had chased them. She did not know it had been Don Coyote. She could not have recognized him through the dust.

Now her car was drawing ahead. Thrilled, perhaps, at what she thought was an encounter with bandits, she was riding on to Carson, blissfully ignorant of the identity of the man who had sought to stop her.

# CHAPTER XXXIX

IF Don Coyote was to act, he knew that there was no time to be lost. Chandler's car was rapidly drawing ahead. If it got away, it might beat them in to Carson City by hours. He came to a decision abruptly and barked an order to Soapy.

"Let him have it, Soapy! His tires, if you can! His gas tank! Anything, only stop him!"

The fleeting machine was more than a hundred feet away. Don Coyote knew that only an expert marksman could hit a tire at that distance, particularly in view of the speed of their own car and the poor visibility. But he felt suddenly confident as Soapy leaned over the side of the automobile and took aim. He'd seen Soapy shoot before. There was that German sniper in the tree at St. Mihiel. Two hundred yards away he'd been, and Soapy had got him with a pistol. It had taken three shots but—

The little man's revolver barked. "Got one of 'em! Soapy exclaimed proudly. "See it go flat?"

Don Coyote couldn't see. His eyes were blind with dust. He wondered that any one could see. Wonderful eyes Soapy must have! He'd thought his own were pretty good.

The cars roared up the grade. Soapy shot four more

times and flashed Lawrence a triumphant grin. "Got both rear tires. I'll save de last shot. If he don't stop, I'll let him have it where it'll do de most good."

"No, no, Soapy! You can't shoot him. You're square with the law now. You got to stay that way."

For a hundred yards or more Chandler's car bumped along on two flat tires. Then it slowed down and came to a halt at the side of the road. Chandler's hands were in the air even before they drew up to him.

"What's the meaning—" he began angrily, and then broke off as he recognized the dust-smeared face of Don Coyote. He stared hard at the younger man for a moment and then said calmly: "I think you'd better explain yourself, Lawrence."

"Don't worry, I will! Plenty!" Don Coyote cried as he leaped out of the tonneau.

He was not looking at Chandler; he had hardly heard the man's words. His eyes were all for Gayle. He had never seen her so beautiful. Her cheeks were flushed with excitement; her brown eyes were wide and sparkling. There was relief in them, too. For she must have read something in his confident, deliberate manner. Don Coyote bowed.

"Sorry to bother you, ma'am," he smiled, "but I got somethin' to say to Mr. Chandler and I'm afraid you'd hamper my vocabulary. Would you mind gettin' over in my car? I won't be long. Please?"

It thrilled him to see how she accepted his suggestion without comment, without question.

"See here, Lawrence, this is going too far," Chandler

began angrily as Lawrence started to help the girl from the automobile. "This lady is not going to leave my car."

Chandler put out his hand to stop her and received a sharp blow on the wrist for his pains.

"You keep your shirt on!" Don Coyote growled.

"I have no intention of taking it off!" the other snapped. "But I'll be damned—"

"You are already! But there ain't no use in tellin' the world about it," Lawrence came back.

Graciously he helped Gayle into the tonneau of Monohan's car and ordered the latter to turn around and drive down the road a hundred yards. "Get plenty far away," he said. "I don't want to shock this li'l lady if I happen to let loose."

Very calmly he stood in the road, rolling a cigarette, while Monohan swung around and drove down the hill. Then he turned to Chandler, lit his cigarette and announced coldly:

"Chandler, we got the goods on you. Ben Burke is out."

Beyond a faint drawing in of the lips, the other displayed no emotion.

"What's more, he's sane and he's made a complete confession. An' that ain't all. I been in conference with the sheriff an' the district attorney all morning. There's a warrant out for your arrest on charges—" this very slowly—"on charges of conspiracy, arson and attempted murder."

Chandler's eyes narrowed. "You're bluffing."

"Am I?" Don Coyote snapped. "All right! I dare
yuh to come back to town an' face 'em. I dare yuh!"

Chandler's jaw snapped shut and he made no reply.
Don Coyote took a puff on his cigarette.

"You got one chance of keepin' this thing under
cover. I happen to know that if yuh pull out o' here
and don't come back, the charges won't be pressed."

"Pull out! You're crazy! I have thousands of dollars invested around Chandler City. Do you think I
am going to desert my holdings? Do you think—"

"I ain't thinkin' anything," Don Coyote interrupted
coolly. "That's up to you. Your attorneys can dis-
pose of your holdings or they can handle 'em for yuh.
Suit yourself. But if you do come back—it means a
trial sure as shootin'. The whole story will come out.
You'll be disgraced, whether you go to the pen or not.
An' I might say that the evidence is pretty strong, when
you consider what Burke knows an' a few other men,
like Johnson, might be induced to tell. Seems to me
you're gettin' off easy, just clearin' out an' nobody the
wiser."

Don Coyote knew his man, knew the pride that was
his, the pride of race and family and social position—
and he knew that he could come to only one decision.

"What about Miss Dorrington?" Chandler demanded
at last.

Don Coyote smiled. He could tell from Chandler's
tone that he was already beaten, that he was trying to
recover one last chip from the wreck of his fortunes.

"Miss Dorrington is goin' to marry me this afternoon," Lawrence answered most casually. "You don't reckon she'd have any more to do with a rat like you, do yuh?"

Chandler stiffened and immediately relaxed. For several moments he stared at Don Coyote and there came at last into his eyes a light that might almost have been admiration. He laughed, bitterly, and slowly shook his head. He spoke quietly, addressing his remark to the immobile back of his chauffeur.

"Lawrence, a man would go to hell and back again to win Gayle Dorrington. Wouldn't he?"

There was humility in Don Coyote's voice, humility and understanding, as he answered: "I reckon he would, Mr. Chandler."

Chandler sighed deeply and turned away. "Baxter, get to work on those tires. We've got to make Reno to-night."

That was all. Don Coyote started down the road. He had won. But, oddly, he felt few of the emotions of the victor. Chandler had been right. Almost any man, even the best of 'em, would go to hell and back again to win Gayle Dorrington—and who could blame 'em?

Don Coyote climbed into the tonneau and took his seat beside Gayle.

"Slats plugged the hole in the radiator," Soapy grinned over his shoulder. "We can make it to the nearest farmhouse an' fill up wit' water an' get back to town. Let's go, Slats!"

Then, very obviously and deliberately, he turned his

back on them. The car moved off down the hill. Don Coyote sought the small hand that rested on the seat beside him. The answered pressure on his own left him inarticulate with happiness. For miles neither spoke—there was so little that needed to be said.

"Chandler has gone for good an' all," Lawrence remarked casually at last. "We got the goods on him. He's been fightin' your dad all along. He wanted—" Don Coyote checked himself. After all, he had won. Why shouldn't he be magnanimous? "He wanted to bust your dad an' get possession of the Buckaroo. It's a rich mine. Millions! I was talkin' to your dad. He hit the ore chamber this afternoon. Millions!"

"Don!" It was almost a cry of anguish.

He looked at her for the first time in miles, smiled gently into her eyes and pressed her hand very hard. "Yeh! S'fact. Honest. Millions."

There were tears in her eyes now. "Oh, Don Coyote! You dear boy!"

"Me? I didn't do anything."

"You've done everything!"

"No! I ain't done nothin' at all. Just been havin' a good time, playin' hunches an' buttin' into things that wasn't none o' my business, like that feller I been named after. Pickin' up that li'l ridin' gauntlet, for instance."

He reached into his breast pocket and slowly drew forth a small, worn glove. "Know it?" he asked.

"Of course! You took it when you left the mine. I knew all the time."

He nodded, gazing tenderly at the bit of leather in his hand. "You been a right kind li'l ol' glove, you have. They's been times when I cussed you out, li'l glove. They's been times when I wished I'd never laid eyes on yuh. They's been times when you've made me think I was all kinds of a fool. They's been times when you made we wish that that blamed name of Don Coyote had never been pinned on me. They's been times—but aw, what's the use? Next to this li'l lady sittin' here at my side, you're the nicest li'l thing that ever drifted across my trail. You are that, li'l ol' glove. Yes, ma'am."

**THE END**

www.ingramcontent.com/pod-product-compliance
Lightning Source LLC
Chambersburg PA
CBHW030939260626
47169CB00002B/538